D0051996

MINT JULEPS, MAYHEM, AND MURDER

"A nifty mystery . . . Fans of TV's Air Force Wives will especially appreciate Ellie, a smart crime solver who successfully navigates the challenges of military life."
—*Publishers Weekly*

"Some cozies just hit on all cylinders, and Rosett's Ellie Avery titles are among the best. Her books recall the early Carolyn Hart."
—*Library Journal*

"Tightly constructed with many well-fitted, suspenseful turns, and flows like a country creek after an all-day rain."
—*Shine*

MAGNOLIAS, MOONLIGHT, AND MURDER

"Rosett's engaging fourth Mom Zone mystery finds superefficient crime-solver Ellie Avery living in a new subdivision in North Dawkins, GA . . . Some nifty party tips help keep the sleuthing on the cozy side."
—**Publishers Weekly**

GETTING AWAY IS DEADLY

"No mystery is a match for the likable, efficient Ellie, who unravels this multilayered plot with skill and class."
—*Romantic Times Book Reviews* (four stars)

"*Getting Away Is Deadly* keeps readers moving down some surprising paths—and on the edge of their chairs—until the very end."
—*Cozy Library*

STAYING HOME IS A KILLER

"If you like cozy mysteries that have plenty of action and lots of suspects and clues, *Staying Home Is a Killer* will be a fun

romp through murder and mayhem. This is a mystery with a 'mommy lit' flavor. . . . A fun read."
—*Armchair Interviews*

"Thoroughly entertaining. The author's smooth, succinct writing style enables the plot to flow effortlessly until its captivating conclusion."
—**Romantic Times Book Reviews** (four stars)

MOVING IS MURDER

"A fun debut for an appealing young heroine."
—*Carolyn Hart*, author of the Death on Demand mystery series

"A squadron of suspects, a unique setting, and a twisted plot will keep you turning pages!"
—*Nancy J. Cohen*, author of the Bad Hair Day mystery series

"Everyone should snap to attention and salute this fresh new voice."
—*Denise Swanson*, nationally best-selling author of the Scumble River mystery series

"An absorbing read that combines sharp writing and tight plotting with a fascinating peek into the world of military wives. Jump in!"
—*Cynthia Baxter*, author of the Reigning Cats & Dogs mystery series

"Reading Sara Rosett's *Moving Is Murder* is like making a new friend—I can't wait to brew a pot of tea and read all about sleuth Ellie Avery's next adventure!"
—*Leslie Meier*, author of the Lucy Stone mystery series

"Mayhem, murder, and the military! Rosett is an author to watch."
—*Alesia Holliday*, author of the December Vaughn mystery series

THE ELLIE AVERY MYSTERIES
By Sara Rosett

MOVING IS MURDER

STAYING HOME IS A KILLER

GETTING AWAY IS DEADLY

MAGNOLIAS, MOONLIGHT, AND MURDER

MINT JULEPS, MAYHEM, AND MURDER

MIMOSAS, MISCHIEF, AND MURDER

MISTLETOE, MERRIMENT, AND MURDER

Mistletoe, Merriment, And Murder

Sara Rosett

KENSINGTON BOOKS
http://www.kensingtonbooks.com

KENSINGTON BOOKS are published by

Kensington Publishing Corp.
119 West 40th Street
New York, NY 10018

ISBN-13: 978-0-7582-6921-8
ISBN-10: 0-7582-6921-8

First Mass Market Printing: October 2012

10 9 8 7 6 5 4 3 2 1

Printed in the United States of America

To Glenn

Chapter One

"Look at me, Mom," squeaked a voice beside me. I glanced up from the green frosting I was slathering on a Christmas tree–shaped sugar cookie and saw my five-year-old son, Nathan, wearing the pale blue bed sheet that I'd made into a shepherd costume for the annual children's Christmas pageant. I had accomplished this sewing feat despite the fact that I'm not exactly handy with a needle and thread. Until a few weeks ago, fabric glue had been my go-to option when it came to creating Halloween costumes, but the pageant with its numerous rehearsals coupled with Nathan's rather energetic nature called for something sturdier. I was still stunned that it had worked. I'd actually made sleeves. I was grateful that zippers would have been anachronistic.

With the loose folds that draped around his neck and the strand of rope that Mitch had found in the garage for a belt, Nathan had looked authentically pastoral. Now, though, Nathan had the neckline hitched up over his head into a tight-fitting hood that dropped almost below his eyes. He held his shepherd crook—a converted broomstick—horizontally in a fierce two-handed grip. "Luke, come over to the dark side," he said in a breathy whisper and swished his "light saber" back and forth.

I closed my eyes for a moment, half frustrated and half entertained. "Honey, I don't have time to play Star Wars right now." We'd had a marathon viewing session of the original *Star Wars* trilogy after Thanksgiving dinner this year and the movies had made a huge impression on Nathan. "Remember, I've got company coming. Daddy's taking you and Livvy to get a pizza, so you need to go change."

He whipped the hood off his head and his dark brown eyes, so much like Mitch's, sparkled. "Really?"

"Yep. And, no, you can't take your shepherd's crook with you," I called out after his retreating back.

With a quick glance at the clock, I went back to frosting cookies, slapping the icing on as fast as I could. I had two hours before the squadron spouse club descended on our house and I still had to make the cider, move chairs, start some music, light candles, check the bathroom for toothpaste blobs in the sink, and wrap my present.

Livvy strode into the kitchen, her ponytail bouncing. At least she wasn't in her angel costume. She had a book in the crook of her arm, her butterfly-shaped purse slung over her shoulder, and a coat of clear lip gloss on her rosebud mouth. "I don't see why I can't stay here," she said as she plunked down on a bar stool. She'd had a growth spurt during the summer and I still couldn't believe how tall my eight-year-old was. She tugged at the cuffs of her sweatshirt, which was sprinkled with sparkly snowflakes. "I mean, I understand why

Nathan and Dad have to go—they're boys, but I'm a girl. I should get to stay, too, right?"

"Well, honey, it's all grown-ups. Truthfully, I think you'd be bored. We're just going to eat and talk."

"And open presents," she said accusingly.

"Another reason you can't stay," I said gently. "You don't have a present for the gift exchange and everyone has to have one for the game to work."

"But they're just white elephant gifts," she said quickly. "You said the rule was they had to be worth nothing and as horrible as possible."

Of course she was quoting me exactly. Our kids had excellent recall for statements Mitch and I had made—certain special selections only, usually having to do with promises of ice cream and other special treats. Christmas was just weeks away and Livvy and Nathan were in agony. It seemed each day another package arrived in the mail for the kids from our far-flung extended families. It wasn't easy for them to watch the presents pile up and know it would be weeks before they could open anything. "I could find something in my room to give away," she said in a wheedling tone.

"I'm sure you could, but you're not staying tonight. You're going with Dad," I said in a firmer voice. The lure of opening a present—even a white elephant gift—was a heavy draw for her, but since no other kids had been invited, I didn't think it was right to let Livvy stay.

"But, Mom—" The garage door rumbled up. Rex, our rottweiler—who might look intimidating, but had a sweet temperament and would slobber all over anyone who'd let him—shot through the kitchen, scrambling across the tile, then the wood floor, legs flailing. He met Mitch at the door with his typical enthusiasm, wiggling and whining a greeting. Livvy hopped off her bar stool and gripped Mitch's waist to hug him and Nathan flew into the kitchen shouting, "Dad's home! Dad's home! We're going to get a pizza!"

Mitch hugged the kids, scratched Rex's ears, and gave me a kiss, all while setting down his lunch box and leather jacket. He told the kids to get their coats on while he changed out of his flight suit. A few minutes later, he was back in the kitchen in a rugby shirt and jeans, reaching over my shoulder for a carrot stick. "Looks good in here," he said.

I was shaking red sprinkles over the cookies before the frosting set, but I paused and glanced into the living room and the dining room. Sweeps of evergreen garland dotted with tiny white Christmas lights, red bows, and creamy white magnolias decorated the mantel of our gas fireplace. The Christmas tree stood in the corner of the dining room by the window with an assortment of gleaming ornaments interspersed with the homemade ornaments that the kids had made at school. Fat vanilla and cranberry candles in islands of evergreen were scattered over the tables and a potpourri of tiny pine cones, holly, and evergreen scented the air. "It does look good," I said, half surprised. "I've been so focused on checking off each item from my to-do list that I haven't stepped back and taken in the whole picture."

"Imagine that. You, focused on a to-do list," Mitch said, and I swatted his arm with the dish towel.

He dodged the flick of the towel as I said, "It looks great *because* I focused on that list." Mitch had some . . . issues with my list-making habits. He preferred the looser, more relaxed approaches to life. I liked to know exactly where I was going and what I had to do to get there.

He held up his hands in mock surrender. "Right. You're right. Without the list, we'd be lost."

"That's right," I said, smiling because I knew he was humoring me.

He grinned back and let the subject drop. We'd been married long enough that we both knew that neither of us was going to change our outlook on life. Agree to disagree, that was our motto—at least it was our motto where to-do lists were concerned.

He bit into a cookie, then asked, "Tell me again why you're hosting this thing? I thought you'd sworn off squadron parties after my promotion party."

I cringed. "Don't remind me," I said grimly. That promotion party was a squadron legend. "I said I'd host this party in a moment of weakness. Amy was supposed to do it, but her mom went into the hospital." I squared my shoulders. "This party is going to be different from the promotion party—nice and normal. Dull, even. Just good food, conversation, and presents."

"No flaming turkey fryer?" Mitch asked with a straight face. I rolled the dish towel again and he moved out of my range.

"No," I said as I went back to arranging the cookies on a platter. I transferred the platter to the dining-room table. Mitch followed me and began massaging my shoulders.

"I'm sure it will work out fine," he said, all teasing gone from his tone.

"Thanks." I felt my shoulders relaxing under his fingers. I wasn't a natural hostess. I worried too much and spun myself into knots. His arms closed around me. It felt so good to lean into his sturdiness. Five more weeks, I thought, then immediately banished the thought. Mitch's turn for a deployment was coming up in January and I was doing my best to avoid thinking about him leaving—I hated when he had to leave for months on end—but the deployment was always there in the back of my mind.

I heard the kids coming down the hall and twisted around for a quick kiss. "Y'all better hit the road. The spouses will get here soon and I still have to change," I said, lifting my shoulder to indicate my flour-spattered sweatshirt and worn jeans.

"I could help you with that," Mitch said with a wicked gleam in his eye.

Out of the corner of my eye, I could see Livvy standing in the kitchen, attempting to juggle her mittens. Nathan was running in circles around Rex, who was patiently watching him despite having his stubby tail stepped on.

"I don't think so," I said. With a significant glance at the kids, I lowered my voice. "I doubt that would speed things up."

"That's the whole idea. Speed is overrated," Mitch whispered before he glanced up at the sprigs of mistletoe I'd hung from the chandelier with red ribbon, then gave me a lingering kiss.

"I see your point," I said. "We'll have to finish this . . . discussion . . . later."

"Yes we will," Mitch said before herding the kids out the door to the car.

I hurried off to change into my favorite deep green sweater with the oversized turtleneck collar and a pair of tailored pants. I managed to get through the rest of my to-do list before my best friend, Abby, arrived.

"Don't panic," she announced, opening the front door. "I'm early. Here." She handed me two poinsettia plants. "I have more in the car." She spun around, her dark, curly hair flying over the fuzzy edging of the hood on her coat.

She'd brought ten plants, which we spaced around

the house for the final touch of festiveness. Once those were in place, she made a final trip to her car and returned with a present and a peppermint cheesecake. "I'm so looking forward to this," she said, stripping off her coat and gloves. With her generous smile and curvy figure, she looked spectacular in a white sweater, black pencil skirt, and high-heeled boots.

I deposited her gift under the tree along with my hastily wrapped present and asked, "The third-graders are getting to you?" Abby taught at the nearby elementary.

She rolled her eyes to the ceiling and managed to look both worn-out and guilty at the same time. "They're so sweet, but eight hours of knock-knock jokes? And then when I get home, all Charlie wants to talk about is how much better front-loaders are than dump trucks."

"Is Jeff out of touch again?" I asked. Abby's husband, a pilot like Mitch, was currently on a deployment to an unnamed location in the Middle East. Communication between the deployed location and spouses at home was generally pretty good. There were morale calls, which were usually filled with static and an annoying time delay that made conversation challenging, but it was always good to hear that familiar voice on the phone. And now online video made staying close so much easier, but there were often stretches of time when the guys couldn't communicate for days, maybe weeks, at a time, depending on what they were doing.

"Yeah. I haven't talked to him for four days. There's nothing going on—no bad news, so I know he's just on a mission."

I nodded. You became quite good at reading between the lines of newscasts when you were a military spouse. "Tonight should be a good break for you. I promise there won't be one knock-knock joke. Come on, you can stir the cider and talk about anything you want while I light the candles," I said, leading the way to the kitchen.

"Enough about me, for now. This smells divine." Abby leaned over the simmering saucepan. "What's going on with you?"

I picked up the candle lighter from the counter and flicked it on. "I didn't get the organizing job for the schools." I'd heard through Abby that the North Dawkins school district was looking for an independent contractor to create and implement paper saving strategies throughout the district to help them cut costs.

"Why not?" Abby asked. "You're the best organizer in North Dawkins. How could they *not* hire you?"

I focused on the small explosion of flame around the wick of one of the candles as it lit. "No, up until a few months ago, I was the *only* organizer in North Dawkins. That doesn't mean I was the best."

Abby gave the cider a vigorous stir that sent it sloshing around the pan. "You're the best. I know how hard you work. And you're good. Don't get down on yourself. They probably had to delay the decision, or they lost the funding for it in the budget cuts—that happens all the time."

Another wick flared. "Gabrielle Matheson got the job."

Abby sucked in a breath. "No! How do you know? She didn't call to gloat, did she?"

I moved to the candles in the living room. "No, I don't think even she would be that tacky."

"I wouldn't put it past her," Abby murmured.

Freshly divorced and with two kids in college, Gabrielle had supposedly moved from Atlanta to North Dawkins for a fresh start. I knew her sister, Jean Williams, through the squadron spouse club. Jean's husband had retired from the air force, but Jean still attended some spouse club events—"the fun ones, anyway," was how she put it with a smile. Gabrielle had told everyone that she'd moved to North Dawkins so she could be near her sister, but I knew there was another reason. Atlanta was thick with organizers, but there was only one professional organizer between Macon and Valdosta—me. Or, there had been only one until Gabrielle arrived.

Gabrielle had called to introduce herself. Networking, she'd said. Her southern accent had oozed through the phone line, "Us professional organizers have to stick together."

I'd jumped at the idea, thinking it would be great to have someone in town to knock around ideas with. I'd even pitched my latest service to her, consulting with new organizers and helping them set up their businesses. I'd hoped this new venture would take off and I could eventually transition to full-time consulting so that when our next move came, I wouldn't have to start over from scratch again with zero clients. So far, I had two "newbie" organizers in two different states that I was working with long distance, via e-mail and social networking.

"Oh, honey," Gabrielle had said with a throaty laugh. "I don't need your help. I'm an old hand at organizing." She'd immediately switched to a new topic. "I think we should start a local chapter here," she had said, referring to the national association of organizers that we both belonged to. "Since you're so busy with your established clients—and I know you have little kids, too—I'd be happy to be president. Don't worry, you don't have to do anything. I'll take care of everything."

She'd signed off quickly and I'd been left with my

mouth open and a dial tone buzzing in my ear. In the two months since she'd moved to North Dawkins, Gabrielle had managed to vacuum up quite a few of my new client leads and she'd also poached one of my most affluent regular clients, Stephanie, who, at one time, had my number on her speed dial. Two weeks after Gabrielle moved to town, Stephanie had called to let me know she wouldn't need me anymore.

"That's three jobs now where she's beat me out," I said, exasperated, as I returned to the kitchen and pulled mugs out of the cabinet for the cider.

"Here. Let me do that. You don't want to chip anything," Abby said. "How did you find out you didn't get the school district job?"

"Candy called me." I'd met Candy when I created storage solutions for a nonprofit group where she worked. She was in her forties, wore huge hoop earrings that always matched her clothes, chomped on gum nonstop, and had a bossy, tough-love kind of personality. She'd left the nonprofit and was now working in the school district office as an administrative assistant. "All she could say was that the director didn't pick my proposal. She asked me to call her back tonight, but I don't think I'll have time." I glanced at my watch. It was almost six.

"Oh, go. Call her. I'll get the door if anyone comes while you're on the phone," Abby said.

Candy answered on the first ring. She sounded slightly out of breath. "Just walked in the door from work. Now, you didn't hear this from me, and I can't say much, but I thought you should know what's going on. You're a good sort, the kind to get run over in a thing like this, so . . . officially, Gabrielle got the job because she has more hours available to work each week. Theoretically, she can get it done faster and she had a refer-

ence from a school in Peachtree City, which never returned my calls, so I couldn't verify she'd worked for
them. She supposedly ran an organizing seminar for
the teachers and revamped the school's workroom,
which counted as more suitable experience than the organizing you've done for individuals."

"But even if I don't have experience organizing for a
school—"

"I know, honey, I know. I've seen you work. You
would have known exactly what to do. Anyway, that's all
neither here nor there. What really made the difference was as soon as Gabrielle came in the office she
schmoozed old Rodrick. That first morning, she just
happened to have brought an extra latte, vanilla and
skim milk, no less."

Rodrick Olsen was the superintendent. Candy's
voice took on a gushy tone. "And wasn't that the biggest
coincidence in the world? That she'd brought Rodrick's favorite? And didn't Rodrick look sharp in his
pinstripe?" Her voice lost its sickeningly sweet exagger-
ated southern drawl. She was spot-on in her imitation.
Back in her normal, rather gruff voice, Candy said,
"Gawd, it was sickening. And he ate it up, let me tell
you. She suggested lunch at The Grille, so she could
completely understand all *his needs.*" There was a clank-
ing, which I assumed was Candy's big hoop earring clattering against the phone in her agitation. "So there you
are. Just wanted you to know what you're up against—
flirty schmoozing."

My heart sank. "I can't do flirty schmoozing. And I
don't want to have to do that to get jobs."

"Don't worry, honey, she's the type of woman that
men fall all over themselves for, but women will see
right through her, just like I did. What goes around,
comes around. Just be aware of what you're up against

when you're both competing for the same job and the person making the decision is a male."

The doorbell chimed. "I've got to go. Thanks, Candy."

"Sure thing," Candy said. "You be sweet now."

Despite the plunge in my self-confidence, I had to grin at Candy's signature southern good-bye. "Bye, Candy."

Petite, pixielike Nadia, with her short, brown hair and elfin face, followed Abby into the kitchen. Nadia was one of the most intensely perky people I knew, which I figured was an asset for a first-grade teacher. She and Abby taught at the same school. Nadia was carrying a glass pan of fudge and had her camera bag slung over her shoulder. She was the official squadron photographer, but her photographs went way beyond the amateur level. She'd recently sold some of her photos of the local pumpkin patch to a regional magazine. She wore a cranberry-colored boiled wool jacket with black piping over a snowy white shell and black skirt. Personally, I thought she took coordination of her clothing a little too far—she and her two daughters always matched, down to the hefty bows that she placed in their hair. I was sure that if the girls had been with her tonight, they would have been in some sort of burgundy taffeta party dresses complete with matching bows.

"There's been another one, did you hear?" Nadia asked as she handed the fudge to Abby and carefully set her camera bag on the counter.

"Another what?" I asked.

"Break-in," she said, clearly delighted to have the scoop on us. I didn't know how she did it, but Nadia always had the latest news on . . . well, just about everything. I thought she probably would have made an excellent investigative reporter, if she hadn't liked teaching so much.

"Another spouse?" Abby said. "Who was it this time?"
Nadia's expression turned somber. "Amy. They got
in while she was at the hospital with her mom."

Tips for a Sane and Happy Holiday Season

A niche industry has grown up around holiday organization. There are endless plastic boxes and
bins designed specifically to hold holiday decorations. The only downside to these organizing aids is
the expense involved. Sometimes it seems you can
spend just as much on storing your holiday decorations as on the decorations themselves. Here are
some cheap and easy storage solutions that won't
break your budget:

- Use Styrofoam egg cartons to store small, delicate
  ornaments.
- Look for plastic cord wrappers in the hardware
  section of your local superstore, which will usually
  be cheaper than the cord wrappers in the holiday
  section. Use these cord wrappers to wind lights,
  tinsel, and garland. Or, make your own cord wrappers out of sturdy pieces of rectangular-shaped
  cardboard.
- Save original ornament packaging and reuse at the
  end of the season.
- Wrap wreaths in plastic trash bags to prevent
  them from getting dusty, then hang in your storage
  area.

Chapter
Two

"How terrible," I said.

"That's low," Abby said, emphatically. "Can you imagine targeting someone whose mother is in the hospital? Who would do that?"

Nadia and I exchanged a look. "It has to be someone in the squadron, doesn't it?" I said, voicing what we were thinking.

"It could all be a coincidence," Nadia said, doubt edging her voice.

"You guys worry too much," Abby said. "Before this, there have only been two break-ins on base and one in North Dawkins. That's not a pattern. That's coincidence."

"Still, I don't like it. Robberies don't happen on base very often. And, how likely is it that each one of those break-ins was at a house where the husband was deployed?" Nadia asked with a frown.

"Not every break-in," Abby countered. "Amy's husband isn't deployed."

"But she and Cody were away in Atlanta, with her

mom, at the hospital. That means someone knew her house would be more vulnerable, like the others."

"It is strange," I said. "When did it happen?"

"At night, like the others," Nadia said, raising her eyebrows. "They drove to Atlanta in the evening. Amy came back the next morning to pick up a few things and found the back door open."

Abby rolled her eyes. "Isn't that when robberies usually happen—in the dead of night?"

I ignored her. "Do you know what was taken?"

"I heard a laptop computer, MP3 players, and some cash," Nadia said.

"It does sound like the others," I said. The other robberies had all taken place during the night and small but valuable electronics and money were taken.

The doorbell rang and I hurried off to answer it. I swung the door wide and said, "Hi, Marie."

Her head was nowhere near the door frame, but she ducked a little anyway as she stepped inside. I guess being six-foot-two probably made you overly cautious about door frames. Marie said hello softly and stopped short in the entryway, like she wasn't sure what to do. She pushed a swath of her long orangy-red bangs out of her eyes and looked around the house. Her slightly protruding eyes seemed to widen even more. "Your house is lovely . . . so pretty . . . so clean. I don't know if I want you coming to my house tomorrow, after all," she said with a nervous laugh.

Despite being in her late twenties, Marie had the gangly arms and legs of a teen, which didn't really go with her more stocky midsection. It was horrible, but every time I saw her I was reminded of the Sesame Street character, Big Bird. It had to be a combination of her height, her soft-spoken manner, and the mismatch of her stringy arms and legs combined with her thicker core. I quickly tried to banish that association from my mind. You know you've been watching too much children's television when it starts to influence how you see people.

"Oh, don't worry. This is definitely not the normal state of our house. There are usually toys and books everywhere." I had an organizing consultation scheduled for tomorrow with Marie and I was afraid that with her timid and hesitant manner, she might cancel. "Come have some food and let me take your gift and coat."

After a slight hesitation, she reluctantly released the red package. I wondered if she was thinking about leaving, claiming some forgotten appointment or errand, but then she smiled nervously and handed me her coat. I sent her into the kitchen and made a mental note to check on her later to make sure she was having a good time.

Everyone seemed to arrive at once and soon the sound of conversation and laughter began to drown out Mannheim Steamroller's "Deck the Halls." I was in the kitchen chatting laboriously with Marie—yes, she and her husband had been assigned to the squadron almost a year ago; yes, they liked it here; no, she didn't like it that he was deployed; yes, she was looking for a job—when I heard Abby call my name, I excused myself, glad for the interruption.

I hurried through the crowded room to her. "What's wrong?" I asked.

Abby was frowning. "I wanted to warn you. Gabrielle is here."

"What? Why would she be here?"

"Jean brought her," Abby said. My eyebrows shot up and Abby hurriedly said, "What could I do? They came in with a big group. I couldn't let Jean in and turn her sister away, could I?"

"No, but I wish you had." I knew I was being unreasonable, but I couldn't help it. "Abby, that woman is sabotaging my business. I haven't even told you what Candy said about her."

"Oh, Ellie, sugar," a syrupy voice, dripping with long southern vowels, sounded behind me, "Your house is—um—charming. So cute and domestic. It must be just perfect for your little family. It's so nice of you to host this party at the last minute, even though it's quite a squeeze in here. And I love all this neutral paint. It must make decorating a breeze."

Wow—had she just said my house was too small and that it was bland? I gritted my teeth, determined to be nice. I would take the high road.

Jean was standing slightly behind Gabrielle and I thought I was seeing double for a moment. I hadn't realized how strong a resemblance there was between the sisters. I'd met Gabrielle at a chamber of commerce meeting, so I knew what she looked like and I'd had plenty of interactions with Jean through the squadron, but I hadn't seen them together. Side by side, they looked not just like sisters, but more like twins. There were differences in their style of dress and—more prominently—in their attitudes, but they were both the same height and had black hair, green eyes, and heart-shaped faces with high Slavic cheekbones.

Jean stepped around Gabrielle and handed me a plate of brownies iced in swirls of chocolate frosting. "Hi, Ellie. I invited Gabrielle along tonight so she can meet more people." Jean's dark hair, which was threaded through with strands of gray, was pulled back into a low ponytail held in place by a rubber band. Under her quilted down coat and wool scarf of neutral brown tones, she wore jeans and a green sweatshirt embroidered with elves.

In contrast to Jean's unfussy clothes and faint makeup, Gabrielle looked incredibly stylish, if a little overblown, in a Christmas ribbon–red wrap dress with a plunging neckline and black heels. Her makeup was thorough and flawless, her dark hair—no glint of gray anywhere—floated about her face in luxurious waves, and the scent of lilies drifted around her.

"Um, yes, I know. Here, let me put those gifts under the tree. Help yourself to some food," I said as I escaped. Really, how could I have thought they were alike? Now that I looked at them, I kept seeing differences—Jean had plain, short-trimmed fingernails. Gabrielle's long, acrylic nails were polished a glossy red. After introducing Gabrielle to everyone, Jean filled a plate with food and plunked down on the couch beside Nadia. Gabrielle avoided the food, except for a few carrot sticks. There was also a sensual air about Gabrielle that was completely absent from Jean. The plunging neckline of the dress, the flowery scent, and the way she held herself—one hand on her thrust-out hip—looked almost as if she were expecting a photographer to pop out and snap her picture.

Impatient with myself, I shook my head. *Stop being catty,* I told myself, and went to get more napkins. I couldn't help but notice that Gabrielle was the center of attention wherever she was. She drew people to her. There was a sort of energy and sparkle about her. No wonder Rodrick had been captivated by her.

Everyone had arrived and the party was in full swing. I cruised through the house, chatting and making sure everyone had food. Abby was slowly herding everyone into the living room so the gift exchange could begin. I filled a plate for myself and hurried into the kitchen to get a mug of cider. The kitchen was empty except for Gabrielle and Marie, who were on the far side by the breakfast table. Gabrielle, who had her back toward me, pressed a business card into Marie's hand. "You should give me a call." Gabrielle spoke quietly, but I could still hear her. "My hours are much more flexible than Ellie's and I'll give you a twenty percent discount on whatever she quotes you."

Marie shot a guilty glance at me, then said, "That's okay—I've already got an appointment, with Ellie, I mean. I'll just keep that." Marie shifted around the back of the table and quickly escaped into the living room.

Furious, I slapped my plate and mug down on the counter and marched over to Gabrielle. "I can't believe you did that." I was so angry my hands were shaking and there was a tremble in my voice.

Gabrielle glanced languidly over her shoulder at me, then turned to face me with a little sigh. "Ellie, sugar," she said in a long-suffering voice, "don't be upset. It's just business. A little friendly competition."

Words burbled up inside me, but when I'm upset, I get tongue-tied and all I could do was sputter, "Friendly? That's not friendly!"

"There are plenty of clients to go around for both of us," she said in that infuriatingly calm tone.

"Then why are you poaching mine? You're intentionally going after them, I know it!"

"I can't help it if they're not satisfied with your services, now can I?"

The muscles in my core tensed and I felt my face flush. "What you're doing is wrong. You and I both know that." I stepped toward her. "I'm a nice person, but I will *not* let you do this to me."

Gabrielle's gaze shifted from my face to the living

room. Our house had an open floor plan and I suddenly realized everyone in the living room could see us arguing. The only sound in the room was the faint strains of "Silent Night" playing in the background. *Great.* I briefly closed my eyes. Everyone had probably overheard us, too.

"Don't worry, y'all," Gabrielle called, addressing the room. I opened my eyes to see that she'd swept by me, picked up my mug of cider, and was strutting into the living room. "Just a professional disagreement—Ellie and I could go on all day debating decluttering strategies."

Every head swung back toward me and I managed to force a smile to my lips. "I think it's time to start the gift exchange."

Abby jumped up. "Right! Okay, here's the rules. Everyone draws a number . . ."

I tuned Abby out and busied myself cleaning up the kitchen. By the time I came back inside from emptying the trash, I felt calmer, and embarrassed, too. I couldn't believe I'd let Gabrielle get me so riled. From now on, I would avoid her.

I slipped into the living room and watched the gift exchange until it was my turn to open a present. The game was complicated and involved options for swapping gifts and strategies to hang on to the gifts you wanted. I kept losing the gift I opened, a stationery set embossed with prints of holly and mistletoe. Most of the envelopes were missing, which was why it was a white elephant gift.

There were only a few presents left when Gabrielle opened a package that contained a flat box made of rough wood with a long opening a few inches wide near the bottom. "What is it?" she asked. "A birdhouse?"

"Sort of," a spouse new to the squadron, Cecilia,

replied. She was four months pregnant and worked out each day with the neighborhood stroller brigade, which despite having the name "Stroller Brigade," was a neighborhood workout open to anyone who wanted to join. The stroller was optional and it was such a good cardio workout with a mix of lunges, squats, and push-ups for toning that I still joined them when I could. I had to hand it to Cecilia. There were some days when the power-walking workout left me exhausted. If I had tried to do that workout while I was pregnant, someone would have probably had to wheel me home in one of the strollers. But Cecilia always powered through the workout. She adjusted the portable—and broken—sewing machine that was on her lap. It was the gift she'd "won." She pushed her glasses up her beaky nose and said, "It's a bat house."

I laughed out loud, along with everyone else, over the strange present.

"What?" Cecilia said. "Bats eat mosquitoes—they're really good to have around." An outdoor girl who'd grown up on a farm, she was still upset that she couldn't ride a horse while she was pregnant.

By the time the dust had settled and the game was over, I'd lost the stationery set for good and was the owner of a three-inch-high Lucite paperweight. It was shaped like the classic round-cut diamond with a flat top and faceted sides that narrowed to a sharp point at the bottom. I recognized it. It had been a giveaway from a local insurance agent. His firm, Jim Excel Insurance Associates, was etched onto the top of the "diamond" along with a phone number. We'd had one a few years ago and, after taking it away from Livvy and Nathan several times because the point was so sharp it could cause major bodily injury, I'd tossed it in a box of charity donations. Now I had a new one.

"Oh, but that means I'm left with the bat house," Gabrielle wailed with a pout when she realized she couldn't swap with anyone else.

I thought the bat house was *so* deliciously appropriate for her. Every witch needs a few bats, right?

Nadia shook her head over the white elephant gift she'd won, a jigsaw puzzle of intricately detailed butterflies, which were repeated over and over again to make the puzzle even more difficult. There was a helpful note jotted on the box that stated several pieces were missing. "This one is way too hard for the girls—four hundred pieces—and it's missing pieces. Imagine how frustrating that would be, to get to the end and not have all the pieces after all that work."

Abby held up her prize, a wooden duck decoy, and said, "Well, at least I can decorate with this." Trust Abby to come up with the white elephant gift that could legitimately be turned into home decor. She had great instincts when it came to arranging furniture and accents. I was sure she'd find a place for the duck on her mantel or on a bookshelf and it would look spectacular and no one would ever guess it had been a white elephant gift.

I turned to Marie, who'd won a figurine of an elf with a chipped nose. The hat was held on with a piece of tape. "Guess you can't decorate with that."

I expected her to laugh and agree with me, but she said earnestly, "I'll find a place for it. I'm sure I can use it."

I wasn't quite sure what to say to that. How could you use an elf figurine? And a broken one, at that? Unless she planned on turning it into one of those funky found-art pieces that recycled trash into sculptures, I couldn't think of anything.

Hannah, the low-key squadron commander's wife, won a small painting with flaking paint and an elaborate frame. Unlike the last squadron commander's wife, who'd become a close friend of mine, Hannah was so self-effacing and quiet that it was easy to overlook her, so I was almost surprised when she called for everyone's attention at the end of the party. "Don't forget the squadron Christmas party is coming up. It'll be at the Peach Blossom Inn and we're having a gift basket auction to raise money for a terrific local charity, Helping Hands."

People began to drift back to the kitchen to grab another quick bite of food or refresh their drinks, but the party was waning. It wouldn't be long before I was distributing coats and waving everyone off. I breathed an internal sigh of relief, a reaction to getting through the party with no major mishaps, except for the spat with Gabrielle, but that was nothing compared to the flaming disaster of our last party.

I relaxed into a newly vacated seat next to Jean and asked how her husband liked retirement. Simon's last assignment had been at the squadron and he'd had a big retirement party during the summer.

"Loves it. He absolutely loves it." She leaned toward me, confidingly. "I was so worried that he would go stir crazy with all that time on his hands, but he got involved with Helping Hands and between that and golf—he's always busy."

"What is he doing for Helping Hands?" I asked. I knew the local charity, located behind our church, had an annual food drive and ran a food bank all year long. They also built homes for low-income families. It was nothing like the scale of Habitat for Humanity, but I thought building even one or two houses a year was quite an accomplishment.

"He started out helping in the food pantry three days a week. It was like pulling teeth to get him to go with me the first time, but once he got involved, he

loved it. He's on the board as the financial manager
now and does just about everything. And," she leaned
in a little closer, "Helping Hands just got a significant
donation." She raised her eyebrows for impact. "Significant. It's really going to help. This year has been rough
for so many people with the economy tanking the way it
has. Donations have been down all year, but now it
looks like we'll be able to break ground on two new
houses. Simon will probably have less free time than
when he was on active duty."

"That's wonderful about the donation," I said. "And
you're still doing your online resale business?" Jean
combed through garage sales and other online auctions for items she could resell through her own online
storefront.

"Yes." Jean held up the white elephant gift I'd brought,
a beat-up set of Hot Wheels toy cars, and said, "These will
probably go fast."

"You're kidding."

"No. I'll put up a couple of nice photographs and
price them right. They'll probably be gone in a few
hours. In fact, a lot of this stuff that people think is
trash could sell," she said.

Hannah held up the painting. "Even this?"

"Maybe," Jean said. She didn't sound so sure. "I
could give it a try. Want me to list it?"

"Sure."

Nadia and Cecilia handed off their gifts to Jean and I
added the paperweight to the collection. An hour later,
I was practically shoving Abby out the door. "I should
stay and help you clean up," she said.

"You already did. All I have left to do is start the dishwasher. Now, go on, you've got a babysitter to pay. And
don't forget to lock the house up tonight!"

I couldn't hear her reply, but it sounded a bit like, "Yada, yada, yada."

By the time Mitch came home and we got the kids in bed, then did the final post-party sweep of the house and talked a bit about our days, it was nearly one in the morning. I'd just relaxed into my pillow when the phone rang.

Abby's voice had a tremor in it as she said, "Sorry to call so late. Don't panic. Everything's okay, well, except that I've been robbed."

Chapter
Three

"Robbed?" I sat up in bed. "Someone broke into your house?"

Mitch clicked on the lamp. I mouthed, "Abby," at him so he'd know who I was talking to.

"It happened about forty-five minutes ago. I heard glass shatter and called nine-one-one. Whoever it was . . . they were gone before I got off the phone."

"Oh my God, Abby,"

"I know. It was horrible, but we're okay and the only thing they took was my cell phone and the GPS. I hate to ask this, but do you think Mitch could come over and board up my window? Jeff has some wood in the garage, but I'm hopeless with the tools. I don't even know where he keeps the drill. There's a cordless one . . . somewhere. I know it's a drive for him and I could ask someone else here on base, but I hate to call and wake anyone else up. Not that I wanted to call you, because I know now I'll never hear the end of this since you were right about the break-ins and I was wrong, so . . . you know . . . anyway, could he come over?"

"Yes, of course." Abby might say she was okay, but I knew when she was jabbering away like this, it meant she was extremely upset. I relayed the request to Mitch; he nodded, and climbed out of bed. "You and Charlie should come back here tonight." I glanced over at Mitch as he pulled an Air Force Academy sweatshirt over his head. I tilted the phone away from my mouth. "Okay with you if they stay here?"

"Sure, yeah. Jeff wouldn't want them there by themselves."

"In fact, pack some clothes and stay with us until Jeff gets back."

"Oh, I couldn't do that—"

"Abby, come stay with us. It's only a few more days until Jeff returns, right? So stay here with us until then."

"Well, maybe just for tonight."

Thursday

"Nathan, brush your teeth and get your backpack," I said as I slapped peanut butter and jelly on slices of whole wheat bread at seven-thirty the next morning. My eyes were puffy and an ominous pulsing in my temples indicated that a headache wasn't far off. I shoved the sandwiches in plastic bags, then grabbed apples and mozzarella cheese sticks to add to the four lunches I was packing. "Livvy, let Rex inside for me."

Dressed in a blue sweater, jeans with rainbow patterns stitched on the pockets, and tennis shoes, Livvy tossed her backpack down by the door to the garage and jogged to the back door, her ponytail bouncing as she moved. At least I had one kid ready to go. She opened the door to the backyard and Rex trotted inside. He paused, sniffed the air, and shot off in the direction of the living room. A puff of white streaked from under the coffee table and ricocheted into the kitchen. Rex jerked to a stop and reversed course, skidding across the slippery kitchen tiles. Abby's cat, Wisk, vaulted through the air and used the island countertop as a springboard to reach the top of the refrigerator. Rex crashed into my legs, then scrambled back to his feet. He moved back and forth in a half-circle around the refrigerator, nose in the air, barking at full volume. Wisk seemed to expand to about twice his normal size as his fur puffed out.

I grabbed Rex by the collar and dragged him to his kennel in the laundry room, telling him, "You're a good watchdog, but you can't eat Wisk." I felt bad leaving him in his kennel, but I had to get the kids off to school. Wisk paced back and forth on top of the refrigerator, then settled into a tentative, watchful crouch on the high perch, keeping a close watch on the laundry room. Rex's whines were dying away, but I doubted Wisk would move from his spot anytime soon. I certainly wasn't about to try and get him down.

Nathan and Charlie had been huddled over their empty breakfast plates, leaning toward a pile of Lego blocks that covered the kitchen table, but now they were laughing as they tried to reenact the chase. Nathan had been surprised to find Charlie curled up in a sleeping bag on his bedroom floor this morning. Both Livvy and Nathan had slept through the arrival of our unexpected guests. It had taken about two seconds for Nathan to go from sleepy to giddy. His friend was in his house at seven in the morning—what better time was there to play with Legos? Who cared about a little thing like getting to school on time? Livvy was playing it cooler than Nathan, but I could tell she loved the company, too, especially Abby, who Livvy thought was the most interesting and fun person around—way more fun than me.

"Nathan," I said sternly. "Teeth—now! You're riding to school with Charlie this morning, so you better get moving. You don't want to make them late."

"You, too, young man," Abby said as she emerged from the guest bedroom dressed in a nice sweater and slacks. Both boys grabbed their Lego blocks and headed down the hall. "Sorry about Wisk," Abby said, "He's so fast. He was out the bedroom door before I even realized it."

"That's okay. Rex is fine where he is for now. Are you sure you should go to school today?" I asked Abby as she picked up the plates and rinsed them at the sink.

"The insurance agent can't meet me until this afternoon and the security police on base have done everything they can. They checked for fingerprints and there weren't any. I might as well go to school—you know, keep things as normal as possible for Charlie. It will keep my mind off it, too."

I nodded as I downed two ibuprofen, then sent Livvy to look for her school library book. Rex's barks were still ringing in my ears and magnifying the pain in my head. "You don't need to check the house again to make sure nothing else is gone?"

"After I calmed down last night, I looked around. They just took what I left on the kitchen counter. I think they scooped up everything there, then left as fast as they came in."

"Thank goodness they left when they did."

She shivered. "I know. I'm glad I hadn't gone to bed yet. Can you imagine how creepy it would be to have slept through a break-in?"

I nodded and said, "It seems like a big risk to take for just a few things."

Abby shrugged. "Well, one of them was my snakeskin purse, so that could have been a big haul if they'd gotten my credit cards and checkbook. And, the duck decoy. They got that, too. Just swept up everything on the counter."

"Your snakeskin purse? That was your favorite." Abby had found the slouchy tote at a discount store and she carried it all the time. "You didn't say anything about your purse last night—only the GPS and your cell phone."

"I know. I remembered after I called you. I'd been carrying the snakeskin purse, but I changed to a clutch before I walked out the door for the party. I left the snakeskin purse on the kitchen counter and I guess they scooped it up with everything else."

I said, "Too bad you didn't just carry the same purse all day yesterday."

"The snakeskin didn't really go with my outfit."

"Gray snakeskin doesn't go with black and white?" I asked.

"No, too casual," Abby said.

"I think you could have pulled it off," I said. I always deferred to her in matters of clothing, but purses were my department—I loved them. They were my one extravagance. I couldn't get excited about the latest clothing trends, but I did know my designer handbags and scoured the online auction sites and garage sales for bargains. Abby's snakeskin purse hadn't been designer, but it was unusual and stylish and, as far as I could tell, unique. I couldn't find another one like it anywhere.

Abby closed the dishwasher door and said, "In fact, if I didn't know you so well, I'd suspect you broke in. You really liked that purse."

"True. I did love it, but even *I* wouldn't go that far

for a purse—despite the fact that you did get the absolute last one in the whole state of Georgia. Any hope of the police finding it or the other things?"

"No, I don't think so. The security police weren't very optimistic. So there goes my sunglasses and my new Urban Decay lipstick. I didn't move everything to the clutch."

"Well, at least they didn't get your wallet," I said as I stuffed lunches in backpacks.

"That'll teach me to put everything away," Abby said. "I came in from the party and dumped everything on the kitchen counter. I always do that, you know."

I nodded. Abby was quite a bit more relaxed than I was when it came to controlling clutter. Actually, clutter didn't bother her at all. I made a mental note not to look in the guest room. I was sure clothes and shoes would be flung all over the place.

"So why didn't they take your clutch?" I was sure she'd left it on the counter, too.

"It had fallen down onto one of the bar stools on the far side of the counter. They probably didn't even see it. That was lucky." She settled her large tote bag with her school work on her shoulder. "It's got to be a disappointing haul for them—maybe they'll quit after this. I mean, how much can you get for a GPS, a cell phone, an almost empty purse, and a beat-up duck decoy? One of the security police guys said the thief is getting sloppy."

"Really? Compared to the other break-ins?"

Abby nodded. "Apparently, at the other houses, the locks were picked."

"I hadn't heard that," I said.

"I know. I overheard two of the security police officers talking about it."

The boys burst into the kitchen at the same time Livvy came out of her room, holding her book high like a trophy. "Found it," she announced.

"Get your coats. Time to go," Abby said, herding everyone toward the door. And suddenly the house was quiet, except for an intermittent low whine from the laundry room. I glanced up at Wisk, who regarded me with a steady, somewhat superior blue gaze.

Abby stuck her head back in the door. "I forgot to tell you. I called Cecilia and she's going to take care of Wisk for me until Jeff gets back. I figured two unexpected houseguests were more than enough for you to handle. She'll swing by this morning and get him. All you have to do is put him in his carrier and leave him on the back porch. Bye!"

The door slammed shut. As the garage door rumbled up, I eyed Wisk. Was it my imagination or did he seem to have a "bring it on" look in his eyes? I walked casually toward him. He flicked his tail once and was gone, a white smudge splashing through the kitchen and down the hallway.

This might take awhile.

An hour later, wearing a long-sleeved white crewneck sweater to cover the scratches on my arms, I parked in front of Marie's house. Neither Wisk nor I had liked it, but Wisk was now stowed in his carrier and ready for Cecilia. I grabbed my tote with my organizing brochures, climbed out of the minivan, and checked my khaki slacks for cat hair. Marie lived in Wiregrass Plantation, a neighborhood heavy on white pillared porches and red brick with sweeping rooflines. The area had once been a pecan grove and the massive trees dotted the neighborhood with gridlike precision. The bare, gnarled branches created an interlocking canopy overhead.

Having grown up in the wide-open plains of Texas, the ranks of trees I saw in Georgia still awed me. These trees were different from the pine tree farms that grew along the local highway with the trees packed close together, each of them growing straight as an arrow. The twisty branches of these tall, widely spaced pecan trees spread wide, some of them so large that the canopy of one tree would shade a whole lawn in the summer. Craning my neck back to look at the shards of blue sky visible through the interwoven branches, I made my way up the short flight of steps to the porch and rang the doorbell, holding the lapels of my kelly green, hip-length raincoat. It was a clear, sparkling cold day and I wished I'd worn a heavier coat or at least zipped the lining into the one I was wearing.

Marie's neighbor, an older man in a red-and-black plaid flannel jacket and an Atlanta Braves baseball cap was outside, untangling strands of Christmas lights. A ladder leaned against one of the pecan trees in his yard and coils of extension cords were lined up on the driveway. He saw me and I waved. He nodded his head in greeting, his hands full. I waited a few moments, then rang the bell again.

Maybe she'd forgotten. I stepped back and looked over the front of the house. All the blinds were closed tight and there was no flicker of movement or shadow that I could see in the Palladian window over the door. I was reaching for my cell phone when the door edged open a few inches. Marie unlocked the glass storm door and stepped outside. "Hi, Ellie. Sorry, I was in the back."

"No problem," I said, and moved toward the door,

but Marie didn't budge. She stood, shoulders shifted to one side in a half slump with her hands clinched together at her waist. She looked . . . scared, I realized. "Marie, are you okay?" She kept her gaze fixed somewhere around my knees and nodded her head a few degrees. "Are you sure? If it's a bad time, I can come back later," I said, and then instantly wished I could take that back. I wanted this job, if only to beat out Gabrielle. If I left now, I doubted Marie would ever call me back.

Marie swallowed hard. "No," she said in her soft voice and shook her head so that her orange, fluffy hair trembled. "Come in," she said, and then she disappeared back through the small opening, slightly ducking her tall frame as she went in the door.

I pushed on the front door to open it wider, but it didn't shift even a centimeter. I frowned and poked my head inside. I saw stuff.

Piles and piles of stuff. I blinked, my heart sinking.

Things were stacked everywhere. It looked as if a waist-high tide of debris had flowed into the room and hardened in place, a sort of modern-day Pompeii. As I looked closer, the mounds of stuff resolved themselves into haphazard stacks of individual items. Some of the stacks were mostly clothes or shoes, but others were random masses: a tea kettle tilted precariously on a pile of boxes, a tennis racket jutted out of a bewildering stack of magazines, umbrellas, hangers, and . . . were those Star Wars figurines? I realized I was staring and that my mouth had literally fallen open. I shut it with a snap as Marie said, "Sorry about my untidiness. I just can't seem to . . ." Her voice trailed away and I really looked at her for the first time since I'd edged in the door. Tears sparkled in the corners of her eyes. She looked so vulnerable and miserable.

I realized how hard this was for her. I hoped my face hadn't betrayed my shock. It probably had. I wasn't prepared for anything like this, but I arranged a smile on my face and did the only thing I could think of—I fell back on the little spiel I'd given so many times. "Okay," I said briskly, "I have a few questions to go through with you that will help me figure out how I can help you." I forced myself not to look at the heaps lining the hall. "Is there somewhere we can sit down and talk?"

Marie nodded. Relief seemed to edge into her face. "Let's go in the kitchen," she said, and I followed her down the small trail that was just wide enough for one person. The narrow hall opened into what I guessed was the living room. Piles of objects ranged around the room, obliterating walls and furniture. A small space was carved out around a large-screen television and a loveseat. "Watch your step here," Marie advised. The trail we'd been walking ended as Marie stepped up about a foot onto a layer of junk that coated the entire living-room floor.

Marie walked sure-footed over the uneven stratum and I followed more slowly, arms outstretched to keep my balance. As I half walked, half climbed through the room, my gaze fixed on individual items—a black sock, a box of light bulbs, a stereo speaker, an antique doll with a china face, a dented Scooby-Doo lunch box.

Stuff and stuff and more stuff. It boggled my mind. Where did Marie get all this in the first place? I knew she and her husband, Cole, had moved here about a year ago. There was no way all this stuff had arrived here in moving boxes. They would have blown their weight allowance by thousands of pounds. But how could she have accumulated all this in under a year?

What had I gotten myself into here? I couldn't organize this. This went beyond clutter—this was hoarding, I thought, already trying to compose a graceful way to bow out of this job, because this wasn't an organizing job. This was a situation that required a mental health professional. Of course, I couldn't say it that baldly and I was here for a consultation. I should complete the consultation and then ease my way into stepping back from the job.

"Here we are," Marie said as she ducked down so she didn't hit her head on the kitchen door frame. A few things from the living room had spilled over into the kitchen, but for the most part, the kitchen floor was clear. I breathed a little easier, relieved to get out of the chaotic part of the house. The kitchen wasn't completely normal, though. The edges of the cabinets and the walls were lined with low stacks of canned goods, large containers of laundry soap, and economy-size packages of paper towels. It felt a bit like I'd wandered into a discount-store warehouse.

The counters were stacked with more of the same type of items—a twelve-pack of Dove soap perched on a case of Raisin Bran Crunch cereal and an extra large jar of salsa. The oven was free of debris as was a tiny corner of the countertop beside it, which was probably where Marie prepared her food. She led the way to the kitchen table, which had some empty space in front of two chairs. The rest of the table was covered with a mishmash of china teacups and tiny commemorative spoons. I sat down and gently moved spoons with the words, "Yellowstone" and "Twenty-second Olympiad" over to make room for my papers.

"So let's go through my questions," I said as Marie sat down gingerly. She looked wary, as if she might spring up and run out of the room at any moment, but as I worked my way through my standard questions in a matter-of-fact voice, she seemed to relax. Normally, I'd take a look at the areas a person wanted me to work on, but I decided to skip that step. I wasn't up to another climb through the living room and I didn't know if Marie could handle showing me more of her house. This was also the point when I'd talk with clients about different options, gauging how involved they wanted to be in the organizing. It always required some involvement, but some people simply wanted me to start them on the right track and then they would complete the job themselves, while others preferred to have me do the majority of the work. I mentally crossed those questions off my list. Working solo on Marie's house would be a never-ending job that I wasn't equipped or staffed to handle.

I put my pen down and licked my lips. "Marie, I'm going to be honest with you." Her face, which had been looking more comfortable, tightened. "Your . . . *situation* is more than I can manage—"

"I know," she jumped in. "I know it's a big job, but, please, I need your help." She leaned a gangly arm across the table and picked up a spoon. She focused on it as she spoke. "I know I need help. I've been seeing Dr. Harper—she's a psychologist—and she recommended I hire a professional organizer. She had a list of people, all from Atlanta, but they'd charge me to drive down here." She shrugged, her finger tracing the grooves on the spoon. "But it wasn't that, not the money. It was that I couldn't stand to have a stranger sneering over me, judging me. That's why I asked you. I knew you wouldn't do that. You might not understand why I do this, but you'd never make me feel like a . . . I don't know . . . a failure, I guess." She glanced at me quickly, then looked away, her eyes wide and scared.

"Marie, that's nice of you to say," I faltered. I wanted

to say no, I couldn't help her—because I really couldn't. This was way beyond my organizing abilities. "But I don't think I'm the person you need. I don't have the skills to help you."

She placed the spoon back in line very carefully. "I'm alphabetizing them, see? I'm going to get a cabinet and put it on the wall. Display them. I've been looking for a cabinet at yard sales, but haven't found one yet." I nodded, not quite sure what to say, but she didn't wait for a response from me. "I'm trying. I'm really trying." She waved her hand at the spoons and the teacups lined up so carefully. "Cole's deployed. He's been gone for five months and if he comes home and sees the house like this . . . well, I don't know what will happen. I was always messy, but it was never this bad . . . Anyway, I have to do something. I'm afraid if Cole comes home and sees all this . . . he'll . . . well, I don't know what he'll do. It was getting out of control when he left for the deployment . . . Back then, it was just the dining room that was packed with stuff. Since he left . . . things have overflowed. I didn't know where to put it all, so I just stacked it in the living room, but now that's overrun, too." Marie paused for a second, then said quietly, "Back before Cole left on the deployment, he told me he couldn't live like this," she glanced guiltily out to the living room, then quickly looked back at me. "Please, just talk to Dr. Harper before you say no. Would you do that?"

I looked at the debris creeping into the kitchen from the living room, then back at her tense face and her fingers clinched around the small spoon.

"Okay. I'll talk to her."

Tips for a Sane and Happy Holiday Season

Entertaining

Make entertaining and hosting houseguests easy. Give yourself permission to save time and cut your stress level. Use plastic plates and cups instead of the fine china, especially if you'll be the one doing all the washing up! You don't have to bake everything from scratch, even if that's the way it's always been done. Pick up a pie or rolls from the bakery so that you don't have to spend the whole holiday in the kitchen.

Chapter
Four

"I'm glad I had a cancellation and you were able to come over immediately," Dr. Harper said in a gravelly voice as she gestured toward a chair upholstered in pale green. Her silver-gray hair was parted in the middle and hung straight to her shoulders, framing a face that proclaimed she loved the sun. Her curtain of hair briefly swung forward, screening her deeply tanned and wrinkle-scored face as she took a seat.

"Yes, it was good timing for me, too." I'd called her office when I left Marie's house and driven straight there when she said she could see me. I had a follow-up appointment with another client at noon, but Dr. Harper's office was close enough that I could work in a stop. Her office, a frame bungalow, was located in a neighborhood that sprang up near the base during the building boom after World War II. Now, almost all the houses had been converted to business offices and discreet signs for attorneys, accountants, medical specialists, and dentists dotted the lawns.

I settled into the chair, which was positioned on a rug of cream-colored shag with enormous loops. A low, dark wood table with a pot of African violets separated the matching chairs. The chairs faced a large window, which looked out over a mammoth elm tree that dominated the backyard. Behind us, the room was decorated in various shades of white and green with splashes of purple and orange on the pillows and in the abstract artwork on the walls. There was a white desk facing two ivory slip-covered chairs, a few low, white filing cabinets, a round table with four chairs, and a soft green sofa with bright pillows scattered across it. The effect was cheerful and sterile at the same time.

"So, Marie." Dr. Harper put her palms together. She was wearing jeans and a stylish, loose, gray shirt with tight sleeves pushed up to her elbows, revealing tanned arms and age-spotted hands with short, unpolished nails. A long scarf patterned in yellow, gold, and royal blue touched the floor as she leaned forward in her chair. "I'm afraid I can't get into specifics . . ."

"I don't want you to. That's not why I called you."

"Why then?" She gazed at me, waiting. She almost succeeded in masking the undertone in her voice, but not quite. There was something there . . . impatience? Irritation? But her face was clear and blank. Maybe I was wrong.

I cleared my throat, suddenly feeling a bit like we'd somehow gotten off on the wrong foot. "Marie asked me to talk to you. I had an initial organizing consultation with her this morning and, to be honest, I don't think I'm the person to help her."

"Why is that? You're a professional organizer."

"Yes, but her problem isn't clutter."

"That's why I'm here. I'll help her with the deeper issues. She needs you to guide her in the actual cleaning out and organizing of her belongings."

Yes, there was something there, a faintly superior attitude that rankled me, just a bit. No wonder Marie hadn't wanted to use one of the organizers Dr. Harper recommended. I was feeling slightly disapproving vibes coming from her and I hadn't done anything but sit down in her office. "Have you seen her house?" I asked, a bit impatient myself.

"Yes. It will be quite a job. I'd figured you would be anxious to get the job organizing for Marie. It will be a tremendous amount of work. Many hours involved."

"That's not why I'm here. The amount of work—" I paused and looked up at the ceiling, "it would be massive, but I'm not concerned about that. Of course, new clients are essential to me as a business owner, and I always want to grow my business, but I don't think I'm the right person to help Marie. I'm not trained to handle this type of client. I deal with clutter, not mental health issues. It seems to me that Marie needs an expert in this type of thing. That's not me."

She narrowed her eyes and pursed her lips together, then sat back abruptly in her chair. "I think you're exactly the right person."

"What?" I was so sure she was going to say the opposite that I was caught off guard.

"Yes. You don't want the job and that's why you're precisely the best person for it."

"What are you saying?"

"You're concerned for Marie. I can see you understand how delicate her situation is—that is a very important part of dealing with a case like this. You won't go in like a drill sergeant and tell people to shape up and order them around. I think you have the sensitivity to deal with her carefully. She told me you're not a close friend, so I expect you'll be able to hold the line where it needs to be held and not give in to her when she needs a boundary."

A smile split her face, a real smile, deepening her wrinkles, and I felt as if she'd abruptly switched her opinion about me. "I'll confess, I had a friend I wanted Marie to use as her organizer. I've worked with this woman before and she's terrific. When Marie told me she'd asked you instead, I was wary. If I seemed a bit hostile, I apologize. I thought you'd want details on Marie's background. *Why* she's the way she is. People are morbidly curious about these things—look at all the television shows focused on hoarding and junk." She shook her head. "Sorry, I'll save my voyeur lecture for another day. The other essential thing about you is that you don't want to milk the project forever. That's critical for Marie. Some organizers would see working for Marie as a cash cow, a never-ending project. It is essential that you help Marie get started. Train her to thin her possessions, then classify and organize her belongings so that she can carry on without you. Set her on the path, give her the skills she needs, then let her continue on her own."

I tilted my head and said thoughtfully, "Teach a man to fish . . ."

"Or organize, in this case," Dr. Harper said, looking pleased. "That is the goal. Of course, it will be challenging and you may not feel like you're making any progress at the beginning."

"Where would you suggest we start?" Even as I asked the question, I thought, am I crazy to even be contemplating taking on this job?

"How do you approach your other organizing jobs?"

"We define goals, then break the large project up into smaller, achievable projects."

"Sounds excellent."

* * *

Thirty minutes later, I was back in my car cruising
through the gently rolling terrain toward my next appointment, wondering if I'd made the right decision.
After I left Dr. Harper's office, I'd called Marie and told
her I would work with her. We set a time for a meeting
at her house on Monday. She sounded more nervous
than relieved. Dr. Harper had made it sound so simple.
Just show her what to do. Start her on the path. I could
do that, but I was nervous about this job, too. It had
been a long time since I'd worried about how I would
do an organizing job. But focusing on the new job, even
if I felt uncertain about how it would turn out, was better than battling with Gabrielle for clients. I stifled a
sigh, thinking that I really had to do something to patch
things up with her. There was a chamber of commerce
meeting coming up and I knew Gabrielle would be
there. I wouldn't put it past her to do something nasty
and undercutting there. I called her and when her
voice mail came on, I left her a message, asking if she'd
meet me for a cup of coffee.

I switched my attention to the scenery since it was so
much more soothing to look at the gently undulating
land than to think about Gabrielle. I was on the state
highway that ran from the base to the southern side of
North Dawkins. The recent development boom was rel-
egated to the area between the base and the interstate
to the west. Big box stores and strip malls with sandwich
shops and evening karate classes had sprouted up and
filled the space between the older homes near the base
and the newer development farther west. This area, to
the south of North Dawkins proper, was mostly rural. I
cruised past the slender pine tree farms and occasional
driveways leading to houses set far back from the road.
Every once in a while, I'd pass a low brick wall announc-
ing a subdivision of new homes. These little pockets of

suburbia had been popping up all over the south side of North Dawkins until the economy took a nosedive. Development had stopped abruptly.

I came to the turn with a little grouping of businesses. Farther down the road were the elementary school, the post office, and the church we attended. Unlike the new strip malls that had grown up quickly near the interstate, this patch of development had been here for years and years. The hardware store was a permanent fixture in the community. You could still buy nails by the pound or just drink a cup of coffee and sit in the rocking chairs positioned under the deer heads mounted on the walls. Unlike the hardware store, which I didn't think had changed since it opened in 1932, Crooner's flea market across the street had a new look. Instead of forlorn pieces of beat-up—or possibly antique—furniture sitting outside in sun and rain as the grass grew up between them, there was now a new sweep of gravel in front of the two freshly painted clapboard bungalows. Curly font on the new sign out front read, PEACHTREE ANTIQUES. CROONER NAVAN, PROPRIETOR.

I drove past the hardware and antique stores, then turned into a strip mall that had seen businesses come and go for as long as the post office and hardware store had been in existence. Currently, a gas station, a dress shop, and a pack-and-mail store were located in this small strip mall. A fitness center, Fit Lifestyle, was located in a large, dark blue steel building beside the strip mall. I swung into a parking lot and answered my ringing phone as I got out of the car. It was Abby calling to tell me she didn't have to stay late after school and she could bring the kids home. She blew out a sigh and said, "The more I think about the break-in, the more it freaks me out. Someone really is targeting military families."

I paused with my hand on the glass entrance door. "But it sounds like the break-in at your house was different than the previous break-ins—it didn't fit the pattern. The one at your house was messier, clumsier than the others, with all that broken glass and noise. All the other break-ins were at homes where the spouse was deployed, or like with Amy, out of town."

"That's all true, but it doesn't make me feel better. I'm still glad you twisted my arm and made me stay with you. Okay, so enough about that scary subject. How's your day going?"

"I think I'm insane. I just agreed to organize—" I stopped abruptly. "I can't say anything else." I couldn't talk about the state of Marie's house. Clients let me see things—clutter, messes, and disorganization—that they normally hid. I'd never talked about the state of clients' projects before and I wasn't about to start now. The overwhelming scale of work needed at Marie's house had thrown me out of my normal reticence and I'd almost slipped up and revealed more than I should to Abby.

"Organizer–client privilege?" Abby asked with a note of laughter.

"Something like that." I didn't think I'd be able to keep the fact that Marie was my client completely quiet, but for now I wouldn't say anything. Later, I'd have to come up with some vague response to why I was spending so long working with Marie, but I'd figure that out when the time came. "I have to go anyway," I said as I checked my watch. I saw it was nearly twelve o'clock. "I have a follow-up appointment with Paige MacIntyre at noon."

"Ah—the controversial belly dancing queen. Tell her I said hello. I still can't believe people were so upset with her. Anyway, I have to run. Lunchroom duty."

I hung up and stepped inside Fit Lifestyle.

Paige had opened the fitness center six months ago with the goal of offering a variety of classes ranging from the typical—gymnastics for kids, yoga, spinning, weight training—to the more innovative—belly dance, Hula-Hoop, and a triathlete training camp. Thinking the best way to promote her new business was to emphasize the unusual classes, Paige had touted the belly dancing and Hula-Hoop classes, even getting a quarter page write-up in the local newspaper complete with a picture and the headline "Dancing Queen."

There had been an initial pushback from the community, which consisted mostly of the question, *What kind of place is this?* A rumor of pole dancing lessons didn't help and it wasn't until Paige opened the fitness center for free for a week that the rumors vanished and people began to understand that Paige wasn't opening a seedy dance club that would make property values plummet. After walking on the treadmills, climbing the StairMasters, and watching a few kids' gymnastics classes, everyone calmed down and, paradoxically, started bragging about their "cool" fitness center. I'd heard the rumors and the bragging in the carpool line at the school and was still amazed at the way public opinion could swing.

A coed in a Georgia Tech sweatshirt stood behind a long, chest-high counter that ran along one side of the room. It was draped with gold tinsel, oversized bells, and sprigs of plastic holly. A menorah perched on the end of the counter. I was glad to see that colorful flyers were displayed in slots along the wall near a small flat-screen monitor that scrolled through photos of smiling, sweaty participants along with advertisements for upcoming classes. The setup had been one of my suggestions to get all the stacks of class lists off the counter. Seeing the finished setup gave me a boost.

"Hey, Miz Ellie," the coed said, recognizing me from my many visits during the previous months. I dredged my memory bank for her name—remembering names is not a strong suit of mine—and after a few beats came up with it. "Hi, Courtney. I'm here to see Paige."

"She said for you to go on back to her office when you get here. She's finishing up a class and will be there in a minute."

"Thanks." I passed the counter and walked into the large, high-ceilinged room that was the heart of the fitness center. Uneven bars, a balance beam, and a vault ranged around a spongy blue gymnastics floor, taking up most of the echoing space. Mirrored workout rooms lined one side of the building. A group of people with flushed faces was meandering out of one of the rooms, sipping from water bottles and chatting as they made their way to the locker rooms. Paige was in the lead and moving much faster than anyone in the group. She had a bin of yoga bands tucked under one arm and a row of Hula-Hoops clattering in the crook of her other elbow. A few resistance bands were looped around her neck like oversized stethoscopes. "Ellie," she boomed as she loped across the large space, her Dorothy Hamill haircut fluttering. "Good to see you."

Paige was built like a tank—solid, with angular shoulders and a core of steel. Despite her size and impressive resume—she'd been a championship volleyball setter in college and had almost made the Olympic track and field team—she wasn't imposing. It was just the opposite. She was bubbly and energetic.

"Come on back," she said, catapulting to the back corner of the building. "Sorry I'm late. Don't know what happened. That last class just flew by. We didn't even get to do the whole ab sequence."

"You're not late. It's just now noon," I assured her,

but Paige wasn't listening. She was already on to a new topic. She moved at practically the speed of sound, which had been a challenge when I'd worked with her. Unlike some of my clients who I had to motivate and cajole, I could hardly keep up with Paige.

"So is this like those make-over shows," she said, "where they check in after a few months to see if the people are still organized or if they've gone to pot again on their own?"

"No, nothing like that at all," I assured her.

"Don't sound so worried," she said as she paused at a row of shelves and slid the bin of yoga bands into a labeled slot and dropped the Hula-Hoops and the resistance bands onto nearby hooks mounted on the walls. "This staging area is a lifesaver," she said, patting the bins as she darted by them. "Love 'em! Come on in," she said, pushing the door to her office wide. She grabbed a zippered, gray knit jacket off the back of her chair and pulled it on over her red workout top and black yoga pants. She dropped into her swivel chair and waved her hands around the room. "See . . . everything is where it should be." She swept her hand over her clean desk like a game show hostess. "Impressive, isn't it, compared to how you found things?"

"Yes, wonderful. I just wanted to check with you to make sure you were happy with the job I did. Have you had any problems . . . any issues that have come up since we finished?"

"Are you kidding? You were a star. Everything is fine."

"Great. That's really great," I said, sitting back in the chair. After I'd lost Stephanie to Gabrielle, I'd decided some damage control—damage prevention?—was in order. I'd been checking in with established clients to make sure all was well.

"Although there is one thing . . . ," Paige said, and I sat forward.

"Yes, whatever you need. I can work you into my schedule this week, if you need it."

Paige handed me a neon green flyer with a class list. "You should join." She said it with a smile and quickly added, "I know you already said no, but I want you to take that flyer. I know you have your neighborhood stroller workout group. But you never know . . . it's getting cold and you might like to work out indoors. Meet a few new people. Network. You know, expand your business while toning your body. I'd give you a plug after class. There's a business card stapled to the back for some free classes. Come try it out."

"Always persistent, aren't you? Okay, I'll try to work it in, but it may not be till after Christmas."

"You and everyone else," she said, standing up. "January is going to be packed around here."

My phone buzzed. I saw it was Gabrielle. "I'd better take this," I said.

Paige waved her hand. "Go ahead. Use my office, if you want. It's time for Tiny Tots Tumbling, my most challenging class. Keeping the attention of three-year-olds is the ultimate workout, let me tell you. I'll look for you in class," she called as she left.

Even with her languid southern accent, Gabrielle managed to make her voice curt as she said, "I got your message. I don't have time to stop for a cup of coffee with you. My day is completely scheduled."

"Well, maybe another day. I really think it would benefit us both to work some things out. We each want to present a professional image and make good impressions on clients," I said.

A noisy sigh came over the line. "I do that. You're the one accusing me of stealing clients."

Because you did. I bit back the quick retort. "Look, it's not going to do us any good to rehash that argument. I'd like to find some common ground. How about tomorrow?"

"No, I don't have any free time then."

"What about this weekend?"

"You really are a ballbreaker, aren't you? Who would have thought it? Okay," she said, in a tone of voice that indicated she'd rather have a root canal. "I am zipping over to Jean's house to pick up some organizing materials. She's close to your house. You can meet me there. Do you know where Jean's house is? I can't stay for more than ten minutes. We can talk while I load my car."

This wasn't the sort of conversation that I wanted to have standing in the street, but I supposed it would be better than not meeting. "Fine. Yes, I know where she lives. I'll be there."

Chapter
Five

Jean lived in Shadow Ridge, a newer subdivision located down the road from the fitness center. I drove through the quiet neighborhood with empty driveways and open lawns speckled with deflated Frosty and Santa decorations. The icicle lights and multiple extension cords festooning the houses looked a little garish in the sharp sunlight. I parked in front of Jean's brick house at the end of a cul-de-sac. A flat-fronted, boxy two-story with four windows on each side of the front door, it had small wreaths with red bows on each window. Garland twisted around the two pillars framing the front porch and a wreath of poinsettias and magnolias decorated the front door. The driveway leading to the three-car garage was on the right-hand side of the house. The house sat at an angle on a small rise, so that the driveway sloped up and around, almost hiding the garage from the street, but I could see one of the garage doors was open and a small, black SUV was visible inside. It must be the one I'd seen Gabrielle driving with the magnetic signs attached to both sides that proclaimed, GET ORGANIZED WITH GABRIELLE, along with her picture.

Leaving everything in the minivan except my keys, I climbed the steep incline of the driveway, feeling a little awkward since neither Jean nor her husband, Simon, had invited me over. Jean might be home, but I had no idea about Simon. I knew he volunteered at the Helping Hands charity, but I didn't know how much of his time it took up. He might be golfing on the neighborhood course.

"Gabrielle? Jean?" I called as I stepped into the sudden darkness of the garage and pushed my sunglasses up on my head. No answer. It took a second for my eyes to adjust. The bay beside the black SUV was empty. Outside, the wind was picking up. It whistled around the corner of the house and sent some dry leaves skittering, but inside the garage it was toasty warm. "Gabrielle?" I called again into the silence, scanning the workbench with tools hanging neatly on a corkboard above it. Stacks of boxes ranged along one wall. There was a fluorescent light on in the third bay of the garage and a space heater, humming away, keeping the garage toasty warm. The third bay was filled with tables and boxes. It must be for Jean's online auction business, I realized, when I saw the stacks of flattened boxes and jumbo tape dispensers. I always love to see how other people organize their space and this looked like a great setup.

I stepped closer and saw three tables that formed a U shape. On the farthest side away from me, a small, white photo box was positioned next to a lamp for taking pictures. There was a laptop and a printer, too. Shelves stacked with all sorts of things, from books to toys to clothes and even kitchen utensils, lined the wall above a table. The next table was arranged with packing materials, boxes, and bubble wrap. There was even a clear plastic trash bag filled with foam peanuts suspended directly over the table. A large clamp held the bottom closed. Three boxes sealed with packing tape had printed address labels attached and stood on the table closest to me, ready to be shipped.

I wondered if Jean had done this herself or if Gabrielle had organized it for her. If Gabrielle had done it, then she certainly was a good organizer. Everything was neat and easily within reach. I stepped forward and kicked something—a ball—that I hadn't noticed. It bounced heavily across the floor, hit a plastic bin under one of the tables in Jean's work area, ricocheted back to me, and rolled to a stop by my toe.

I paused. I realized two things almost at once. First, it wasn't a ball. It was the oversized diamond-shaped Lucite paperweight that had been the white elephant gift I'd won and, second, it had something on the pointy end, something dark that was leaving a geometric pattern across the floor and a spot on my boot. I leaned down, touched the tip of my boot.

I rubbed my thumb across my finger, smearing the liquid. I sniffed my fingers and caught the unmistakable coppery smell. It was . . . blood. I stepped back quickly, instinctively heading for the rectangular square of sunlight at the garage's entrance. As I scurried backward, I saw a hand and part of a forearm extended on the floor. I blinked. The creamy pale skin looked so out of place on the concrete floor. Maybe Jean was auctioning off a mannequin?

But it looked so real. The plastic bins under the worktables had blocked my view of it before, but now it was visible, since I'd shifted position. Hesitantly, I walked forward, not sure why I was moving so slowly. I wanted to get out of the garage, but if it wasn't a mannequin . . . if Gabrielle had slipped and fallen . . . maybe an accident . . . if she needed help . . .

I skipped over the dark smears on the concrete and

moved around a box on the floor. It held the white elephant gifts—I caught sight of the ugly picture frame,
the bat box, and the sewing machine. I rounded the
end of the tables and saw a woman lying face down, one
arm extended out from her body. Dark hair splayed
across her shoulders and the floor in an almost perfect
circle as if she'd struck the ground and hadn't moved. I
sucked in a gulp of air and backed away when I saw the
bloody concave wound in the back of her skull.

I clamped my hand across my mouth. "Oh my God,"
I whispered against my fingers. It was Gabrielle. Her
face might be turned away, but I recognized the loose,
dark hair and fitted, boiled wool jacket with matching
red skirt. Gabrielle had worn it to the last chamber of
commerce meeting. She'd made every head turn when
she walked in the room that day. This was no accident
and there was nothing I could do to help. At least, I didn't
think there was anything I could do. I forced myself to
crouch down over her extended arm and feel for a pulse.
There was not a flutter of movement. I stood up quickly
and backed away, flexing my hands open and closed as
I took deep breaths, my thoughts skittering from one
direction to another. How horrible for Gabrielle. I hadn't
liked her, but this . . . this was terrible.

Oh God, I was going to have to tell Jean. Was she
even home? No, call nine-one-one first, then find—

A voice sounded behind me. "Ellie! There you are.
Let's make this quick."

I jerked around and watched a dark figure come into
the garage from the brightness outside. The glare of
the sunlight backlit the woman and my heart raced
even faster. As she walked into the garage, the fluorescent light evened out the shadows and I saw it was
Gabrielle in a thick sweatshirt, designer jeans, and three-
inch-heeled boots. Stunned, I couldn't speak for a mo-

ment and gaped at her. "But you're . . . How . . . ?" Then suddenly my brain snapped into gear. I looked at the black SUV in the garage and saw that it didn't have advertising signs on the sides and it was a different style—sleeker—than the one I'd seen Gabrielle drive, so it must belong to Jean and Simon. It wasn't Gabrielle who'd been in the garage. She'd just arrived. The dead woman was Jean. It had to be. I hadn't looked at her face. I'd only assumed from the clothes and her dark hair.

I surged forward. "No. Don't come any closer. We've got to go outside." I sped toward her, my hands up like a cop stopping traffic.

"Ellie!" she said sharply, dodging past me. "What is wrong with you? I've only got a few minutes and I need to get my supplies and get on the road. Our little chat will have to wait—"

"Gabrielle, don't go over there." I reached out and grabbed her arm with my left hand, but she twisted away and walked through the trail of blood, smearing it without noticing as she moved toward Jean's work area. "Wait!" I called, going after her. "It's Jean—"

"Really, Ellie!" she said, exasperated. "You've got a lot of nerve, ordering me around—," she broke off as she rounded the tables. In seconds, her face shifted from bafflement to dawning horror. She dropped to her knees and pulled on Jean's shoulder, rolling her over.

The way the body moved, slowly, heavily at first, and then slapped to the concrete with a dull thud turned my stomach. "I'm calling nine-one-one," I said, backing away. With one arm under Jean's neck and shoulders, Gabrielle pulled Jean's head into her lap and leaned low over her face, murmuring to her as she wiped the hair back from her forehead. She kept repeating, "Hang on. Hang on, Jeannie. Hang on."

I had to scurry outside and get my phone from my purse, which I'd left in the van, then I had to look at the number on the mailbox so I could give the dispatcher the correct address. That was when my legs started to shake. I made my way back up the driveway, feeling as if I'd run a marathon. There was nothing I could do to help Jean at this point, so I collapsed onto the sidewalk to wait for the ambulance.

Chapter
Six

I was standing beside the empty ambulance nearly an hour later when Gabrielle emerged from the garage, her jeans splattered with a dark stain. The little cul-de-sac was full of official cars and people milling about. Someone had called Simon and he'd arrived shortly after the ambulance. He'd flung his car into the drive-way with a squeal of brakes and run into the garage, not even bothering to close the car door. I hadn't seen him since, but assumed he was in the house somewhere.

A few neighbors were looking on from down the street and talking to a reporter from the *North Dawkins Standard*. I knew he was a reporter because he'd shouted at me, asking if I'd tell him what had happened. I'd shaken my head and moved away. After I'd called nine-one-one, I'd made two more calls. I'd phoned Abby first, giving her the barest details of what had happened so she'd know why I wasn't at home when school let out, then I'd called Mitch. He'd been as shocked as Abby had been and said he was leaving work right away. I felt steadier after talking to him.

There were times when his calm, measured attitude drove me crazy, but today it was just what I needed.

I'd been interviewed by the responding officer from the sheriff's department—Shadow Ridge wasn't within the city limits of North Dawkins. An empty gurney with a body bag waited as the officials investigated. The shakiness I'd felt as I'd waited for the ambulance had subsided. My hands weren't trembling anymore and my heartbeat had returned to normal, but I still felt off kilter.

"There she is." Gabrielle's voice, angry and taut, cut across the low, professional tones of the people moving around the cul-de-sac. "Her. She's the one who was here."

I realized with a start that she was pointing at me.

Gabrielle marched down the driveway to me. A young man in a navy blue jacket and chinos quickly followed her, catching up to her as she arrived at my side.

"Her," she said again, jabbing her finger at me. "She was in there. Her name is Ellie Avery and—"

"I know who she is," he said.

"Hello, Detective Waraday," I said. I'd met Detective Dave Waraday a few years ago when I got involved in a search for a local woman, Jodi Lockworth, who'd gone missing. Waraday hadn't been happy I was involved in that case and that same displeased frown that I'd seen so often was again on his baby face. He was one of those people who was going to look like he was in his twenties long after he'd turned the corner of the big three-o. His straight, brown hair was still dark and thick, his face was still unlined, and he had the fresh-scrubbed quality of the all-American star quarterback. But there was something in his face that was different . . . a weariness? Or maybe it was wariness. It had to be hard to deal with murder day after day. I'd recently seen his photo in the paper. He and Colleen, a high school science teacher I'd met while helping with the search for Jodi, were engaged. Should I congratulate him on his engagement? No, this was definitely not the time, I decided.

"Mrs. Avery," he said. "And you're here because . . ."

"I found her. I found Jean."

Gabrielle surged toward me. "No, you didn't find her. You did that to her—you killed her." Waraday quickly stepped between us and maneuvered Gabrielle back a few steps.

I was so shocked I could only stare at her and gape.

"Ms. Matheson," Waraday said, "you need to wait inside with Mr. Williams."

"She was in there. That was her white elephant gift— the diamond paperweight was hers—and look at her shoes! There's blood on them—"

"Ms. Matheson!" he said, his voice so commanding that I jumped a little in surprise. "You have to go inside." When she didn't budge, he forcibly turned her around and, holding her upper arm, walked her toward the house as she struggled to free herself. He signaled for another officer, who came over and escorted Gabrielle to the front door, where she shot a dark glance at me.

Waraday returned, adjusting the navy jacket with the words *Dawkins County Criminal Investigation Division* stitched on it. He shot a glance at my boots. "Come with me," he said shortly, and escorted me away from the stares of the people in the cul-de-sac. I followed him up the incline of the driveway. Instead of going into the garage, he kept walking into the unfenced backyard. A large swath of yellow grass ran right up to a thick line of bare trees. Faded brown and golden leaves carpeted the ground under the trees. The house was situated deep in the Shadow Ridge development and there was nothing around it except for its two neighbors on the cul-de-sac.

The stretch of forest extended unbroken in all directions—except for about a quarter of a mile to the right, where I could faintly see the outlines of a line of houses, another development butting up against this one. We were close enough between the Williams' house and the house next door that we were sheltered from the wind, which had started up again and was pulling at my coat and hair.

Waraday pulled out a notebook and very formally took down my name and address. As I gave the information, I twisted my boot. There was a large, dark splotch on one toe. Waraday asked, "How well did you know Mrs. Williams?"

It took me a second to process his use of Jean's last name. "Not that well. We were more acquaintances than friends. I saw her at spouse club activities and would talk with her there, but we've never met outside of the spouse club. Her son is older—in college. I have more interactions with the women who have younger kids." I realized I was babbling away, probably telling him more than he wanted or needed to know.

"Did Mrs. Williams have any enemies? Anyone who'd want to hurt her?"

"No," I said quickly. The idea was preposterous. Who would want to hurt Jean? "No, I don't think so. She wasn't the type of person who generated . . . animosity." Unlike her sister, I thought, but kept that to myself. "Jean was nice. That's such a bland word, but she was always pleasant, always smiling. She liked to bargain shop. She turned that into a home business. That's about all I know about her. And I guess she was close to her sister, although they have very different personalities, she and Gabrielle. Gabrielle moved here after her divorce so she could be near Jean." I didn't want to talk about Gabrielle, so I quickly added, "I know she liked to paint, too. Oil paint. She was taking classes. She mentioned that once at a spouse coffee."

"When was the last time you saw her?"

"Last night at the spouse Christmas party. We talked for a few minutes after the gift exchange."

"About what?"

"Um . . . about Helping Hands. Simon, her husband, is on the board. The squadron is doing a fundraiser for Helping Hands, a basket auction. She probably set that up."

"Did she seem different in any way? Stressed or worried or anything unusual?"

"No, she acted like she always did—friendly and pleasant. If something was wrong, I didn't notice, but, again, I don't—didn't—know her that well. You'd have to ask someone closer to her, like Gabrielle or Hannah."

"Hannah?" Waraday raised his eyebrows, pen poised.

"Hannah Jenkins, the squadron commander's wife. She seemed to know Jean better than I did."

Waraday's attention shifted from his notebook to my face with an intense searching look. "Why are you here at the Williams' house today?"

"Gabrielle asked me to meet her here."

"Why here?"

"She said her schedule was packed and she didn't have much time, but we could meet here for a few minutes because she had to pick something up. She said something about storing things here at Jean's house. Some organizing stuff."

"Gabrielle Matheson is a professional organizer?" Waraday asked.

"Yes," I said, my heart sinking. This was going to be bad. There was no way I could avoid or gloss over our professional competition and the argument we'd had. Waraday was thorough. He'd find out.

"And why were you meeting?" he asked. There was a clatter as an EMT pushed the empty gurney up the driveway.

I swallowed, pushing down a flashing memory of how Jean had looked when I found her. It wouldn't do any good to hide anything. Jean's family deserved to know what had happened and I wasn't going to waste Waraday's time beating around the bush. "Gabrielle and I had an argument last night at the squadron spouse Christmas party. She's stealing my established clients—undercutting what I charge and poaching new clients. She was trying to—" I broke off, realizing I sounded like my kids when they try to justify themselves after they've broken a rule. "Never mind what we argued about. What's important is that we did argue and later I wanted to patch things up, so I called her today and asked if she'd meet me. She told me to come here."

Waraday still hadn't written anything in his notebook, but he was watching me carefully and I knew he was taking it all in. "Did anyone else witness this argument?"

"The whole squadron spouse club."

"I see. Was Mrs. Williams involved in it?"

"No," I shook my head. "Jean wasn't anywhere near us. It was just between Gabrielle and me."

"So you argued over professional issues yesterday. You called today and set the appointment," he summarized, and I nodded. "What time did you arrive?"

"It was probably about twelve-fifteen or twelve-twenty or so. I'd just met with Paige at Fit Lifestyle and came directly here. It only takes a minute or two to get here." I described how the garage had been open and that I'd assumed the SUV inside belonged to Gabrielle.

Waraday jotted something down, then asked, "So you thought Ms. Gabrielle Matheson was in the garage?"

"Yes, I didn't notice that the SUV didn't have the advertising signs on it and once I was in the garage, I saw Jean's setup for her business and was looking at that." I shrugged. "It's a fantastic setup, so I wanted a closer look. I figured Gabrielle was inside and I would knock on the door to the house or call her on my cell phone after I had a quick peek at Jean's work area. But then I kicked something—the diamond-shaped paperweight— and I saw it had . . . something on the pointy end. I wasn't sure what. The lighting was a bit weird in there, all the sunlight from the one open garage door, but the rest of the garage wasn't brightly lit except for Jean's work area. I was in the shadowy part in the middle.

"Anyway, I didn't realize it was blood right away. I touched my boot and then after I sniffed it, I knew. That's when I saw her hand. That was all I could see, an outstretched arm on the ground." I stretched my arm out to illustrate. "The rest of her body was behind some plastic bins. I couldn't see it. I went over to see if she was okay. I thought she'd fallen . . . but she hadn't. I checked her wrist for a pulse, but with her head . . ." I stopped and swallowed. "Anyway, Gabrielle came in— scared me to death because I thought it was Gabrielle on the floor—but then I figured it out, that it was Jean who was dead. I tried to keep Gabrielle from seeing Jean, but she shook me off. That's when I called nine-one-one."

I paused, hoping I'd given a fairly coherent account. He'd let me run on, not interrupting me, only occasionally scribbling a note. He asked, "The paperweight, it was yours?"

"Well, I won it at the party. It was one of those gift exchange things. I didn't want it, so I gave it to Jean. Lots of people gave their gifts to her after the party was over so she could try and resell them through her business. That's what she does—*did*, I mean—resell items at on-line auctions."

"I see," Waraday said.

At his flat tone and blank face, my stomach twisted. He hadn't written off Gabrielle's accusation, I could see that in the speculative look he was giving me. Jean's blood was on my shoes, my fingerprints were on the paperweight that killed her. Suddenly, I was afraid. Maybe I shouldn't have told him everything. What if . . . what if he thought I did it? No, it was all circumstantial . . . wasn't it? My palms felt slick and, despite the chilly breeze whipping through the air, I felt overheated.

"Lots of people have those paperweights," I said quickly. "Our insurance agent gave them away a few years ago, so I'm sure they're all over North Dawkins. We actually had one, but I thought it was too dangerous to have around the kids. I was afraid they'd put some-one's eye out . . ." I trailed off abruptly.

"So the paperweight will have your prints on it?"

"Yes, I suppose so. I held it at the party, after all."

Waraday stared at me for a long moment, then his gaze dropped to my feet. "I'm going to need those boots."

I had to drive home in my socks. One of the EMTs took pity on me and gave me a set of paper booties to wear over my socks, but my feet were still freezing by the time Waraday told me I could go. I hadn't lingered. I pulled into our garage and parked beside Mitch's car, my heart fluttering in near panic as I thought about what I'd told Waraday and how the situation must look to him.

I'd called Mitch, when Waraday released me, and told him I was on my way home. He'd beaten me here, but there was no sign of Abby or the kids.

Mitch met me at the door and I went into his arms, leaning against his solid, comforting presence. "The kids and Abby should be here any minute," I said into his shoulder as Rex wiggled around, bumping into my legs.

"Abby's taking them for ice cream after school. What happened to your shoes?"

"Waraday took them. They're evidence," I said, frustrated with myself. I burrowed into Mitch's shoulder. "I'm so stupid. Why did I have to go on and on and on?"

Mitch rubbed his chin across my hair. "What did you go on about?"

"Everything!" I leaned back in his arms. "I blabbed away and now Waraday thinks I killed Jean."

"Why?"

I broke out of the embrace and paced into the kitchen, giving Rex a routine rub on his head. He trotted off, his welcoming duty seen to. I stripped off the hospital booties and stuffed them in the trash. "Because Gabrielle accused me of killing Jean."

I could tell I'd stunned him into silence. Mitch wasn't the type of person to speak quickly, without thinking. He usually considered before he spoke, but right now he was speechless. He walked slowly to the kitchen, crossed his arms, and leaned against the door frame.

"I happened to kick what was obviously the murder weapon so there's blood on my boots—her blood. And my fingerprints are going to be on the diamond that killed her." I was striding around the island as I talked.

"Two questions," Mitch said, his tone calm, his face frowning. I caught sight of my dim reflection in the microwave. My hair, which had been tossed by the wind, was a chaotic mess and my eyes were wide with fear. I ran my fingers through my hair, combing it behind my ears, and took a deep breath as Mitch asked, "One, you're sure it wasn't an accident?"

"Yes, there's no question. It was murder. Someone bashed in the back of her skull," I said, pacing to the end of the island and back again. "With a diamond-shaped paperweight, like the one we used to have—do you remember it?"

He nodded. "Ah, that was my second question."

"What?" I paused in my circuit of the island. "Oh. Right. I see. How could a diamond kill someone? It can if it's a heavy Lucite paperweight about three inches high with a sharp point." I stopped pacing and looked back at him. "It was horrible, Mitch. Whoever did that to her . . . I can't imagine . . ."

I trailed off, gripping the back of one of the bar stools to steady myself as the mental image of Jean's body flashed into my mind again. I felt breathless and light-headed. Mitch unfolded himself from his leaning pose and came over to me. "Sit down," he said, pulling out the bar stool and guiding me into it. "Your hands are freezing and you're shaking. You need food."

He put hot water on to boil, then rummaged around in the refrigerator. I was generally the food person in our house. I cooked and Mitch cleaned up, but I suddenly felt so drained I didn't think I could move. Mitch assembled a peanut butter and jelly sandwich for me, ordered me to eat it, then set a steaming mug of hot cocoa beside my plate.

I didn't think I could eat anything, but a whiff of the chocolaty aroma wafted up and I reconsidered. I devoured the sandwich and sipped the cocoa as fast as I could. Mitch watched me eat, sipping from his own mug. I felt better after I ate, more normal and grounded.

I realized my toes were freezing so I went to the bedroom, slipped on my thick house shoes, and returned to the kitchen.

"Thanks."

Mitch raised his mug. "Just give my girl some chocolate and she's fine."

I had to smile as I hopped back up on the bar stool. "That is usually true." My good humor faded as quickly as it came. "Except this time, I don't think chocolate is going to fix everything."

I went back to the beginning and told Mitch everything that had happened, winding up with Waraday's confiscation of my boots. "That's when he told me he needed my shoes. To test the blood, I assume. Then I was fingerprinted and my hands were photographed." I took another sip of the cocoa to ward off the chill that was again creeping through me. "They took a sample of the blood that had dried on my finger, too." I tilted my mug, watching as the dregs of my hot chocolate puddled on one side. "This is really bad, Mitch. I got the feeling that the crime scene people wanted to take my clothes, too—something about blood spatter—but there wasn't anything on them so Waraday told them to leave it and go back to processing the garage."

Mitch wiped his hands down over his mouth. "You just told them all this . . . everything?"

"Well, yes," I said, shifting on the bar stool. I leaned forward, bracing my arms on the countertop of the kitchen island. "It seemed like a good idea to tell Waraday everything. You know he would have found out about the argument that Gabrielle and I had, anyway. Honesty is the best policy and all that."

"Your argument with Gabrielle doesn't give you a motive to murder Jean. It's unrelated," Mitch pointed out, logically.

"Yes, but patching up the argument with Gabrielle was the reason I was there. I'm not going to just drop by Jean's house in the middle of the day."

Mitch nodded, his gaze fixed out the window on the bare tree branches dancing in the breeze. "You don't have a motive, though. You didn't have a reason to kill Jean."

"Why would anyone want to kill her? She was such a sweet person. I don't understand it." I twisted my mug around by the handle. "But I could tell that Waraday viewed me as more than a coincidental bystander who happened to find her."

"Why did you think that?" Mitch asked, watching me over the rim of his mug.

"He didn't like it when I got involved in the search for Jodi or that mess with Colonel Pershall. He thought it was odd that I was interested in those cases. And now to find me at the scene of a murder with blood on my boot and hands . . ." I rubbed my forehead. "I thought if I explained it—the blood and fingerprints—he'd understand. It *is* a reasonable explanation, and it's the truth. It's exactly what happened, but that didn't seem to matter." I shrugged. "It was like driving in that ice storm I got caught in when we lived in Washington State. I was moving along the road just fine and then before I realized what happened, I was sliding diagonally, pumping the brakes, and turning the wheel, but it did absolutely nothing." Fortunately, I'd drifted into a huge snow bank at such a low speed that no damage was done that time, but now . . . I had that same out-of-control feeling and was worried the outcome wouldn't be so harmless.

Mitch put his mug down with a click. "I'm going to call Legal, see if the JAG can recommend an attorney in North Dawkins."

Tips for a Sane and Happy Holiday Season

Gift Wrap

To take the hassle out of gift wrapping, create a gift wrapping storage container with everything you need. A narrow, long plastic bin works well. Place wrapping paper in the bin and reserve space for bows, ribbon, gift tags, tape, and scissors. Gallon-size, zippered, plastic bags are great for storing these smaller items if you don't want to purchase additional plastic containers. Flatten gift bags and tissue paper and store on top of wrapping paper, or if you have a large number of gift bags, create a separate bin for bags and tissue paper.

Chapter
Seven

Friday

It had been easier to pretend that nothing was wrong after Abby and the kids arrived home and I was caught up in the normal weeknight chaos of math problems, spelling words, and cooking dinner, but I moved through the routine actions with the weight of worry pressing down on me. I couldn't quite put out of my mind the awful way Jean had died and I couldn't keep from jumping every time Rex barked as a car surged down our street or a car door slammed. Mitch, Abby, and I had rehashed everything last night after the kids had gone to bed, as we waited for a call from Mitch's lawyer friend, the JAG, which was military lingo for Judge Advocate General. They were the military lawyers who worked at the base. But the call didn't come and we'd all eventually gone to bed. I hadn't slept much.

The next morning, I was in the middle of another crazy rush to get everyone dressed, fed, and draped with appropriate backpacks and lunch boxes when the phone rang. I stepped around Abby, who was zipping

Nathan into his coat, and reached for the phone. Rex pranced, tongue lolling out one side of his mouth, through the kitchen with Charlie trailing alongside of him, halfheartedly trying to jump on his back. I waited for them to clear my path. How could two more people—one of them child-size—make the house seem so much more crowded?

"You made the news," Nadia said as soon as I answered.

"No." My heart plummeted as I remembered the reporter trying to interview me. "Well, maybe a lot of people won't see it—newspapers are dying, right?"

"Not the paper. You're on the local television news."

Livvy tugged at my sleeve. "We're going, Mom."

"What? Hold on, Nadia," I said, and leaned down to give Livvy a hug and Nathan a quick kiss on his head.

"Boys, you're in the back," Abby shouted as she heaved her tote bag on her shoulder and the kids disappeared through the door to the garage.

"Nadia says it's on the news." I rushed into the living room and dug in the couch cushions for the remote. No one ever put it back in its place in the ornamental box on the coffee table. "Hold on," I said, flipping throw pillows over. Just because one person in a family is organized doesn't mean everyone will be.

"*You're* on the news," Nadia corrected in my ear. "We're watching it in the teachers' lounge. "They had a teaser before the commercial and your picture was definitely on camera. I thought you'd want to know. I've got to go—I have a conference in five minutes, but I want all the details later," she said before hanging up.

Finally, I found the remote and clicked to the news channel. Abby walked over, her hand hooked into the straps of her tote bag, keys jangling as she walked.

"Jean Renee Williams was found dead early yesterday

afternoon in the Shadow Ridge subdivision," a female voice said as a wide shot of Jean's cul-de-sac filled the screen. The shot narrowed and focused on the open garage door, then panned to the driveway where I stood talking to Detective Waraday. My face was pale and with the wind flinging my hair around until it practically stood on end, I looked like I'd been Livvy's test subject in her static electricity show-and-tell project. "A sheriff's department spokesman said the body was discovered around noon yesterday. Cause of death has not been released and investigators wouldn't speculate on whether or not the killing is linked to the recent rash of break-ins around the county. This North Dawkins woman, Ellie Avery, is believed to be a person of interest in the case." The shot switched to a grainy close-up of me with my wild hair. "Neighbors are shocked," the female voice continued as I dropped down onto the couch, devastated that my picture and name were on the news. Person of interest! I wasn't a person of interest. I was a bystander, a witness.

The video cut to a close-up of a bald man with oval glasses. "How do you feel, knowing a woman was murdered in broad daylight in your neighborhood?" the unseen reporter asked, then angled the microphone to the man.

"Scared. We're all scared. This isn't the sort of neighborhood where things like this happen—" I hit the MUTE button. I knew word of Jean's death and my involvement in its discovery would spread quickly, but now I doubted there would be anyone in all of the county who didn't know about it.

Abby squeezed my shoulder and said, "I've got to go. Call me if you need me, okay? You've got my new cell phone number?" She'd bought a new one last night.

"Yes. Right," I said, standing up and clicking the television off. "Thanks for taking the kids again today." Her head was tilted as she studied me with a concerned look. To lighten the mood, I said, "I could get used to this—having you chauffeur the kids around. It's almost like having a live-in nanny."

"Um-hum. It's the least I can do, since you're letting me mess up your guest room and most of your house so I can get a decent night's sleep." Her face turned serious. "Don't brood all day. Do something. Get out of the house. I'm sure the lawyer will call you back soon."

"I will. I have a few follow-ups and it's my turn to volunteer at the food bank today."

"Good," Abby said. "Don't skip it. You'll feel better if you don't mope all day."

"Yes, ma'am," I said with a mock salute.

"Peanut butter, aisle three," I muttered to myself as I consulted a list taped to the top of the waist-high counter that served as the front desk of the food bank. Abby had been right. Getting out of the house and doing something completely different was exactly what I needed. The lawyer friend still hadn't called, but I shoved that thought aside to deal with later. If there was no word from him by this afternoon, I would make some calls of my own. But that was for later. Right now I was up to my elbows in food that needed to be sorted before the food bank opened later this afternoon.

I balanced the three jumbo containers of store-brand peanut butter in my arms and walked down the concrete floor to the correct aisle, where I stacked them on the shelf beside containers of varying sizes and brands. The food bank received donations from local restaurants, but a large amount of the food they distributed came from individual donations. I smiled as

I scanned the shelf, noting that there was everything from a small two-ounce jar of crunchy organic peanut butter to an extra large thirty-ounce jar of plain Peter Pan peanut butter. I loved the uniqueness of it. The mishmash of jars and flavors showed that individuals were digging in their home pantries or dropping extra food into their grocery carts to help hungry people.

My phone vibrated in my back pocket as I went back to the counter for the next load. It was a text message that read, Can't meet next week. Sorry! Will reschedule. Nancy.

"Not another one," I muttered as I tapped out an upbeat reply.

I didn't feel upbeat. Nancy had been my only other new client lead besides Marie. I'd tried to follow up with two other previous clients—part of my maintain-my-client-list campaign—but one person had been too busy to take my call and sent word through her secretary that she was fine and she'd call if she needed anything else. Translation: the old don't-call-me, I'll-call-you ploy. I had a feeling she wouldn't be calling me anytime soon. The other woman's voice had gone strained as she muttered something about seeing me on the news. She couldn't get off the phone fast enough. So, now, not only were my established clients avoiding me, my potential clients who'd expressed an interest in a consultation were cancelling on me, too.

I jammed the phone back in my pocket and sorted another load of food, this one mostly spaghetti noodles, sauce, and cereal. I checked my watch. I had another two hours before the food bank opened its doors for afternoon pickup, but I hustled, sorting the last of the donations onto their designated shelves, because I had to pick up the kids from school today.

The wind buffeted the steel frame of the building,

the only noise besides the low music that came from an old radio on the counter. I knew that Emily, the volunteer coordinator for Helping Hands, was at the back of the warehouse in her office. But I hadn't seen her since she set me to work and disappeared to her office in "the headquarters" as she laughingly called it, behind the aisles of food where flimsy walls separated three stripped-down offices.

The food bank was located in the quiet grassy meadow behind the church we attended, North Dawkins Community Church. Surrounded on three sides with parking lots, the church was a modern blend of natural wood and glass with a large lobby area that contained a coffee bar with free high-speed Internet and a scattering of comfortable chairs and high-topped tables. A cross was placed high on a lobby wall lined with field-stone. The church was a longtime partner of Helping Hands and when the nonprofit lost their lease after their original building was sold, the empty lot at the back of the church seemed the perfect place for the food bank. There was access from the church parking lot, yet the location was sheltered and private since it wasn't in direct view of the road, which was a very big deal.

I'd learned that anonymity was important to some people who came to the food bank, especially to people who'd been hit hard by the economic slowdown and who had never had to ask for help before. Lots of people didn't want to be seen coming and going from the food bank, or even parking in the food bank parking lot. The warehouse building with a swath of gravel for parking was the first phase for the food bank—an initial low-cost way to get set up—but I'd heard that plans were in the works for a more permanent building at the same location.

The Boss's version of "Merry Christmas, Baby" came on and I turned up the volume before extracting a Hershey's kiss from the small supply I kept in the pocket of my fleece vest. I popped the chocolate in my mouth. A girl needs her energy.

The door flew open and Diane, the food bank manager, hurried inside on a burst of cold air. She held a large cardboard box in her arms and used her foot to kick the heavy steel door closed. "Oh, it's you today, Ellie! And, look, you've already finished sorting the donations. Great!" She set the box down on the counter, then smoothed her short, brown hair off her fine-featured face. Diane was in her midthirties and seemed to have boundless energy and enthusiasm, which reminded me of Nathan's kindergarten teacher—all sunny smiles and upbeat positive reinforcement, which I was sure was essential when you worked with volunteers, but her attitude did occasionally make me feel as if she were going to tell me it was time to finger-paint. I'd worked with her a few other times when I volunteered, but I didn't know her all that well.

I expected Diane to head for her office, but instead she draped her arms over the box and leaned toward me. I noticed that her eyes were pink and swollen. "Ellie, you were there, weren't you? I saw you on the news." Her upbeat tone had dropped away.

"Apparently you and every organizing client I've ever had," I said. I had no idea so many people watched the news in the morning.

"Well, it was on the front page of the paper, too," Diane said with a grimace.

"My picture?"

"Yes, well, it was an inset. The big picture was of Jean from a spouse function at the base a few years ago, but you were there, too, in a kind of collage beside another photo of the open garage."

"No wonder," I muttered.

"Not good for business, I guess?" she asked.

"Afraid not."

She twisted her lips to one side and looked speculatively toward the back offices, then shook her head. "I'd help you out, if I could. Lord knows, we could use some organization in the office, but financially we're stretched to the limit as it is."

"Thanks, Diane," I said, touched that she wanted to hire me.

"All that stuff on the news is nonsense, anyway. I know you didn't do it," Diane said, and I felt slightly better. At least one person who wasn't related to me or one of my closest friends believed I wasn't a murderer. It wasn't much, but I would take whatever I could get at the moment. Diane lowered her voice, "What happened? Can you talk about it?"

"I guess so. No one told me not to."

"We haven't heard anything, except what's been in the news—and that's practically nothing. A detective came by this morning and asked us all questions, but he didn't tell us anything about what happened. All we know is that yesterday, Simon hadn't been back from lunch long before he got a call and went flying out of here. Gravel literally sprayed the building when he pulled out of the parking lot. He didn't say one word to anyone, just ran out the door."

"Maybe one of the neighbors called him," I said, because I couldn't imagine that the police or sheriff's department would notify someone of a loved one's death over the phone.

"So what happened?"

"I walked in their garage and saw her on the floor.

She was already . . . gone. She'd been hit on the back of the head."

"Oh, you poor thing," she said sympathetically. "How terrible. What did you do?"

"Well, there wasn't much I could do. I did check for a pulse. Then Gabrielle got there and I called nine-one-one." It was the condensed version of the story, but I figured that was enough detail.

"Hit on the head," Diane murmured as she straightened up and absentmindedly opened the flaps of the box. "Hard to believe. Why would someone do that to Jean? Jean! Of all people."

"Did you know her well?"

"No, not really. We met for lunch every so often . . . we weren't close friends. But I am shocked. She wouldn't hurt a fly, now would she? What could have happened that someone would do that to her?" Diane was speaking more to herself than to me, so I didn't answer. I began unpacking the items in the box she'd brought in—dried beans, bags of rice, and cans of peaches. She continued, "I had no idea when she didn't show up yesterday . . . I thought she'd forgotten."

"You were supposed to meet her yesterday?"

Diane nodded. "One of our occasional lunches. But when she didn't turn up, I figured she got busy or forgot. I called her and left a message, but I suppose she was already . . . gone by then. Such a loss for Simon," she continued. "You know, he's only been here a short time, but he works so hard and does so much. We really feel it with him gone today."

"Is he here a lot?"

"Oh, yes. Every day. And he didn't just work on the books and round up new donors. He's not afraid to get his hands dirty. Anytime the doors are open, he's out here packing boxes, carrying food for people to their cars. I really was amazed at how quickly he's become integral to Helping Hands." She ran her hand over the plastic bag of kidney beans, smoothing it flat. "I was hoping you'd say that it was an open-and-shut case . . . that the police knew who did it."

I picked up the cans of peaches and said somewhat bitterly, "I sure hope it's not an open-and-shut case, at least not right now, because I seem to be the only suspect they've got."

"Oh, dear. Then I really do have to say something. When I saw you on the news, I thought that they can't seriously think you'd do something like that. But I can see by your face that you're really worried." She hesitated, then said, "I don't want to make any trouble. Simon *is* on the board . . . but if they really don't know who did it and they're leaning toward you . . ."

"What is it, Diane?" I set down the cans.

"It's his lunches," she said reluctantly. "I wasn't even going to say anything, but I suppose I have to now."

"What about his lunches?"

"Well, he says he's going to lunch every day around eleven-fifteen and he's gone for an hour, but then he comes back after twelve-fifteen, closes his office door, and eats a sack lunch in there."

"Okay," I said slowly. "He's running errands during his lunch break?"

"To the same place, every day? I don't know what he's doing, but he's certainly not going to lunch. I happened to leave right after he did a few weeks ago, not so soon that he noticed me, but close enough that when I pulled into traffic, I noticed I was a few cars behind him on the state highway. He didn't go to lunch. He turned into that strip mall."

"Maybe he had a package to mail on the way to lunch?"

"It's possible," Diane said in a doubtful tone. "Then,

a few days later, it happened again. I left shortly after him and he went to the same place. I didn't really think about it until I came back that day. I tapped on his door and saw him with a sandwich at his desk. I'd asked him earlier that day what he was doing for lunch and he got this weird look on his face—oh, I don't know how to describe it—like he was worried and sort of scared. It was strange. Why would he look like that? It made me curious, especially when he kept specifically saying he was going to lunch and then he'd secretively eat a sandwich in his office later. I saw him make that same turn into the strip mall again later that week. I don't know why I didn't just say something, ask him what he was doing, but I didn't, probably because I could tell he didn't want to talk about it. He had the same jumpy reaction when I asked him if he wanted to go to lunch with Emily and me."

"Maybe he's going to that fitness center to work out." I said. "It's right there by the strip mall."

"Then why wouldn't he say so? Why make a point of mentioning lunch—and he does make a point of saying he's *going to lunch*—but then eat in his office later? It's weird."

"You'd better tell the detective investigating the case. His name is Waraday, Detective Dave Waraday at the sheriff's office. I'm sure he'll be contacting you anyway since you called Jean right before she died."

"Yes, I suppose I'd better."

"So he was 'at lunch' yesterday shortly before he got the phone call and left?"

"Yes, just like every day. He was back from lunch—or wherever it is that he goes—when he got the phone call."

"You never followed him to see where he goes?" I asked.

"No," she sighed. "I thought about it, but I always have some errand to run on my lunch hour—the bank or the dry cleaner or the grocery store. I don't have time to trail along after him to see what he's up to—and it would be peculiar, wouldn't it? Following someone that you work with. I'd decided it really wasn't any of my business and I wouldn't worry about it, but now . . ."

"Yes, now you'd better mention it."

She nodded. "Right. I'll do it now. The detective left his card. I'll call his cell phone. You can handle the rest of these things?" she asked.

"Of course," I said, again picking up the canned peaches. She headed for the back offices and I focused on sorting the rest of the food, thinking that Simon was probably doing something totally innocent, but at least it would give Waraday something else to look into besides me.

A few minutes later, I signed out on the volunteer log and reached for my purse and coat, glad that I'd finished early and would have plenty of time to make it to the school for pickup. My phone rang as I shrugged into my coat. I didn't recognize the number.

"Ellie, this is Paige." Her voice was hurried and nervous. "I just finished talking to a detective—he wanted to know all sorts of things about you. He said it was a murder investigation, the woman who died from a blow to the head. I heard about it on the radio this morning. Are you okay?"

I felt a contraction, a squeezing, in my chest. "For the moment. Was it Detective Waraday?"

"Yes, that was his name. What's going on?"

"I found Jean, the woman who was murdered. He's checking my alibi. I told him I was with you right before I found her." I couldn't believe I was talking about an alibi. Was I really saying that sentence? But I suddenly realized I *had* an alibi. A wash of relief flooded through me.

Paige's voice almost squeaked as she said, "You're kidding me—he's checking up on *you?* Are you serious? Now I wish I hadn't told him anything."

"No, I'm glad you talked to him. Thank goodness I had an appointment with you. I didn't have hardly any time between when I talked with you and when I found Jean. That's such a tiny window of time—that has to count for something," I said, then felt some of the relief seep away as I realized I had no idea when Jean was killed, so I didn't really know if I had an alibi or not. She certainly hadn't been dead long when I found her. Had her wrist been cold when I touched it? I couldn't remember. I suppressed a shiver and focused on what Paige was saying.

"Well, I still think he's an idiot to even suspect you," she continued. "I mean, come on. You're too neat and organized to do something as messy as conk someone on the head. Talk about untidy. I mean, not that I think you'd murder someone in a neat way . . . oh, you know what I mean. You'd never murder someone."

"Thanks for the vote of confidence," I said, grinning. "Remind me not to put you on my defense team. You didn't say any of that to Waraday, did you?"

"No," she said, her voice dismissive. "Although, why he was so interested in your clothes, I don't understand."

"My clothes?" I asked, picking up my purse.

"Yes. He wanted to know exactly what you were wearing, right down to your shoes. It's a good thing I've got an excellent memory—and I really liked that sweater you were wearing. Where did you get it, by the way?"

"It was a Christmas present. He's making sure I hadn't changed clothes," I said, and closed my eyes briefly.

"What?" Paige asked.

"He wants to make sure I hadn't changed clothes because, you know . . . whoever murdered Jean probably had some blood on them." And it had to be more than a spot on their shoes, I thought fiercely.

Paige said, "Guess it's a good thing you wore white that day."

Tips for a Sane and Happy Holiday Season

Simplifying Holiday Cards

If you send Christmas cards through the mail, use a spreadsheet program to create a mailing list. Then you can print address labels in a snap. Cut the cost of paper and postage with social networking and e-mail. Look for free online newsletter templates or use templates in your word processing program to create an instant update with a fun, eye-catching layout.

Chapter Eight

The first thing I saw when I stepped out the door of the food bank into the gravel area that served as a parking lot was a patrol car from the sheriff's office. It was parked beside my minivan. The door swung open and Waraday stepped out. I gripped the two-by-four railing of the wooden platform that topped the three steps leading down to the parking lot. The heavy door to the food bank thudded closed behind me. I wanted to spin around and retreat back inside.

I didn't want to talk to Waraday. My palms suddenly felt sweaty despite the cool day and my heart was bumping quickly in my chest. He was checking on my movements, following up on where I'd been yesterday. I was a suspect.

As much as I wanted to dash back inside, I couldn't. I had to get to school to pick up the kids. And he'd already seen me. "Mrs. Avery," he said, walking toward me. "A word with you?"

I took a deep breath to calm my crazy heartbeat and made a move to brush past him. "I'm sorry. This isn't a good time. I have to get to the school."

"We can talk here or we can talk at the sheriff's office."

I paused. I didn't want to go to his office. And I certainly didn't want to go there without a lawyer. The sheriff's office was in a county government complex and the county jail was there, too. I licked my lips and cautiously said, "Okay." I knew it was probably not a good idea to talk to him here without a lawyer, but since I didn't have one at the moment, it seemed like I should at least hear what he had to say. I didn't want to make him mad or give him a reason to say I'd refused to cooperate.

"You said that when you first saw the body in the garage you thought it was Gabrielle?" The sun was directly behind his shoulder, so I couldn't see his face very well, but his voice and manner were straightforward, not intimidating or hostile, which I took to be a good sign.

"Yes," I said, squinting in the bright sunlight, trying to make out his expression.

"Why was that?"

"I was expecting her. She was the one who asked me to meet her there." Could he hear the slight tremble in my voice? It was very quiet. The food bank and the bulk of the church building behind me cut off most of the noise from the busy road. A bird, wings stretched wide, glided in lazy circles in the sky overhead.

"What was she doing when you got there?"

"You mean Gabrielle? She wasn't there when I got there." The bird swooped lower. It was a vulture.

"What was Jean doing?"

"She wasn't doing anything," I said, puzzled at his line of questioning. "She was lying on the floor. I didn't see her right away."

"Tell me again about this conflict between you and Ms. Matheson."

The quick change in the direction of the conversation seemed odd, but it really didn't surprise me—I knew any conflict would attract his attention and he'd keep pursuing it. I suppressed a tiny sigh at having to go over the details again—it was painful enough to know that Gabrielle had bested me on the professional level and I didn't really want to dwell on it. Besides, it had nothing to do with Jean's death, but I answered anyway. "We argued because she lured away an established client of mine and she was undercutting my fees, trying to beat me out when it came to potential clients."

"I understand one of these jobs you lost to her was for the North Dawkins schools."

"Yes, that's right." Since I couldn't really see his face, I focused on the vulture, which was making another pass overhead. It tipped its wings and glided out of sight in a quick descent into the wall of forest in the distance.

"Why did she get it and not you? You're the local— she's the newcomer. Makes more sense that they'd want someone with a track record in the area."

Did he know about Gabrielle's underhanded methods? I believed everything Candy had told me about Gabrielle using sex appeal to get the job, but that information was basically hearsay—just Candy's opinion. I didn't want to drag Candy into this situation and I knew that Gabrielle would insist that it was nothing but her organizing talents—not any other *talents*—that got her the job, so I said, "I don't know how they make their decisions at the school admin office. All I know is I didn't get the job."

"When did you learn this?"

"Wednesday. I got a phone call."

"And when did you learn Gabrielle got the job?" Waraday asked, and I felt a frisson of worry trace up my spine. Why was he so focused on the job? It had nothing to do with Jean's death.

"The same day."

"I see. That must have made you mad," Waraday said, his voice somehow taking on a more sympathetic tone.

"Well, yes," I said cautiously, because his sudden abandonment of the straightforward Q-and-A session felt weird. He'd never been solicitous before. "I was upset. It would have been nice to get the job, but there are other jobs."

"And that very night Ms. Matheson went after another of your potential clients, Marie Forrstead," Waraday said.

"Yes, that was what brought everything to a head. I felt I had to stand up for myself. But I shouldn't have lost my cool like that."

"But it's understandable," Waraday said, nodding. "Yep, I can see how you'd be upset, and when you walked in to the garage and saw her standing there the next day, you lost it again, didn't you?"

I blinked at him a few times. "What? What do you mean?"

"When you walked in to the garage and saw Mrs. Williams standing with her back to you, you assumed it was Ms. Matheson. You were angry. You had every right to be—it's common knowledge in the school administration office that Ms. Matheson emphasized other—*assets*, let's say—to get that job and she was lowballing you on prices. Yeah, I can see how you'd be upset. Furious, even. That's how one person from the party described you, Mrs. Avery. Maybe that fury came rushing back when you saw the tall, dark-headed woman in the garage . . ."

"No, no, it wasn't—" I shook my head, thoughts twist-

ing around in my brain. "No! It wasn't like that at all."
He thought I'd mistaken Jean for Gabrielle. He thought
I'd killed Jean. Motive—he'd constructed a motive for
me, his main suspect, and twisted the facts around to
support it. I felt breathless and a little dizzy. "I didn't see
anyone when I walked in the garage."

"But you said you saw an arm on the ground."

"Not until later." I reached out, gripped the wooden
railing of the steps to steady myself. "I didn't see anyone
when I first walked in." My thoughts were still swirling. I
fought to get them in order, to make sense as I spoke. "I
didn't do it. I didn't hurt Jean and I didn't think she
was Gabrielle because I didn't *see anyone in the garage.*"

"Until later." Sarcasm laced his tone now.

"Yes. A few minutes after I walked in, I saw the arm
and rushed over there."

Waraday stared at me for a few moments. I held his
gaze, my heart pounding. Was he going to arrest me?
Who would pick up the kids? Why had I ever opened
my mouth without a lawyer? Finally, Waraday said,
"You've always had an unhealthy interest in criminal activity, especially murder. That's not normal."

"I didn't seek this out," I protested. "I wish I hadn't
been there. Goodness knows, I wish I hadn't been
there."

"Um-hmm," he murmured in a dismissive way. "But
you were. You always seem to be there. Right in the middle of everything. There's too much coincidence in
your life, Mrs. Avery, for me to write you off or to believe everything you say. And a word of advice . . . it's
not going to do you any good to get your friends to call
with bogus leads to distract me."

"Are you talking about Diane?" I asked, looking up at
the doorway with the Helping Hands logo. She certainly hadn't delayed in calling Waraday. She must have

made the call immediately after our conversation. "I didn't ask her to call you."

"Right. But you do know she called me and I bet you know exactly why she called—Mr. Williams's lunch activity, right?"

"Yes. She asked if I thought it was important. I told her to call you because I didn't know if it was important or not—that you'd sort it out," I said.

"Yes, it's sorted. In fact, it was sorted yesterday. Mr. Williams has a hobby he didn't want anyone to know about—hula-hooping."

I was stunned. "He *hula-hoops* every day at lunch?" I asked hesitantly.

"Yes," Waraday said. "A whole class at Fit Lifestyle vouched for him—says he always shows up and then returns directly to work." Did I see a ghost of a smile on Waraday's face? Surely not . . . but it was kind of funny . . . a retired military guy—a pilot, no less—taking Hula-Hoop classes. No wonder he wanted to keep that quiet. If any of his old buddies found out, they'd have a field day. The amount of kidding he would get about hula-hooping would be astronomical, I was sure. The guys were notorious for ragging on each other and playing practical jokes. If he'd still been in the squadron and the guys found out, I'm sure he would have found a Hula-Hoop on his desk or draped over the antenna of his car, and heard endless jokes about it. Even though he was retired, I knew he continued to do things with the guys from the squadron, just like Jean had continued to come to spouse club activities. Mitch had mentioned that Simon dropped in at the office occasionally and Abby said he'd played golf with Jeff awhile back. I could see why he wouldn't broadcast his hobby.

"That's . . . surprising," I said.

"Apparently, it's all about core strength," Waraday

said. Yes, there was certainly a flicker of humor in his eyes. He must have forgotten who he was speaking to for a few seconds, but he quickly returned to his serious demeanor. "It's irrelevant." His face straightened into official lines. "And confidential. Don't go spreading that tidbit around. I'm warning you, Mrs. Avery. I won't let you push this investigation into wasting time and resources. Stay out of it."

"Stay out of it," I murmured to myself as I pulled to a stop in the carpool line at school. Thanks to being waylaid by Waraday, I was at the very back of the line. The way he'd gone on about how he thought I'd mistaken Jean for Gabrielle and all the prodding about me being angry . . . well, I wasn't sure how the conversation was going to end. I'd been half afraid he was going to order me into his car and take me to the sheriff's office right then and there, despite his insinuation that if I talked to him there, he wouldn't do that. But in the end, after he'd dropped the bombshell about Simon and hula-hooping—*hula-hooping!*—he'd told me he'd be in touch. Then he'd climbed the stairs and gone into the food bank. I'd stood there for about one second before I darted over to the minivan and got out of there as fast as I could.

A knock on the window startled me and I hurried to unlock the car. One of the school aides was standing beside the car with Livvy, Nathan, and Charlie lined up on the curb. As they scrambled in, Nathan announced, "Mom, Brandon can't come over and play today."

The after school play date had completely slipped my mind. "Something must have come up," I said. "Maybe he can come over next week," I added, seeing Nathan's disappointed face in the rearview mirror.

"He can't," Nathan announced flatly. "His mom came to get him on the sidewalk today and said he can't *ever* come over to my house."

As I maneuvered through the curving lane and exited the parking lot, I caught a glimpse of Brandon's mom. She was fastening the seat belt around Brandon, the back door of the car open. She saw me and I waved. I couldn't slow down—it was strictly against protocol and I'd probably get rear-ended—so I rolled slowly by her. She glowered back at me and my spirits took a nosedive. Clearly, she'd seen me on the news.

"Shepherds! Over here. All shepherds line up over here," called Molly, a Sunday school teacher, as she herded ten boys to one side of the sanctuary and put her fingers to her lips. I didn't envy her. Keeping that many five- and six-year-old boys calm and quiet was almost impossible. I was seated at the back of the room on one of the padded chairs that linked together to form rows. I leaned over, checking to make sure Nathan was in the group he was supposed to be in and that he was fairly quiet. He was shooting Charlie very expressive looks, but they weren't talking so I sat back in the seat and fiddled with my phone.

No messages. No missed calls. Nothing. Truthfully, I wasn't quite sure what to do with myself. Normally, I'd have taken the time during the evening pageant rehearsal to return phone calls or run a quick errand, but I had nothing on my calendar, except my meeting with Marie on Monday. No clients to prepare for, no organizing supplies to buy—we were a long way from that stage with Marie—and no e-mails to catch up on. Abby was picking up a pizza for dinner tonight and would meet us back at the house when rehearsal was over, so I didn't even have to fix dinner.

A plastic-wrapped plate covered in frosted cookies appeared before me and a deep voice said, "Merry Christmas."

I looked up to see Gary Donahue standing beside me. "Monica made enough cookies to feed an army," he said, lifting the plate slightly. "Would you like some for your house?"

"Yes, of course. Thank you," I said, taking the plate. "Merry Christmas to you, too. Here, sit down. Is Claire down there?" I asked, looking to the front of the sanctuary where parents, teachers, and kids were moving up and down the stairs in a sort of organized chaos.

"Yep. She's the innkeeper's wife. Disappointed as all get-out that she doesn't get to tell them there's no room at the inn."

I spotted a sullen-looking Claire, her fair hair slipping out of its barrettes, standing on the opposite side of the room from Nathan. Gary was a police officer in the city police department and, after my conversation with Waraday earlier, I would have wanted to avoid any other law enforcement types, but Gary was our friend. He and Monica sat a few rows behind us most Sundays at church, and Gary was a part-time reservist with the air force, so he and Mitch had a lot in common. "Where's Monica?" I asked.

"Still baking. My folks are coming in next week and she's turned into Martha Stewart." Gary kept his gaze on the kids being steered into place. "Figured you could use some holiday cheer," he said, pointing to the plate of cookies.

Of course, he knew about the murder and the investigation. Even though he was with the city police, not the sheriff's office, he would have heard about it. "You got that right. Not exactly a joyous time for us right now."

Gary nodded, but didn't comment. We watched the kids move through the Christmas story, then there was a moment of absolute silence, a burst of static that startled everyone, and, finally, the opening notes of "Away in a Manger" came over the speakers. Molly raised her arms and nodded to the kids. A few wobbly voices filled the air, then a few more, until all the kids realized they were supposed to be singing and everyone joined in.

Quietly, Gary said, "I hear that the detective likes you for the murder."

"I know," I said miserably. Waraday had made that quite clear this afternoon. *He likes me for it.* Those words echoed around in my head, obliterating the soothing Christmas carol.

"Just wanted to make sure you knew."

"Yeah, I know," I said, a depression settling over me. Waraday had his sights set on me. "What can I do? I've already given him a ton of ammunition. I was trying to help his investigation, but he's using everything I've told him against me."

"A lawyer would be a good step, I think," Gary said mildly, his attention still fixed firmly on the kids.

He doesn't want anyone to know he's talking to me about the case, I realized. I had to get a grip on myself and keep my voice down. Gary could probably get in big trouble for talking to me about the case even if his office wasn't investigating it, but I knew why he was doing it. He was a friend. I swallowed the sudden lump in my throat and shook my hair back away from my face as I, too, looked determinedly to the front. The rows of chairs were mostly in the dark and I doubted anyone had noticed me nearly falling apart. "That's finally taken care of. I won't be saying anything else without T. Randall Hitchens around."

"Good. He's good. You'll be fine."

"It's good to hear your vote of confidence, but I don't feel reassured." I'd spoken to T. Randall Hitchens's secretary and to him for a few moments. He was soft-spoken and I had the image of an elbow-patch-wearing professor in mind when I thought of him—not exactly the firebrand defense lawyer I'd been hoping for.

Gary cleared his throat and spoke in an even softer voice. "I also heard—through the grapevine, you know, nothing official—but I heard there were no prints on the murder weapon."

I shot a glance at him out the corner of my eye. His arms were crossed over his chest, his hands tucked up under his arms, head bobbing slightly to the beat of "Little Drummer Boy."

"Then that means . . . that my prints aren't on it. Someone wiped it clean? Used gloves?"

Gary shrugged. "Your guess is as good as mine, but that fact combined with T. Randall Hitchens gives you a pretty good chance, even considering the detective's focus on you."

I sagged back against the chair, feeling like I could breathe again. There was no physical evidence to tie me to the murder—well, except the spot of blood on my boot. And Waraday's questions to Paige about my clothes obviously meant that he thought that whoever killed Jean would have a lot more blood on them than one spot.

There was a shoving match going on between the three wise men, so the children's choir director clapped her hands together to get their attention. "Once more," she called over her shoulder to the sound booth in the back as she spun her finger, "then we'll call it a night."

The strains of the carol filled the room again, but I barely noticed.

"And with the prosecutor we've got—." Here, Gary shook his head. "Likes to keep his win ratio up, so unless a case is airtight, he doesn't want to move. I think you'll be okay with the lack of prints and Hitchens on your side."

"There's something I was thinking about today—"

"Just one thing?" Gary said.

"No, I have about a thousand unanswerable questions, but you might be the one person who could help me with this one. Do they know what time Jean died? I felt for a pulse, but I can't remember if she was . . . cold . . . I didn't even notice. I was too freaked out about the whole situation." Gary hesitated, and I said, "It could make a difference, how long she was . . . like that before I got there. I was at Fit Lifestyle up until just a few minutes before."

"It's always hard to pinpoint time of death—lots of things can interfere with it, like the temperature of the room," he said, raising his eyebrows and giving me a quick look.

"There was a space heater in one corner and the garage wasn't cold. Whoever killed her was trying to complicate things."

"Could be. On the other hand, she might have always had that heater on whenever she was in the garage in the winter . . . hard to know. Anyway, I hear Waraday is focusing on the time between noon and twelve-thirty."

"I was with Paige during most of that time," I said with another rush of relief. Two bits of good news at once—it was almost too much to handle. I'd had too many emotional swings in the last forty-eight hours and this barrage of positive news, for me at least, was almost too good to be true. My eyes pricked with tears and I blinked quickly. I had to get a grip. Gary would not thank me if I became a weepy watering pot.

"Thanks for telling me this, Gary. I appreciate it. I might even be able to sleep tonight."

Gary grinned at me. "What did I tell you, Christmas cheer . . . that's what I deliver."

Chapter Nine

Monday

The feeling of relief lasted until I entered the funeral home for Jean's memorial service on Monday morning and walked past Waraday to slip into a seat beside Mitch. It had been a fairly normal weekend. We'd had our traditional Friday night pizza. On Saturday, Abby and I had taken the kids to the park and even worked in a quick trip to do some Christmas shopping. Sunday had been a blur because Jeff came home. We'd spent the day waiting for his flight to arrive in a drafty hangar at the base. Abby had somehow managed to gather up all the clothes and Charlie's toys, and our house had seemed unusually quiet and empty this morning.

I murmured hello to Mitch, who'd driven over from the base, and glanced back over my shoulder. Waraday had his gaze locked onto me and I shivered as I remembered Gary's words. *He likes you for it.* It seemed Waraday hadn't changed his mind. I reminded myself that I had an excellent lawyer—a criminal lawyer, which still amazed me every time I thought of it. I pushed down the worry about how hard a hit our savings account would take when we had to pay him and instead focused on the service.

I was shocked when I saw Simon walking slowly down the center aisle as if the effort of moving was painful. If you'd asked me to describe Simon a week ago, I would have said he was a wiry guy in his midfifties with a quick smile, but today he looked shrunken and frail. In his dark suit, with his face pale and haggard demeanor, I almost didn't recognize him. The times I'd met him, he'd either been in a flight suit or a plaid shirt and khaki pants and he'd always told a corny joke that made the kids laugh. I assumed the young man in his early twenties moving down the aisle beside Simon was his son. He had the same light brown hair as Simon and a similar lean body type, but was taller than his dad. I only caught a quick glimpse of Gabrielle, in a clingy black dress, because she was flanked on each side by two young women with manes of straight, glossy hair and the slimness of youth, who must have been her daughters. A man with curly brown hair and a ruddy face wore a plain white dress shirt, no tie, and dark dress pants. He walked a few steps behind Gabrielle and her daughters and sat as far as he could from the female trio. Gabrielle's ex-husband perhaps?

The service began with a song and I couldn't help thinking what a horrible thing it would be to lose a loved one during the holidays. Wouldn't the season always be tinged with sorrow afterwards? I slipped my hand into Mitch's, knowing that the funeral had to bring back memories of the last funeral we'd attended, for his grandfather. He squeezed my hand and I leaned against his shoulder. Movement up front drew our attention as Simon made his way to the podium.

Obviously working hard not to cry, he made it

through a very nice eulogy in which he described Jean's sunny personality and told how they'd met in college when he helped her extract a candy bar stuck in a vending machine. After he returned to his seat, he broke down in the front row and sobbed quietly throughout the rest of the service. After a short word from the pastor, a reading from First Corinthians, and a prayer, the service ended. I was surprised Gabrielle didn't speak since she seemed to thrive on attention, but she had remained seated with her arm wrapped around one of her daughters. Mitch and I made our way out of the chapel and spoke briefly to the family. I didn't even try and think of anything to say to Simon. Up close, he looked even more traumatized. I shook hands with his son, who said a very correct, "Thank you for coming," and moved down the line to Gabrielle. She stared at me a moment with her puffy, red eyes, and I wondered if it was a huge mistake to have come today. Honestly, I hadn't thought about Gabrielle until I saw her during the service, but she had made quite a scene when she accused me of murder. I'd only been thinking of Jean and how she was one of the nicest people I'd known and I needed to go to her funeral. Maybe it would have been more appropriate to attend, but then slip out the back a few minutes before the service was over. Unfortunately, I didn't think Miss Manners covered proper murder suspect etiquette. I'd just have to wing it.

I said quickly, "I'm so sorry, Gabrielle," and started to move on to the next person, one of her daughters, but Gabrielle put her hand on my arm and stopped me. She continued her long examination of my face. Finally, she nodded once and said, "Thank you for coming."

Her daughter's gaze was flicking back and forth between us and finally settled on her mom with concern, obviously wondering what was going on. Gabrielle shot her a quick glance that I couldn't interpret, then turned to Mitch. I moved through the rest of the family, glad that Gabrielle had held it together, but ready to get out of the atmosphere of sorrow and grief.

I paused on the steps outside to find my keys. It was another bright, crisp day that would have been beautiful except for the funeral service.

"Are you going to the graveside service?" Mitch asked.

"No." I slipped on my sunglasses. "I have that appointment with Marie. I have to get home and change, then go to her house."

"Didn't she come today?" Mitch asked as we moved down the steps to the parking lot.

"No. She didn't really know Jean. They'd only met a few times. Simon had retired by the time Marie moved here, so Jean wasn't doing as much with the spouse club. I called Marie this morning to see if she wanted to reschedule because of the funeral, but she said she didn't want to put off our appointment. I got the feeling she knows if she cancels once it will be hard for her to call me again to set up a new appointment."

I gave Mitch a quick kiss and turned to find Waraday lingering in a group of people behind us. I wondered what he had hoped to overhear. I bet he was disappointed to hear me talking about something as mundane as keeping appointments. He was talking on his cell phone as I left, watching my every movement, and I couldn't help but wonder if I was the subject of his call. I really hoped something would come up to move his attention away from me.

"Okay," I said in a hearty voice, feeling completely out of my depth. Marie and I were standing in the small cleared trail of her entryway, stacks of stuff rising on either side of us. It reminded me of the snow that the plows would pile up along the sides of the road, which I was so amazed to see when we lived in Washington State. There had only been a slight hesitation when Marie opened the door today, which I thought was a good sign, but as soon as I entered her cluttered house, I felt overwhelmed. I took a deep breath and mentally went over the phone conversation I'd had with Dr. Harper before I'd arrived. Be supportive. Go slowly. Don't take over. "Okay," I repeated, and said, "Where would you like to start?"

"Here, I guess," Marie said with a bit of a shrug.

"I think that's a good idea," I said as I put down my tote bag, which contained trash bags, labels, markers, and other essentials. After the funeral, I'd changed out of my black dress and into a sweatshirt, jeans, and tennis shoes. I tried to put all thoughts of the funeral and Jean's death out of my mind. I had a job to do and it was going to be a doozy.

I'd considered beginning in the kitchen, but it wasn't in as bad a shape as the other main living areas and if there was one thing I knew about organizing, it was that it helped if you had a feeling of accomplishment. If we could get the small entry hallway cleared, then Marie would have something to inspire her to keep organizing.

There was a miniscule nod of agreement from Marie as she pushed a strand of her fiery hair behind her ear. Her face looked tight and worried.

"So, here's what we'll do," I said. "We'll start here in this corner and go through each thing in this pile and you'll decide if you want to keep it, give it away, sell it, or throw it away."

"All right," Marie said, ducking her head slightly.

I'd also brought three large plastic bins. I propped them up on the teetering stacks, hoping I wouldn't cause an avalanche, but there was nowhere on the floor to put them. I pulled the first thing off the stack beside me, a long green-and-white golf umbrella. "What about this? Keep, donate, or throw away?"

"I use that," Marie said, almost eagerly. "Keep."

"Okay. Do you have any other umbrellas?"

"Um . . . they're around," she said vaguely. "Maybe the hall closet?"

"That's a good place," I said, and Marie's face relaxed as I put the umbrella in the "Keep" bin. "We'll put that away later. Next," I said, holding up a single blue glove with a hole in the index finger.

"Umm . . . well, I don't know where the mate to that is, but I'm sure it's around here somewhere."

"Maybe," I said. "But since it has a hole, why don't we put it in the throw away?" I watched her carefully for her reaction.

She frowned. "But that could be mended."

"Do you knit? Do you know how to fix it?"

"No," she said reluctantly. "But I could still use it. It's just a tiny hole."

I almost relented, but then I looked at the pile of items that were up next: a lidless teapot, several coats, a couple of mateless shoes, and three-ring binders—and that was just the stuff I could see on the top. Who knew what lurked lower down in the stack? "Marie," I said as gently as I could. "You're going to have to make some decisions. You're going to have to let go of some of these things. You have quite a bit to deal with here. Do you think you're going to use one glove with a hole in it?"

"No," she said in a low voice. I handed her the glove. She looked at it for a long moment and I thought, *this job might end right now if she can't throw away a useless glove . . .*

But she nodded decisively and put it in the "Throw Away" bin.

"Great!" I said, trying to be enthusiastic but not go overboard. I quickly picked up one of the coats, trying to draw her attention away from the glove. I shook out the coat, a nice caramel-colored double-breasted wool coat. "So, about this coat . . . what do you think?"

Two hours later, we'd worked our way through a pitifully small amount of stuff. At least, in my mind, it was only a tiny sliver of the job, but it was a start. And Dr. Harper had said not to focus on the amount of material we moved through, but instead to concentrate on encouraging Marie to develop the skills she'd need to sort and organize on her own. One pile in the entryway was gone and we'd uncovered the edge of a hall closet. In a few more sessions, she'd be able to open the closet door. For a second, I wondered what shape the hall closet was in, but I forced my thoughts away from that potentially scary thought. That was a battle for another day.

I set up our next appointment before I left and encouraged Marie to start on the next pile of stuff on her own. I thought it was important for her to try it on her own. I just hoped I wasn't turning her loose too soon. I pressed my card into her hand before I left and told her to call me with any questions. She gave me a quick wave from the doorstep and ducked her head back inside. I had the feeling she was glad to be rid of me. It had been a challenging day, but I thought we'd accomplished something and I admired Marie. It had to be hard to admit she needed help and then have someone go through her things.

Her neighbor was outside again. Long strands of Christmas lights wreathed his house and extension cords snaked down from the huge trees, then criss-crossed the lawn in a complicated pattern. He nodded at me again as I drove by. This time he was maneuvering several large reindeer out of the garage. I waved back and reached to answer my ringing phone.

It was Dorthea, our neighbor who lives across the street from us. "Hi, Dorthea," I said, always glad to hear from her.

"Ellie, where are you?"

"Only a few minutes away. Is something wrong? Are you okay?"

"I'm fine, but you better come home. I just came in from my walk and there's a car from the sheriff's department in your driveway and a large van. They're standing on your doorstep and they look very impatient—like they want to use a crowbar to get in. I asked what was happening and one of the officers said they had a search warrant."

"A search warrant?" I said, feeling as if I were coming out of a cocoon. I'd been so focused on Marie that I hadn't even thought of the murder investigation for the last couple of hours. I felt almost disoriented. *What could they . . . ?* Oh, my clothes, I realized, remembering what Paige had said about the specific questions Waraday had asked her about what I'd worn the day Jean died. Could they go in my house while I wasn't there? I wasn't sure of the finer points of the law, but I thought they probably could. "Well, don't let them break down the door. And Rex! If they go inside, he'll go crazy. He's in his kennel, but they won't know that."

"I'll take care of it, dear. Don't worry," Dorthea said, then the phone hit a hard surface with a resounding smack.

"Dorthea . . . are you there?"

No reply. The traffic light turned green and I hit the accelerator. I stayed on the phone line and in less than a minute Dorthea was back.

"They found the spare key you keep taped to the bottom of that decorative bench on your porch," Dorthea said. "I told them Rex was in his kennel. Good thing, too, because he was making a racket. I hate to think what might have happened. They are dead set on getting in there quickly. Does this have something to do with that poor woman you found the other day?"

"I'm afraid it does," I said as I pressed harder on the accelerator. "I'll be there as soon as I can."

When I arrived in our neighborhood a few minutes later, I'd already called T. Randall Hitchens's office. I knew Mitch had a late afternoon flight and he was already in the air, so I didn't even try and call him. I kept repeating to myself that I had nothing to hide. It didn't matter if they searched my house, because there was nothing incriminating there. But no matter what I told myself, I couldn't stop the jittery feeling that made my hands tremble. *They were in my house.*

I forced myself to slow down on our neighborhood streets, then stopped the minivan with a jerk in our driveway. I saw Dorthea framed in the big picture window at the front of her house, her face looking worried. I could hear Rex, his deep, steady barks unrelenting. I jogged up the steps and entered through the front door, which was standing open, letting in a cold draft. I automatically shut it, then headed down the short hallway to the master bedroom where I could hear voices. I fell into step behind a short man with a crew cut who wore a tan, long-sleeved shirt and brown pants. I followed him into my bedroom and felt as if I were in some sort of surreal dream. Waraday was standing in the closet and I could see there was at least one more person inside the closet, sliding hangers along the rod with a fingernails-on-chalkboard screech. As soon as the man in brown entered the room, he called out to Waraday, "I got nothing from the washer or dryer—no trace of blood."

Waraday turned toward the man, saw me over his shoulder, and shot a look at him that even I could interpret as *keep quiet.*

"You think I tried to wash blood out of my clothes?" I asked. "How could I have done that? You saw me yourself at Jean's house—I didn't have blood on my clothes."

Waraday didn't reply, just nodded to a female officer, who handed me a piece of paper. It was the search warrant. I tried to scan it quickly, but she motioned me back to the hallway and said, "Ma'am, would you come with me, please?" I wasn't sure if they had the right to keep me from watching them. I was about to protest when the person inside the closet said, "That's it. Nothing else here."

Nothing *else?* What did they have? I stood rooted to the floor, despite the female officer's tug on my arm. Waraday stepped away from the closet and a man followed him out. He held the crumpled sweater and slacks that I had worn the day Jean died, in his gloved hands. They had pulled them out of the clothes hamper. He transferred the clothes to an evidence bag and as he opened it wide, I caught a glimpse of the kelly green raincoat I'd also worn that day.

"Why are you taking those? Even I can see there's no blood on them. And they haven't been washed—they were in the clothes hamper."

"They'll be analyzed. If they're not entered as evidence, they will be returned to you," Waraday said in a formal, measured tone as he gave me a receipt for the items.

"But you'd be able to see if there was anything on them. For heaven's sake, the sweater is white!"

Waraday ignored me and left the room. The man with the evidence bag, the female officer, and the man in brown all followed him out. I stood there, stunned. I heard the front door close and the sudden silence of the house enveloped me. He wasn't about to give up on me as a suspect, I realized, dropping down onto the corner of the bed. Rex's insistent barks were still sounding, steady as a metronome. The doorbell rang, sending him into a new crescendo of staccato barking.

Wearily, I stood up and went to the door. Had they forgotten something? They already had my clothes, boots, and coat. What else could they want? My purse? *My underwear?* I thought sarcastically. Clothes they could have, but my purses weren't going anywhere. I'd been carrying a canvas and leather Prada purse that I'd snapped up at a garage sale for twenty dollars. If it went into evidence, I might not see it for years. And I hadn't even taken it out of the van when I went in to Jean's garage.

But it wasn't Waraday back to harass me—Dorthea was standing on my porch. She'd come over to check on me. Cooing and clucking like a mother hen, she shooed me into the kitchen, made me a cup of tea, let Rex outside, and then sat down across from me with her own cup of tea. I called the attorney's office with the news that the search was over. A secretary who was too chipper for my black mood took down all the details of what had happened and asked me to fax over the search warrant.

"So much for Christmas cheer," I said, hanging up the phone and climbing onto a bar stool. The tea burned my tongue, so I put the cup down. "I thought I was in the clear—that the investigation would focus on someone else besides me, but now it looks like Waraday is more determined than ever to pursue me."

"I wouldn't worry too much, dear," Dorthea said. "He can't manufacture evidence. You didn't do it, after all."

"Thanks for the vote of confidence," I said with a small smile.

Dorthea finished her tea, then said, "Call me if you need anything—anything at all."

"Hopefully it won't be bail," I'd muttered as I closed the front door behind her.

I pulled on a pair of rubber gloves and grabbed the bin of cleaning supplies. I didn't like the thought of strangers in my house, handling my belongings. It made me want to scrub the house from top to bottom. I moved through the rooms, vacuuming and dusting, but I couldn't shake the feeling of vulnerability. Dorthea's words about manufacturing evidence kept going around in my mind. I knew she'd intended to calm me down, but I couldn't help but think that if the murderer realized how tightly the investigation was focused on me, I was a ready-made scapegoat. One carefully planted piece of physical evidence—say, a blood-spattered piece of clothing left in the house or my van—would link me to the crime. And it wouldn't matter how much I protested that I'd never seen that item . . . I shook my head to stop that train of thought. Those ideas wouldn't do me any good. Unless . . . I could find someone who was a better suspect than me.

Tips for a Sane and Happy Holiday Season

Keeping Track of Gifts

Can't remember what you gave your nieces and nephews last year, much less which gifts are age appropriate? You can solve this problem with a small spiral notebook. Jot down everyone on your holiday gift-buying list and what present you give them. Add birth dates of children so you'll always know how old they are. A good place to store the notebook is with your holiday gift wrap.

Chapter
Ten

An hour later, I was vigorously scrubbing the soap scum on the shower wall, still contemplating how in the world I could turn up viable suspects in Jean's murder. I didn't like the exposed feeling of knowing that Waraday was watching me, examining my life so closely. Any hint of a connection to the murder and I knew I'd be in big trouble. Rex, who had been sprawled across the threshold of the bathroom, sprang up and sprinted down the hallway. Faintly, I heard the rumble of the garage door. Abby was here with the kids. Livvy and Nathan both knew the code to open the garage with the exterior keypad. Abby had been parking at the end of our driveway to keep her car off the street, something the home owner's association frowned on. I gave the shower a quick rinse and dried my hands.

The door from the garage to the house flew open and footsteps thudded through the house. It sounded like a miniature army was invading. "Mom, we're home!" Livvy announced unnecessarily.

"Never would have guessed," I said as I patted her on the shoulder. I grabbed Nathan for a quick hug as he dropped his backpack on the peg by the door and shed his coat, all in one swift movement. Livvy hadn't even hung up her coat yet and I could already hear Nathan rummaging in the pantry for a snack. "How was your day?"

She shrugged. "Fine."

I always wanted more details, but I didn't push it. The kids seemed to be the least talkative when they walked in the door from school. I'd get more out of them at dinner tonight. I opened the door to the garage to wave to Abby—Monday afternoon was her carpool day—but she was walking up the driveway, holding Charlie's hand.

"You didn't think I was going to just wave and drive off, did you?" she asked. "Couldn't do that after the day you've had. And I never did get to answer your question. The answer, by the way, is no, you're not crazy paranoid."

Between vacuuming and cleaning the bathrooms, I'd called Abby to tell her about the search and ask her if she thought I was being paranoid.

"What's party-noid?" Charlie asked.

"Paranoid, honey," Abby said. "It means to feel scared."

I handed him a package of cheese crackers and a juice box. "Do you want to watch TV with Livvy and Nathan?"

He didn't even answer, just scooted into the living room where he joined Livvy and Nathan for their allotted thirty minutes of wind-down time.

Abby followed me into the kitchen where I poured us two tall glasses of Diet Coke. I opened a bag of tortilla chips. I'd worked up an appetite cleaning. "The thing is . . . I can't think of anyone who'd make a better suspect than me."

"How can you say that?"

"The problem is that Jean was nice. No one hated her. She didn't have enemies."

"Or get into arguments with people at parties," Abby said, raising her eyebrows at me. I grimaced. "I do see what you mean," she continued. "Jean didn't rile people."

"No," I said with a sigh. "Apparently, she and Simon had a good marriage. Unless you've heard something different . . ." Abby shook her head. "I could ask Mitch if he's heard anything about Simon being unhappy or fooling around," I said uncertainly. Mitch had never been a big fan of my getting involved in criminal investigations. His "live and let live" philosophy was the exact opposite of my "take life by the horns and wrestle it into place" philosophy. Of course, he'd felt differently when he was in danger a few years ago. He'd sure been active then in trying to figure things out, but that was no guarantee that he'd be fine with me snooping around on my own. But if this was as far as I could get with ideas for suspects, he might not have much to worry about, anyway, I thought dismally.

"You'd think Waraday would be interested in Simon. Don't the police always check out the husband first? Isn't that like protocol or something?" Abby asked as she selected a chip.

"Yes, but Waraday told me Simon has an alibi. He was working out at Paige's fitness center." I left out the part about the Hula-Hoop class. We only had about nineteen more minutes before the kids' show was over and I didn't want to distract her from the topic at hand. Hula-hooping would be at least a ten-minute tangent.

We both chewed thoughtfully. Abby finally said, "Jean didn't work anywhere?"

"No. She had her Internet resale business, but I seriously doubt that some buyer would track her down and murder her if they didn't like the shipping time or the condition of their goods."

We ate some more chips. Finally, I dusted my fingers and said, "I can't think of anyone who didn't like her. She wasn't involved in anything controversial, except maybe the debate over what book the book club would read next. I just don't understand why someone would kill her."

Abby swirled the ice in her glass. "I suppose when you figure that one out, you'll know who murdered her."

"I suppose," I said with a sigh, thinking how tragic the whole situation was. I'd made a concentrated effort not to think about the scene in the garage—it only upset me, thinking of how Jean's life had been cut short so abruptly and so senselessly—but the picture was stuck in my mind and I knew I'd never forget Jean's crumpled body lying on the cold garage floor, her red suit a splash of color on the hard gray concrete. I leaned forward. "Why was she wearing a suit?"

Abby put her glass down. "Jean was dressed in a suit?"

"Yes," I said. "Have you ever seen her in a suit?"

"No. Only casual clothes like sweatshirts, T-shirts, and jeans."

"Me, too," I said eagerly as I stood up and paced to the other side of the kitchen. "Even at the Christmas party she wore jeans and a sweatshirt."

"What kind of suit was it?"

I knew Abby was asking if I recognized the style or even the designer, but that was far too fashion-advanced for me. "It was nice—a fitted, boiled wool jacket with a matching skirt."

"That doesn't sound like Jean."

"I know. Gabrielle wore it to a chamber of commerce meeting—that's why I thought it was Gabrielle at first, because of the suit," I said, realizing that I hadn't mentioned the clothing to Waraday. In the stress and confusion afterward I had forgotten all about it. "I probably should call Waraday and tell him."

Abby lowered her chin and gave me a long look.

"Yeah, right. No more chatting with the guy who wants to arrest me." I walked slowly to the other side of the kitchen as I said, "The suit probably was Gabrielle's, don't you think? I wonder why Jean was wearing it? Diane—from the food bank, you know her, right?—she told me she and Jean were supposed to meet for lunch the day Jean died, but I can't really picture Jean dressing up for lunch with a friend. Did she have another appointment afterward? A meeting?"

Abby shrugged. "You could ask her."

"Gabrielle? No, I doubt she'd even speak to me. I thought she was about to punch me at the funeral when we came face to face."

"Well, I better stay a few minutes then to make sure you two don't get into a brawl," Abby said, tilting her head toward the dining room window where I could see a black midsize crossover SUV rolling to a stop at the curb. A magnetic sign on the passenger door read GET ORGANIZED WITH GABRIELLE.

Still in her clingy black funeral dress and high stiletto heels, she marched across the lawn, head tilted down and shoulders squared. Since our garage was standing open, there was no way I could pretend I wasn't home. I opened the front door before she could ring the doorbell. "Hello, Gabrielle," I said. Her shoulders were set as if she was going to stand her ground. I wondered if she was prepared to throw her expensive shoe onto the threshold to keep me from closing the door on her, but then she caught sight of Abby, who was behind me in the living room.

"Don't mind me," Abby called as she reversed the sleeves on Charlie's coat, which had been pulled inside out when he took it off. "We're on our way out." I knew from personal experience that getting a kid out the door required at least five minutes. I should have a read on Gabrielle by then and know whether or not she still wanted to slug me.

"Oh . . . ," Gabrielle said uncertainly, crossing her arms over her chest and stepping back slightly. "I wanted to talk to you, but . . . I guess now isn't a good time—"

She didn't look quite so confrontational. Instead, she looked . . . cold and rather deflated. She hunched her shoulders against the cold as she said quickly, "I wanted to apologize for today at the funeral. Being so hostile. And for the other day . . . what I said." She stopped abruptly, threw her glance upward and shook her head. I realized that she was tearing up. Arms still crossed, she shrugged and made eye contact with me again. "I have this horrible habit of not thinking before I speak and I've got a really short temper—Jean was always telling me to calm down and think—but I never do." She sniffed and blinked determinedly. "Anyway, I lashed out at you and there was no reason for it, except that I was devastated to lose Jean and wasn't thinking straight. I should never have accused you of . . . anything. I'm sorry," she said, edging backward to the porch steps. "I'd like to talk to you about that day . . . give me a call when it's a good time for you."

"Wait, Gabrielle," I said. I'd never seen this contrite, apologetic side of her. She looked so miserable. I couldn't let her walk away. She'd just buried her sister—and she'd apologized. "Now is fine. Come on in. Would you like some hot chocolate or a cup of coffee? You look frozen."

She stepped hesitantly inside. "Coffee would be nice."

I waved for her to follow me into the kitchen. My

path crossed with Abby and Charlie, who was bundled into his coat and had on his backpack. He was so layered that his arms stuck out stiffly. Abby mouthed the word *wow* at me and I gave her the *I know!* signal with my eyes. Abby hugged Gabrielle quickly and said, "We're on our way out—papers to grade, you know. So sorry about Jean. I wish I could have come to the funeral today, but I couldn't get a sub."

Gabrielle nodded, seeming to choke up again. Abby squeezed her arm and said, "Let me know if you need anything."

"Sure," Gabrielle managed to say and Abby whisked Charlie out the door.

"Have a seat at the island," I said, and made coffee while Gabrielle pulled a tissue out of her pocket and wiped her eyes. I called out to the kids that they could watch the next show. There was a muted cheer in reply. I leaned against the counter near the sink.

"Thanks for this." She raised her mug and took a small sip. "And thanks for talking to me. I would have understood if you never wanted to speak to me again."

"That's a bit extreme," I said.

A hint of a smile turned up the corners of her mouth. "That's you all over, isn't it?"

"I'm not sure what you mean."

"Just that you're so normal." She waved her hand around, indicating the inside of the house. "Nothing too excessive, too crazy. You're the perfect suburban mom with two kids, a handsome husband, and a home-based organizing business. You've got it all. You'd never do anything so out of bounds as murder. It's just not *you.*"

"Ah—thanks," I said, not sure if she'd just complimented me or insulted me. It depended on your perspective, I guess. But there was no malice, no vicious little undercurrent in her tone today, not like there had been at the Christmas party when she'd given me the backhanded "compliment" about how cute my house was.

She wrapped both hands around her mug and gazed at me over the rim. "That's what I decided today at the funeral, when I saw you—really looked at you—I knew you couldn't be involved in Jean's death. You just weren't. It's a gut feeling. I always go with my gut. That's another thing Jean warned me about." She transferred her gaze to her mug as she said, "Jean and I were so different. She was quiet and steady, always following the rules. She always read the directions—used to drive me crazy. And she never tried to find our hidden Christmas presents when we were kids." A smile crossed Gabrielle's mouth. "I was the one sneaking down the stairs at midnight after Mom and Dad were in bed, trying to pry off the tape on the presents to see what we were getting for Christmas. I was the wild child, always challenging everything." She seemed to shake herself, then wiggled back in her bar stool and focused on me. "But I know I'm right about you," she said confidently.

I didn't know what to say. *Thank you for not suspecting me? Could you speak to the police on my behalf now?*

Before I could say anything, she continued, "I suppose you think it's odd for me to be here, but I couldn't stand it any longer, the funeral postmortem. Simon, so pale that he looked like something out of a bad vampire movie, and everyone going on about what a lovely service it was and how Jean would have liked it." A little tremor passed through Gabrielle, a shiver of revulsion, I realized, as she said firmly, "Jean *wouldn't* have liked it. She never should have died. She's not supposed to be dead. Talking about her funeral like it was something she would have enjoyed—it makes me want to scream."

She took a breath, then sipped her coffee. "Sorry to get worked up. It just makes me furious the way some people are . . . accepting Jean's death. Like there's nothing to be done, but bury her and get on with our lives. That's wrong. Whoever killed her has to be caught."

I nodded in agreement, hoping she wasn't about to swerve back into accusing me, but she surprised me by asking, "Was your house searched today?"

"Yes," I said guardedly. "How did you know?"

"Of all the idiotic things to do," she said under her breath. Then aloud, she said, "I confronted that investigator, Waraday, after the funeral and asked him pointblank if he was close to catching the killer. He said they were in the process of getting a search warrant, but wouldn't tell me for what, or where they were going to search. I heard later, after the graveside service. Hannah said it was your house. Nadia told her."

"Who'd heard it from Abby, who I called." I should have known by now how news moved with lightning speed through the squadron grapevine. I only had myself to blame that the news was out. Nadia loved to be "in the know." She would have made an excellent investigative reporter. And I couldn't blame Abby because I hadn't asked her to keep it quiet. I hadn't even thought about trying to keep it quiet, but I guess I'd assumed that I'd have a few hours, maybe a day, before it became general knowledge.

Gabrielle set down her mug with a solid click. She looked more revived. Her back was straight and she had the determined glint in her eye that I'd seen during the chamber of commerce meeting when she was going after new clients. "That settles it, then. I have to get involved."

"Involved? What do you mean?"

"I mean, I can't sit by and wait for Detective Waraday

to solve my sister's murder. If he's focusing on you, he clearly needs help."

"While I couldn't agree with you more about the focus of his investigation going in the wrong direction . . . what can you do?"

"I can make sure he hasn't missed anything—other suspects or evidence he should know about. When he spoke with me about the status of the investigation, I knew he was focusing on you. He never said anything specific, but I had the distinct impression that he thought you were the murderer. I was so wrapped up in grief, so *angry* that someone killed Jean, I just accepted it. But then today at the funeral, I looked into your face, really looked, and I thought, that man is crazy. Ellie Avery could no more murder someone than she could flirt with the school superintendent."

Before I could arrange my features into something less stunned—she was admitting to her underhanded methods?—Gabrielle breezed on. "So I need to figure out who else Waraday should be looking at. What do you think? I hear you've got some experience in this sort of thing."

"I have found out a few things in the past that have helped the police, but that doesn't mean we should get involved in this investigation," I said, thinking what a hypocrite I was. Hadn't I just been thinking the same thing—that I better find someone else for Waraday to focus on?

With a flick of her hand, Gabrielle waved away my objection. "We're not going to interfere. We're just going to make sure they find the guilty person."

"Trust me, Waraday won't see it that way," I said.

"Who cares? It doesn't matter if he's upset as long as we find out who killed my sister."

It did come back to that, I thought sadly as I chewed

on my lip. But, I wasn't sure I trusted Gabrielle. She seemed contrite and sincerely apologetic for accusing me of murder, but it might be an act. She didn't exactly have a track record of honesty and integrity, so I didn't completely believe her. But as she said, Jean was dead and Waraday wasn't going to find the killer if he kept looking at me.

"It's easy for you to write off Waraday," I said. "It's me he's after. If I step out of line . . . I know he'd love to charge me with interfering with an investigation and anything else he can come up with."

"Come on, Ellie," Gabrielle said, leaning over the countertop as she pleaded with me. "If we find anything, I'll take it to Waraday. He has to talk to me, anyway. I'm a family member and he has to keep me updated on the investigation. Please?" I wondered if she'd used that same upward, besecching gaze, through thick eyelashes, when she asked for the school district contract.

I carefully set my mug down in the sink and said, "Gabrielle, I really don't think it's a good idea—"

She dropped the pleading look and leaned back. With the manipulative appeal stripped away, her voice was level and serious as she said, "Ellie, I know you don't like me. I can even understand why you'd want nothing to do with me, but you knew Jean through the squadron. I know you weren't incredibly close to her, but you know how sweet she was. Please help me find out who killed her. And, on top of that, you're in a risky position. Do it for yourself. I realize now how reckless that was of me—flinging accusations at you. It certainly hasn't put you in a good position and I'm sorry about that. If we find anything, anything at all, that's got to help your situation."

I stopped chewing on my lip. She was right. I hated

it, but she was right. She was inside the family and had access that I'd never get—except maybe through a conversation with Simon, and I only knew him slightly, so I doubted he would have a heart-to-heart talk with me about Jean's possible killers. And Gabrielle had access to Waraday and the information he shared with the family.

"Okay," I said slowly, "but there's one condition—this is information-sharing only. We don't confront anyone or accuse anyone . . . or do anything else that could get us in trouble."

"That's three conditions," she said, grinning. "Oh, Ellie, thank you." She clasped her hands together. "This is going to be so terrific. I've never collaborated with anyone. We'll be partners. No, wait—partners in crime!"

Chapter
Eleven

"Not partners in crime," I said quickly. How had we gotten off on this? What had I gotten myself into? "More like partners *solving* a crime."

"Don't worry," Gabrielle said, unclasping her hands and jerking her purse into her lap. "I won't get carried away. I promise," she said as she dug around the large Louis Vuitton bag.

Why did I think she threw those words, "I promise," around much more freely than I did? She pulled out a wrinkled sheet of paper. "That's what I remember from the day . . . from the day you found Jean." She slid the sheet of single-spaced text across the island, then pulled out a notepad with a hot pink high-heeled shoe on the cover and opened it to a blank sheet. "Now, I need you to tell me everything you remember about that day," she said as she reached back with both hands and gathered her long dark hair at the nape of her neck, as if she was going to put it in a ponytail, then twisted it together and pulled it over her left shoulder. She picked up a pen and leaned over her notepad.

I blinked. She looked at me, pen poised.

"Okay, well, I thought you were there. That's why I walked in the garage. I saw the black SUV and thought it was yours. I walked in, called out, and when I didn't see you, I went over to Jean's work area. I didn't notice her right away because the plastic totes under the table blocked my view of the floor." I wasn't sure how Gabrielle would react as I talked about what had happened, so I'd been speaking slowly, delaying the part about when I found Jean, but Gabrielle looked up from her writing with her eyebrows raised.

"Go on," she prompted. She'd been so emotional when she arrived, but now she was very businesslike. She seemed to have walled off any feeling and was concentrating on only the facts.

I cleared my throat and said, "I walked farther into the garage and kicked something on the ground—it was the diamond-shaped Lucite paperweight from the white elephant gift exchange. I realized it had blood on it and that's when I saw her hand. At first, it was like it just didn't compute . . . it didn't fit. I thought it was a mannequin or something, but once it registered that it was an actual person, I hurried over there and saw her." I decided to leave out the part about thinking it was Gabrielle who was dead. I wasn't sure that was information my "partner" would like to hear.

Gabrielle nodded, swallowed hard, but stayed on task. "Okay. What happened next?"

"I checked for a pulse, but didn't feel anything. Then you came in."

"Yes," Gabrielle said. "That was . . . there are no words for how horrible it was," she said quickly, then pressed her lips together.

"Gabrielle, let's not rehash that afternoon—"

"No," she said sharply as she ran her knuckle under her eyes to wipe away a tear. "We have to. I have to know. I was so distraught, I didn't notice anything and my memory of what happened isn't good—it's all mixed up. I don't even know how long it took for the ambulance to get there. It felt like hours. And I didn't even see the paperweight that you saw. That's important." She scooted forward on the bar stool, back in control of her emotions. "Now, when you first went in the garage, did you notice anything . . . did you hear anything or smell anything different or unusual, a scent of perfume, anything like that?"

I thought back. It was a good question. "Ah—no. I didn't notice any unusual smell, nothing sticks out in my memory. It was warm. There was a space heater going. That's the only sound I remember."

Gabrielle wrote that down. "I didn't notice that space heater, either. Jean did use it on really cold days, but I'm surprised she had it on when the door was up. Usually she was a stickler about stuff like that—leaving doors and windows open when the heat or air conditioning was running—that was one of her pet peeves. Anything else?"

"No, only the drone of the heater stands out," I said, feeling in some absurd way like I was letting her down with my negative responses. "I wasn't taking an inventory, well, except for her work area. It looked like a wonderful setup. Did you help her with it?"

"Yes. I drove down a few years ago and designed it for her. Okay, tell me about the paperweight. Are you sure it was the same one from the gift exchange?"

"There's no way to know. There weren't any special marks or anything on the one from the party that would identify it. Considering the paperweights were a promotional giveaway from my insurance agent, there are probably thousands of those in middle Georgia. I assumed the one I saw in the garage was the same one I gave Jean after the party because there was a box on the ground near her work area with the other white elephant gifts." I shook my head. "The weird thing is that my fingerprints weren't on it—so maybe it wasn't mine."

Gabrielle tapped her pen against her teeth, then said, "That's interesting. Jean might have cleaned it—wiped it down—she tried to make everything look as good as possible before she photographed it. Or, it might be a completely different paperweight."

"Yeah, but that would mean someone would have to know the paperweight was there and bring one exactly like that . . . and then remove the one I gave to Jean. No, that's too convoluted."

"Doesn't matter how crazy it is. Right now, I'm writing everything down."

"Okay, then say it was mine. There are no prints on it at all now. If Jean cleaned it and removed my prints, then where are her prints? And the prints of the person who hit her with it?"

Gabrielle winced slightly at my words, but said, "It must mean that whoever used it to kill her wore gloves or used a rag to hold it so their fingerprints wouldn't be on it."

"I'm not an expert on legal definitions, but wouldn't that argue for premeditation?"

Gabrielle said, "I think you're right, except how would the person know the paperweight would be there?"

My thoughts shot to the people closest to Jean— Simon and Gabrielle. Both of them would know her routines. Simon would probably have seen the box of gifts between the time Jean brought it home and when she died. At the party, Gabrielle had been around when several of us gave the white elephant gifts to Jean. So Gabrielle would have known what was in the box and she had set up Jean's work area and knew her routines.

I kept my thoughts to myself, suddenly feeling uncomfortable sharing theories with Gabrielle. I didn't really know what her motives were. And even if the police had cleared Simon with his exercise class alibi . . . well, he was still Jean's husband and wasn't the spouse always on the suspect list? He could have had help.

Gabrielle brought me back to the present as she said, "Maybe the paperweight was just a handy object. There are lots of things in garages that are lethal . . ."

"But if it was planned, wouldn't the killer bring a weapon?" I asked, thinking aloud.

"Maybe the murderer was afraid the weapon would be traced back to them. Better to use something from the house itself." Gabrielle said, deep in thought.

I shifted uncomfortably, thinking the murderer wouldn't have to bring a weapon if he—or she—knew one was going to be handy.

A thought that had been lurking in the back of my mind, indistinct and foggy, suddenly came into focus. "You've heard about the break-ins?"

Gabrielle nodded, her eyes widening. "The ones where the victims have been squadron spouses? Do you think it was—what do they call it on those television shows?—a robbery gone bad? Do you think Jean got in someone's way and they freaked?"

"I don't know," I said slowly. "The situation with Jean doesn't really fit the pattern." Gabrielle was scribbling away on her notepad as I ticked off the differences on my fingers. "The other break-ins were at night, they were all at houses where the spouse was deployed, and no one was home. Well, except for one, when the family was away, at a hospital in Atlanta with a sick relative. And the break-in at Abby's house. She was at home."

She tapped the pen against her teeth again, then summarized, "The . . . incident . . . happened during the day and Simon isn't deployed, but he was in the squadron and he is gone quite a bit during the day. Even with all that, it's an angle we have to consider."

"You should ask Waraday about it."

"I will," Gabrielle said.

I heard the wrap-up theme music from the kids' show playing and asked quickly, "Do you know why she was wearing the red suit? It was yours, wasn't it?"

"Yes, it was mine," Gabrielle said, her eyebrows knitting together in a frown, "but I don't know why she had it on. She asked if she could borrow it and I said of course. I never asked her why."

"When did she ask to borrow it?"

Gabrielle tilted her head and looked at the ceiling. "I don't know . . . a few days before, maybe a week?"

"It could be important. Is there any way you can narrow it down?"

Gabrielle shrugged. "I don't think so . . . it's not like I made a note of it or anything. I remember we were on the phone when she asked, but we called each other all the time."

"It wasn't her usual style, not something she normally wore," I said, hoping to jog her memory.

"No. She hated heels, which was such a drag because she never had any shoes that I wanted to borrow," Gabrielle said with a sad smile.

"The suit was the only thing I thought that was strange . . . I wondered if she had a meeting or an appointment. I know she was supposed to meet Diane for lunch, but maybe she had something after . . ."

"Nothing I knew about," Gabrielle said, writing on her notepad, "but I'll see what I can find out."

The kids' show was over, so I sent Livvy and Nathan to brush their teeth, which bought me another few minutes. "What about the people in her life? I can't think of anyone in the squadron who was upset or angry with her. Was there anyone in her family . . . ?" I let my words trail off because Gabrielle was shaking her head.

"No. No one." Gabrielle capped her pen, closed her notepad, and shoved them in her purse. "I've thought about everyone—and I do mean *everyone*—who might want to hurt her. I can't even think of anyone who was mad at her. She wasn't one of those people to arouse emotions. She went through life . . . quietly—I guess that would be the word. She and Simon were happy. She missed Kurt, but was so proud of him, that he'd gotten into Harvard."

I nodded, remembering how excited Jean had been when she told us her son was going away to such a prestigious school. "And how is Kurt?"

"Devastated, now, but before—great. He had a few bumps his first year, but now he's a junior and has really settled in. He's making good grades and has an internship lined up at a brokerage house next summer."

"And the rest of the family?" I asked.

"There aren't any feuds or grudges in the family on either side." She stood up and shrugged. "I can't think of anything. She was in a book club, but I don't think they'd met for several weeks. Some of the women came to the funeral and they all seemed broken up about Jean. I don't think there's anything there, but I'll ask."

Gabrielle left, promising—or possibly threatening— to call me the next day with any news and I was caught in the homework–dinner vortex for the next few hours and didn't have a chance to read her notes. By the time the kids were in bed, I was exhausted. I staggered down the hall and dropped the bedtime story book, *The Best Christmas Pageant Ever*, on the coffee table. I'd been reading the kids one chapter each night and Livvy said she hoped their Christmas pageant was as good as the one in the book. I collapsed onto the couch with Gabrielle's typed notes and the mail. I clicked on the television because the house was too quiet.

It was the first chance I'd had to read Gabrielle's account of where she'd been on the day Jean died. She'd had an interview with a local radio station at seven-thirteen a.m. She'd shared tips for juggling Christmas chaos, as they called it. I probably should have tuned in, I thought. I wasn't doing a very good job of keeping up with our holiday activities.

I told myself not to be a sourpuss, but it still irked me that Gabrielle had waltzed into town and managed to snag my clients *and* local media attention. Not that I'd actively tried to secure spots on local radio and television—I was too busy with the clients I had and with my family to work in anything else. Correction: I *had been* too busy to court North Dawkins reporters. I wasn't now. Maybe after Christmas . . . I shook my head. I couldn't do everything. *Let it go*, I told myself, and got back to my reading.

Gabrielle had left the radio station at eight, driven to a client's house—I grimaced when I saw it was my former client Stephanie—and worked with her until noon. After returning my call, she'd driven to Jean's house where she found me in the garage huddled over Jean's body.

I folded the paper in half, thoughtfully. I'd spoken with Paige around noon. I'd probably stayed there until twelve-fifteen or so, then spoke to Gabrielle and driven the short distance to Jean's house. I'd probably arrived by twelve-twenty at the latest. I mentally calculated the distance from Stephanie's upscale neighborhood to Jean's house. Probably five minutes or so. But then that would mean that we'd have arrived at roughly the same time and I was sure I'd been in the garage at least five, maybe ten, minutes before Gabrielle arrived. I ran my hand down the fold of the paper. What took her so long? I yawned and stretched out on the couch, the mail balanced on my stomach. The last thing I remembered was opening a bill. I must have dropped off to sleep because I awoke to find Mitch leaning over me.

"I hope this isn't a message. We're not sleeping in separate beds, are we?" he asked.

"Uh?" I said inarticulately, taking in the bright television with the late-night talk show glowing behind Mitch, who was in his flight suit.

"You know, the bed is much more comfortable than this old couch," he said, and I woke up enough to recognize the hint of a smile in his tone.

"Yes, but it's not the same without you," I said as I struggled into a sitting position, sending a cascade of bills and empty envelopes onto the floor. Rex, who I was sure had been sleeping curled up on the floor beside me, was walking around the room in a slightly loopy manner, hoping someone would either pet him or put him to bed. Mitch reached down to scratch Rex's ears. "I heard Waraday was out here today," Mitch said.

I scooped up the papers off the floor and rubbed my eyes. It only took a few seconds for the events of the day to come rushing back into focus. "Yeah. Yeah, he was," I said with a sigh. "He took the clothes I was wearing when I found Jean, but I know there's nothing incriminating on them. I think he was trying to rattle me. Don't worry, though. Gabrielle and I are on it. We're going to find some other suspects for Waraday besides me."

"You and Gabrielle? Isn't she the one you don't like?"

Oops. Had I said that aloud? Dang it. I should have known better than to discuss things with Mitch when I was still groggy. If I'd been wide awake, I wouldn't have let anything about my sleuthing slip out. Too late now to go back. "I still don't like her. Don't really trust her, either, but she's got access to Waraday and to Jean's family," I said. "Of course, she hadn't heard any earth-shattering news on either front."

Mitch made a thoughtful "ah-hum" sound.

"You're taking this whole search-of-the-house thing better than I thought. To say nothing of the Gabrielle issue."

"I don't *like* either situation, and I was upset when I heard about the search, but it's not your fault that Wara-day's latched on to you. And, you're right, Gabrielle might know something that would help you out. Besides, I can't be mad at you for doing something that I'm doing as well."

"I'm sure that would make sense if I hadn't just come out of a deep sleep," I said.

"I may have some news later," he said as he reached out his hand and pulled me up.

"Really?"

"Maybe." He wrapped his arm around me as we walked through the living room, Rex sagging along behind us. "I'll know more tomorrow. Let's go to bed."

Tuesday

"Would you like some help with that?" I asked a woman who was struggling to balance a box of canned goods on the handle of her stroller. She tucked a strand of her pale blond hair back behind her ear and sent me a fleeting smile.

"Sure," she said as her son twisted sideways in the stroller, straining against the belt that held him, and let out a scream that reverberated off the food bank's steel walls. I had been unloading a corporate donation from a local restaurant when the front counter got busy. I wasn't scheduled to help out at the food bank today, but I was covering for Cecilia. She'd mistakenly scheduled an appointment with her obstetrician for the same time as her volunteer shift.

As I took the pallet of canned goods topped with a large container of powdered milk, she said, "Sorry about the noise." She was wearing a thin sweater and jeans. Her son, who looked to be about five or six months old, was bundled in a coat and knitted hat that covered his ears. She didn't look like the stereotypical person you'd picture visiting a food bank, someone homeless or down on their luck. She looked like any one of the moms I'd be seeing in a little while at the carpool line, but I'd learned that people from all economic levels were struggling to make ends meet. She expertly held the heavy outer door open with her heel and maneuvered the stroller over the threshold.

"Don't worry about it," I said as I followed her outside and walked with her down the long ramp beside the wooden steps. "I have two kids and I swore my first one was going to be an opera singer. She could hit all the high notes."

The woman smiled and said, "Over here," indicating a large SUV. She opened the back and wheeled the stroller around the side while I loaded the food. The boy's cries went down a notch as she transferred him to the infant seat. I closed the back door as quietly as I could, not wanting to startle him. There were several other cars ranged around the gravel lot with people loading and unloading food, but I did a double take and stared at one older Ford.

That wasn't Simon, was it? I squinted and shaded my eyes. Yes, it was, I realized as I watched his wiry figure arrange food in the back of the Ford. He still looked pale, but he was smiling and, although I couldn't hear what he was saying, I could tell he was keeping up an easy flow of conversation with an older, nearly bald man wearing a short-sleeved shirt and jeans, moving nervously from foot to foot while he waited for Simon to finish loading the food. Simon nodded at the man and shook his hand, indicating he'd close the trunk for him while the man climbed into his car.

The woman collapsed the stroller and I hurried to reopen the back of the SUV for her, surprised at how quickly I'd forgotten the stroller routine. It had only been a few years since I'd lugged a stroller and a diaper bag everywhere. "Thanks again," the woman called as she hurried to the driver's seat. I waved and turned back to watch Simon, intending to wait for him so we could walk in together. He pulled off his thick jacket and placed it on top of the food, then closed the trunk. He patted the car, waved to the man, and made his way across the parking lot. The older man had his eyes on the road and didn't notice Simon wasn't wearing his jacket.

I tilted my head and smiled at Simon as he made his way across the gravel lot toward me. "Helping Hands is doing clothing donations, too, now?" I asked, thinking that it was amazing enough that he was actually back working on the day after his wife's funeral—and then he goes and gives his coat to a needy person. Most people wouldn't be able to see past their own needs at a time like this. Had I seriously considered this guy as a murder suspect?

He glanced quickly over his shoulder at the Ford, which was creeping slowly over the speed bumps in the paved portion of the parking lot near the church. "You weren't supposed to see that," Simon said. "Against policy and all that."

"Don't worry. Your secret is safe with me. How are you doing?" I asked as we climbed the wooden stairs. I could tell from the dark circles under his eyes and the way he was moving—slowly, hanging on to the wood railing tightly and almost pulling himself up each step—that the last few days had taken an emotional and physical toll on him.

He gave a small shrug and turned his free hand up, palm out. "I don't know. I'll tell you later."

"Working helps?" I asked.

"It does." He opened the heavy door and waited for me to walk through first. "Gets me out of the house. I know everyone is shocked to see me today, but I can't sit at home. It's better to be here. At least here I can do something productive and make a difference, even if it is small."

"I can see how that might help," I said.

"Thanks for coming in today," Simon said as I moved back to the spaghetti noodles and he walked to the offices at the back.

The rush was over and the rest of my shift passed quietly and quickly. I buttoned up my coat and signed out. As I reached the door, it opened a crack, then an arm reached through the small opening, grabbed my wrist, and pulled me outside.

Once I realized it was Gabrielle behind the most ridiculously huge sunglasses I'd ever seen, I let go of my death grip on the door frame. "Ellie," she said, "good you're leaving. Just the person I was looking for. Don't you answer your phone?"

I patted my pocket and checked my purse. "I must have left it in the van," I said. "How did you find me?"

There was a second of hesitation, then she said, "I came to drop off a donation and saw your van."

"Do you need help carrying it inside?" I asked.

"No. I'll do it later." She gripped my arm again and pulled me down the stairs. "Come on. I've got something to show you."

"What?" I asked as I followed her across the gravel lot. Her car was parked beside my minivan.

She already had the car door open. "Just hop in. I'll explain on the way," she said.

"I can't. I have to pick up the kids in a few minutes." That wasn't exactly true. I had some time before I had to be at the school, but there was no way I was jumping in the car with her, especially when she was acting kind of weird.

"Ellie," she said with an eye roll that I could see through the sunglasses, "it's only a few minutes away. You'll be back in plenty of time." When I didn't budge, she said. "Fine. Okay. I don't have time to stand here arguing with you. I thought you wanted in on this, but that's okay. I'll call you. Maybe." She climbed into her car and slammed the door.

I checked my watch. I did want to know what Gabrielle had found. I knocked on her window and shouted. "I'll follow you."

She mouthed *whatever* and put the car in gear.

I hopped into the minivan.

Tips for a Sane and Happy Holiday Season

Holiday Shopping

The best time to do your holiday shopping is during the after-Christmas sales. This strategy requires some planning and storage space, but if you hit the sales, you can pick up fantastic bargains. If you have quite a few people you shop for, put a sticky note on each item with the name of the recipient, then store for next year. Store all your gifts in the same area to make it easy to find them months later. If you're not a plan-ahead shopper, you can still pick up a surefire gift at the last minute: a gift card. If you're not sure which store or restaurant the person likes, get them a generic gift card like a Visa or an American Express gift card, or—simplest of all—give cash.

Chapter
Twelve

Gabrielle drove fast and took the turns quickly. In less than two minutes we were turning into Simon's neighborhood. I realized she was taking me to his house. She parked in the driveway and I rolled to a stop at the curb where I quickly checked my phone. Three missed calls, all from her.

I climbed the steep driveway. Gabrielle had already punched in the code on the remote garage door opener keypad and gone inside. I paused in the gloomy garage. I couldn't help but glance over to the last bay, where I'd found Jean. A burst of light flashed in the shadows. I heard the distinctive click of a camera shutter. "Gabrielle, is that you?"

"Over here," she called as my eyes adjusted to the dim light. There were more rapid flashes and clicks of a shutter.

"What are you doing?"

"Photographs," she said shortly as she moved to the opposite side of the garage and took a wide shot. Then she rotated the lens and moved to Jean's work area. She began clicking away, photographing close-ups of the work table and the floor. "I thought it would be best to do our investigation exactly like the cops. Photograph everything, record everything."

"They've already done that."

"I know," she said impatiently. "But it doesn't seem like they're using them. And we don't have those photographs to look at. We need our own photographic record."

"Okay," I said slowly, thinking that she was going a little overboard on the crime scene investigation. "What did you want to show me?"

"In a minute." She'd worked her way around to the other side of Jean's work area and was snapping pictures of Jean's shelves of inventory. "I don't know how long Simon is going to leave this stuff here. He's being funny right now, not touching any of her stuff, but he's acting so strange that he might throw it all out tomorrow. I wanted to get it photographed."

"I saw Simon today at the food bank. He seemed . . . okay." Not the best term to describe someone whose wife had been murdered, but he had been functioning and even interested in helping other people—that had to count for something.

"Yeah, well, maybe he's different when he's there, but here at home, he's definitely erratic—weeping one minute, furious at the world the next."

"Does he know you're here?"

"Of course," she said quickly. "Hey, is that the box you saw with the white elephant gifts?" she asked, pointing to an open cardboard box on the floor.

"Yes, it is." The picture frame, the bat box, and the sewing machine were all in it. I used a knuckle to push the frame aside and look into the box. "Everything else is in here, I think. Would she sort everything on the floor?"

"No." Gabrielle switched the camera off. "She usually put what she was working on over there by the shelves. I've never seen her work with items on the floor." There was a gap under the table about the size of the box.

"I bet she had it stored under the table," I said, pointing to the faint trail of dust.

Gabrielle whipped out her camera and photographed the floor. "I don't think Jean was working with these things. I bet someone pulled the box out, found the paperweight, and wiped it clean before . . ."

I touched the edge of the box, where there were black smears. "I think this is fingerprint dust."

Gabrielle shrugged. "But if the person wore gloves . . ." She cleared her throat. "Come on," she said, and charged over to the door to the house. She was inside before I could say anything.

Reluctantly, I trailed along behind her. This didn't feel right, but I'd never been good at tamping down my curiosity. The doorway from the garage opened into the kitchen, a large room with dark wood cabinets and a huge Formica-topped island with bar stools ranged along one side. There was a box of cereal on the island along with a menu for Chinese take-out and a few crumpled napkins.

Gabrielle picked up the menu and said, "He's ordering take-out when he's got all that food in the refrigerator?" She slapped the menu back on the counter and opened the refrigerator. "He threw it out? All of it?" She yanked the freezer door open, then shoved them both closed rather hard. "I can't believe he'd toss all that perfectly good food." She seemed to remember I was with her and ran her hands down the lapels of her coat. "I can't stand waste," she said.

She certainly was passionate about it, I thought, as I nodded agreement. I hated it when the kids didn't eat all their food, but did I act like that? I wondered. She moved to another part of the kitchen and I scanned the rest of the room.

An oak dining table separated the kitchen from a family room with worn couches and a rather tired-looking recliner. A woman's black cardigan was draped over the back of one of the dining-room chairs and I wondered if it was Jean's. Surely not. It would be kind of weird to leave it out, almost as if she could walk in at any moment and put it on.

Three Christmas stockings dangled from the fireplace mantel and an artificial tree stretched to the ceiling, its branches crammed with all sorts of ornaments. Fragile glass globes nestled next to ornaments made of Popsicle sticks and glitter, obviously made by her son when he was younger.

I looked away from the tree—the whole situation was so sad. I focused on Gabrielle, who was bent over a small built-in desk in the corner of the kitchen. While I'd been looking around, she'd been at work with her camera again, but had put it away. "Gabrielle, does Simon know we're here?" I asked again.

She didn't look up. She closed one drawer and opened the one below it. "He doesn't mind. I had to drop off those sympathy cards," she said with a wave of her hand at the dining-room table where a few pastel sympathy cards were stacked. "We're just taking a quick look around."

"So he doesn't know we're here," I said.

"I'm in and out of here all the time," she said. "Not a big deal."

"But you said Simon has been acting strange. You don't think poking around his house while he's gone might upset him?"

She shoved the last drawer closed and stepped back,

hands on hips. "I don't know. He's . . . skittish. Better that we do this and get it over with. No need to upset him unless we find something. After all, he wants Jean's killer found, too." She'd repositioned the sunglasses that she had pushed up on her head and was looking around as she talked, clearly more interested in whatever she was looking for than in talking to me.

She strode across the family room and opened a door to a hall closet near the front door. She checked the floor, then parted the coats and peered into the back of the closet.

"You said there was something you wanted to show me," I said.

"I was so sure it would be in her desk," Gabrielle said in an undertone. "I thought maybe it fell on the floor when she was putting her coat away, but there's nothing there." Gabrielle moved away from the closet, her forehead wrinkled in a frown.

I crossed the room to the closet. It didn't look as if anything was out of place. A mix of men's and women's coats hung on the rod and a row of matching gray luggage lined the back wall from a large oversize suitcase to a small overnight bag. There was a gap where a small rolling suitcase would have fit. "What are you looking for? The small suitcase?"

"No, Kurt probably took it to school. Her calendar. She had a date book with a nice leather cover. That's what I wanted to show you."

"Maybe the police took it?"

"No, I saw the inventory of the things they put into evidence and it wasn't on it."

"Maybe her bedroom?" I suggested.

"No, I looked there yesterday. Simon blew up." She raised her eyebrows and gave a little shake to her head as she said, "He wasn't upset that I was in her room. He was upset that I was cleaning things out. But, he can't leave all her things as they are forever. He's going to have to get in there and clear them out. I don't know what he's thinking."

"Maybe it's too soon."

She let out a heavy sigh. "Maybe. I guess it's the organizer in me. I can't stand the thought of her things— her clothes, her books, her knitting, even her makeup— sitting around getting dusty like they're some sort of museum display. That's pitiful and not a good way for Simon to live."

"You might give him a week or two," I suggested.

She made a noncommittal noise. "Where else would she put her date book?" Gabrielle asked, returning to her main concern. "The more I think about it, the more important I think that date book is. Jean was very old-school. Her cell phone was positively ancient and she hardly ever used it. She didn't like to be on the computer and only used it for her business. I don't think she ever sent me an e-mail—said it was better to just talk to people, that all that new technology only got in the way of communication and became a time waster."

"She might be on to something there." I tilted my head, thinking about where Jean would go during her day. "Could it be in her car?"

She snapped her fingers and said, "Good idea."

She nearly knocked me over as she rushed back to the garage. I pulled the door to the kitchen shut, then walked across the garage to the black crossover SUV that was so similar to Gabrielle's.

"Found it!" she said, backing out of the car. "It was stuck under the passenger seat." She put the brown

leather date book on the hood of the car and opened it
to December, then went still. "Nothing? The day she
died is blank?"

"Only a note about lunch with Diane."

"Maybe there's something else—a notes section?"

Gabrielle's hands were shaking as she viciously flipped
pages. She slapped it closed and shoved it at me. "Nothing. There's nothing."

I turned the pages, seeing normal entries: book club,
spouse club, dentist, lunch with "G," which I assumed
meant Gabrielle.

"Look at these," I said, pulling out a few folded
pieces of paper from the back. There were a couple of
glossy brochures for apartments and a flyer with a border of holly promoting a move-in special.

Gabrielle yanked them from my hand and quickly
flicked through the pages. "These are left over from
when she helped me look for an apartment," Gabrielle
said, and shoved the pages into a trash can, then stalked
out of the garage. I stood there, contemplating going
after her, but decided to give her a few minutes.

I skimmed through the rest of the sections—phone
numbers and a section of notes that were nothing more
interesting than grocery lists and reminders to return
books to the library. There was one page of numbers
that made me pause.

I walked slowly outside. Gabrielle was leaning against
her SUV, arms crossed. The sunglasses were back over
her eyes, but it looked as if she was staring at the thin
scalloped layer of clouds in the distance. As I walked
up, she said, "I shouldn't have gotten my hopes up. I
just want to know what happened. And for there to be
nothing . . ."

"Well, I don't know if this is something or nothing,
but it's . . . different from everything else in here," I

said as I held out the date book and pointed to a page with two columns of numbers. They ranged from three-digit numbers all the way up to seven-digit numbers.

"What could they be? They're not long enough to be phone numbers."

"I don't know. I'd think they were lists of dollar amounts, but there's no dollar signs or periods or commas."

"If they're about money, then these are huge amounts. That one would be a million dollars," she said, her voice incredulous. "It can't be money. Simon and Jean were fine financially, but they didn't have that kind of money. It's got to be something else."

"Lock combinations?" I said, half joking, but Gabrielle missed my lighter tone.

"No. I don't think lock combinations have three-digit codes." She put the date book on the hood of her SUV and photographed the page, then flipped back and got shots of all the calendar pages. "I'll send you all these photos once I get them downloaded." She looked considerably more upbeat than she had a few minutes ago.

Later that evening, I was pushing a grocery cart through the grocery store. Livvy and Nathan were gripping the sides of the cart, their feet braced on the bottom rack. The classroom Christmas parties were scheduled for later in the week and I was on the list to bring cupcakes for both classes, but I had no cake mix, no frosting, and—ultimate horror—no sprinkles.

Since it was a quick run to the store, I'd gone to the local grocery store instead of the commissary on base. I spotted a familiar figure moving slowly along the last aisle ahead of me. "Cecilia," I called. She twisted around and waved. She wore running shoes, black yoga pants, and a pale yellow workout top. In the formfitting clothes, I could just make out the hint of a pregnant belly. While she waited for me to catch up with her, she took a box of ice cream sandwiches off the shelf and put them in her basket.

"Caught red-handed with the ice cream," she said as I came even with her. She greeted Livvy and Nathan, then said, "I know I should feel guilty about the calories and the sugar, but I want one so bad."

"You've got some fruit in there, too, so I wouldn't beat yourself up about it. Besides," I said as she fell into step beside me, "I bet you worked out today."

"As you can tell," she said, gesturing to her makeup-free face and her pale yellow hair, which was held back with a thin headband, then gathered into a ponytail. "Stroller brigade. We've missed you."

"I know, but the holidays are so busy. I'll get back soon."

"Hey, thanks for covering for me at the food bank. Sorry if it put you behind," she said, crinkling her beaky nose up in an apologetic expression that made her small, circular glasses rise slightly.

"It was no problem. It was the least I could do after you rescued me from Wisk," I said, leaning into the basket, pushing harder to keep up with Cecilia's fast pace as we hurried down the aisle to the checkout lines.

"Oh, that wasn't hard. Gavin takes care of our cats, now that I'm pregnant." She saw me glance again at her basket, which was loaded with multiple boxes of macaroni and cheese along with about twenty cans of soup. "Don't worry, that's not all for me. Food bank donation. Did you get the e-mail?"

I shook my head. "No, I've been so busy I haven't even checked it today."

"Food donations are down this year and they're running low. I figured the least I could do was to pick this up for them, since I missed my slot today."

We separated to go through different lines, then met back up again at the exit to the parking lot. Cecilia pulled her keys out of her tiny shoulder bag. "I'm over this way."

"Me, too," I said, taking long strides and pressing hard against the cart's handle to keep up with her. We were power-walking again.

"Whee!" Nathan called as we bumped along at our fast pace.

Cecilia said, "I still can't believe what happened to Jean. Have you heard how the family is doing?"

"I saw Simon at the food bank and he seemed all right. Not good, but coping."

"Such a shame about her and Gabrielle. I really hope they were able to patch things up before Jean died."

"Wait—there was a disagreement?"

"Well, it sure sounded like it to me," Cecilia said. "I heard them arguing over their lunch at Chili's. I was in the booth behind them."

"When was this?" I asked. Gabrielle had told me that there weren't any feuds or issues within the family.

Cecilia tilted her head as she thought. "A few weeks ago."

"I wonder what they were arguing about?" I said, slowing my pace to match Cecilia's as she neared her white Kia.

"Property. A house they'd inherited. It sounded like Gabrielle wanted to sell it, but Jean was telling her it would be better to rent it out." Cecilia fingered her key chain as she said, "I know it sounds like I was eavesdropping, but they were talking really loud. The more they talked, the louder they got. Gavin and I felt really uncomfortable. We were going to stop by their table on our way out, but then after they argued, it didn't seem like a good idea. They left before us, anyway, so I don't think they ever knew we were right there, hearing everything."

"So they didn't come to an agreement?"

"No! Jean said her mind was made up and Gabrielle said she wasn't going to change her mind, either. Gabrielle stormed out and then Jean left a few minutes later."

"Maybe they did get past it, because they seemed to be getting along at the squadron spouse party."

"I know. It might have just been me, but I thought there was some tension between them." She shrugged as she clicked the button to pop the trunk. "Maybe I was reading into the situation—because of what I'd heard at the restaurant, but they didn't talk to each other much, you know."

"That's true—," I said, then broke off when I glanced inside Cecilia's trunk. She put the grocery bags in and slammed the trunk back in place.

"I suppose we'll never know. Anyway, great to see you," Cecilia said. "Don't forget. Book club at my house this week."

"What? Oh, right. See you then," I said, and slowly pushed the cart down the aisle to my van.

I wasn't absolutely sure, but it looked like Abby's gray snakeskin purse was in Cecilia's trunk.

Chapter Thirteen

I should have said something. Right away. Why hadn't I just said, "Hey, you have a purse like Abby's. I've been looking for one of those. Where did you find it?"

But I hadn't. I'd been so surprised to see the gray snakeskin shoved in the back corner of the trunk that I hadn't known what to say. At least, I thought it looked like gray snakeskin. What if I was wrong? Had there been a glint of silver, shining from behind the thick blanket that covered the rest of the purse—or whatever it was? Or was that just my imagination? Instead of mentioning it casually, I'd done my usual tongue-tied routine and kept silent. Now, sitting in the darkened auditorium, tapping my foot in time to "Angels We Have Heard On High" while watching the kids straggle onto the risers at the front of the room, all I could think about was that possible sliver of snakeskin. What if it *was* Abby's purse? Why would it be in Cecilia's trunk? Could Cecilia have found it somewhere? And why did it look like she'd been trying to cover it with a blanket? But if she didn't want anyone to see it, then why open the trunk when I was right there? She could have easily put the groceries in the backseat of the car.

I shook my head impatiently. There was no way I could work out an answer to that question without talking to Cecilia and I wasn't sure how to approach her. I couldn't casually mention the purse now, especially since I'd only seen a small part of it in the trunk. I couldn't exactly say, "Hey, the other day I thought I saw Abby's purse in the trunk of your car. Did you know it was stolen?" If I could somehow sneak another look, then I'd know for sure. Maybe I could conveniently run into her again the next time she did her grocery shopping. Mysteriously run into her at the library and offer to stow her books in the trunk for her? Too crazy and weird.

I stood up and walked to the back of the auditorium where several parents were chatting. Abby was talking to Nadia. I slipped out the door before she spotted me. I decided not to bring up the possible gray snakeskin sighting to Abby. She was impulsive and, until I knew for sure or came up with some way to figure out if it was her purse, there was no use in mentioning it.

I walked through the lobby area of the church, past the Christmas trees glittering with their tiny lights, swaths of gold ribbon cascading down. I pushed out through the heavy glass doors into the cool, dark night. It was cloudless and tiny pinpoints of light glowed in the inky sky. I wished it would all go away—Waraday, the feeling that I wasn't sure who I could trust, and that premonition, that nagging feeling, that things were somehow going to get worse. I wanted a normal Christmas with my biggest worries being simple things like getting my Christmas cards out on time and finding the perfect gifts for the kids. I didn't even want to think about all those Christmasy items on my to-do list that weren't checked off. I was being a very bad Santa and had to get in gear to make sure I bought the kids' gifts before the stores sold out.

I paused at one of the benches positioned around the front of the church. I could still hear the faint notes of music from inside. The music stopped and I knew the shepherds were making their way from one side of the stage, their "pasture," to the other side where they would find Mary and Joseph and the baby at the stable. I drew in a deep breath of the chilly night air, thinking of the Christmas story and how cozy and snug "the barn" looked on stage, but in reality, it had probably been cold and a bit scary, that first Christmas night. Having her baby in a barn far away from her relatives was probably not how Mary had envisioned the birth of her first child.

I shook my head to myself, thinking how often I wished for some abstract ideal. The picture-perfect Christmas of glossy magazine spreads didn't really exist, not in my life, anyway. I had to accept that and move on. It wouldn't be the end of the world if my Christmas cards arrived late and I knew I'd find wonderful presents for the kids. We were together, everyone was healthy and happy—those were the important things.

I drew in another gulp of the brisk air. It felt good to be outside and absorb the quiet, still night. A silent night, I thought with a smile. But then a pair of headlights cut through the darkness as a car turned into the parking lot. Swerving around the speed bumps, the car accelerated toward the building, then cut sharply to the side, making for the road that curved around the side of the building. I was in the shadows of the wide overhanging portico surrounding the front entry to the church, so I doubted the driver noticed me, but as the car bumped onto the unpaved road that led to the gravel parking lot of the food bank, I could read the sign on the side of the driver's door. GET ORGANIZED WITH GABRIELLE.

Gabrielle certainly wouldn't have been in my plan for a perfect Christmas, but it seemed she was one of the cards I'd been dealt and I needed to talk to her. I stood up and walked down the steps, then turned toward the food bank. The rehearsal had just begun. The kids would be singing and reciting their lines for a while. I had time to catch up with Gabrielle. I needed to find out if she and Jean had had a disagreement. I wasn't sure how to broach the subject, but I really needed to know if she was being honest with me. Was she playing me?

I decided honesty was the best policy. I'd just ask her. I wasn't good at beating around the bush and I was still kicking myself for not just asking Cecilia about the snakeskin purse. I'd ask Gabrielle if she and Jean had had a disagreement. It wasn't that uncommon for sisters to argue—it probably didn't mean anything, but I had to know. I would have trusted what Cecilia said— why would she lie? But, then again, why would she have something that closely resembled Abby's stolen purse in her trunk?

Gabrielle was probably checking on Simon. The food bank had already closed, but I knew Diane would still be there, shutting down computers and turning off lights. Simon was probably there, too. I was pretty sure Gabrielle wasn't picking up a late-night volunteer shift. She seemed more like the type of person who'd organize a fundraiser before she'd stock shelves. And she would be great at raising money, I thought as I walked along, digging my hands into my jeans pockets, wishing I had grabbed my coat. I could see Gabrielle running an auction or Vegas-style casino fundraiser. I'd have to mention it to Diane or Simon and see if they'd consider it.

I heard a car ahead of me coming around the corner of the building, its headlights washing over the thicket of trees beside the road. It wasn't moving fast, but I hurried off the road and continued walking beside the building. The car came even with me and stopped, then the window rolled down. "Ellie, are you okay?"

I was surprised to see Cecilia inside, but then I remembered the food bank donation she'd bought at the store. She'd probably driven here directly from the store, just like we had. In fact, I could have offered to drop off her donation, if I'd thought about it. I'd been so flustered by the possible sighting of the missing purse that it hadn't crossed my mind, but now I was glad I hadn't. I had another chance.

"I'm fine . . . just going to check in at the food bank," I said, leaning down to the window. "The kids are rehearsing for the pageant." I waved toward the church building behind me.

"So that's what all the cars are here for," she said. "Do you want a ride to Helping Hands?"

"No, it's only around that curve. Thanks, though." She glanced at the road and moved her hands on the wheel, preparing to pull away, so I said quickly, "Hey, do you have a gray snakeskin purse?"

Her chin moved up, pushing her lower lip flat, an expression that said she had no idea what I was talking about. "No . . . ," she said, drawing out the word.

"Oh, okay. Someone had one," I said, scrambling wildly to think of some reason I'd be asking her about a purse—this was why I don't do things on the fly. "I wondered if it was you. I was looking for one like Abby's." At least that much was true. "Maybe you've got something similar, something made of gray snakeskin, and I'm just confused . . ."

"Nope. Not me," she said. "See you later." She waved and edged the car away.

No guilty look or betraying fumble for an answer. I guess I was wrong . . . but I really had thought it looked like Abby's purse.

I cleared the corner of the building and the food bank's parking lot came into view. Two empty cars sat beside each other. I recognized Gabrielle's SUV and Diane's Subaru wagon. The door to the food bank swung open and I heard Diane's voice. "I'll get the door for you."

I was about to call out, but Gabrielle followed Diane out the door, carrying a box. A square of light illuminated her face and I saw her glance quickly around the parking lot, as if she was checking for cars. "Thanks," she said. "Sorry to keep you late. Traffic, you know." Her voice had a tone that I'd never heard, strained and . . . almost soft. Her southern accent was still there, but more muted, as if she didn't want to be heard.

Traffic? In North Dawkins? Other than the bottleneck that developed at the gates to the base at seven in the morning, traffic jams were pretty much nonexistent.

"Of course," Diane said in a mild tone. "Don't worry about it." I'd heard her speak that way before with especially skittish clients. "Do you need help . . . ?"

"No. No, I've got it," Gabrielle said as she pushed the button on her remote key chain and the back door to her SUV popped open. "Thanks again. See you later. Well, hopefully not *here*. Not that I don't want to be here," Gabrielle said as she hurried down the steps and put the box in the SUV. I could see that it was filled with food items. A package of spaghetti noodles stuck up over the edge and the light glinted off circles of cans packed into the box. "I mean, I'd love to help out . . . sometime." She sounded breathy and flustered.

Gabrielle was picking up food from the food bank? I was stunned into silence. I'd been about to call out to her, but as it dawned on me why she was there, I hung back in the shadow of the building. Her comments about the funeral food made sense now. She needed food. No wonder she'd been so upset that Simon had emptied his refrigerator.

"I understand. We'd love to have you. Anytime," Diane said, still standing at the top of the steps as she held the door open. I thought there was a little extra inflection in that last word—another layer of meaning. As in, *stop in anytime to volunteer or for food.*

Gabrielle revved the SUV into a quick turn and was out of the parking lot before the door fell closed behind Diane.

Wednesday

The next morning after I dropped the kids off at school, I headed for the interstate that flanked the outskirts of North Dawkins. I merged into the traffic heading north and set the cruise. I'd spent a good portion of the night tossing and turning. For the first few hours, Cecilia occupied my thoughts. Since she'd denied owning a purse like Abby's or anything made of snakeskin, I was at a dead end unless I could get another look in her trunk. But after another sleepless half hour, I couldn't come up with one even slightly plausible reason to get another look.

I signaled and moved to the fast lane to pass a car. I suppose I could have followed Cecilia around and tried to use Mitch's binoculars from his hunting gear to get a long distance look in her car trunk, but that idea seemed chancy at best. If she did have the missing purse, did Cecilia have the rest of the stolen items from Abby's house? The idea seemed ludicrous—Cecilia breaking into Abby's house? But if I was going to go that far in my thinking . . . was it possible that she'd broken into the other houses, too? Maybe even Jean's house and, like Gabrielle had suggested, she'd freaked out when Jean spotted her. Had she then killed Jean to keep her secret life as a burglar quiet? No, I just couldn't picture it.

I'd spent the rest of my sleepless hours contemplating what I knew about Gabrielle. After seeing her obvious embarrassment and unvarnished need at the food bank last night, I'd realized that there was more to Gabrielle than I thought. If she was to the point that she was getting food from the food bank—a move that I was sure from her body language and words was a last resort for her—then she had to be in dire financial straits.

I shifted uncomfortably as I zoomed past the exits for Macon. No wonder she'd gone after my clients. If you couldn't buy food . . . well, that could make you do some pretty crazy things. Of course, it didn't make it right. Desperation wasn't an excuse for bad behavior. And if she was desperate . . . well, people did awful things when they were desperate. I already knew Gabrielle wasn't above using underhanded methods to get clients.

I had to know if there was a conflict between her and Jean and—if Cecilia had been telling the truth about it—how deep the rift was between them. I'd felt all along that I couldn't completely trust Gabrielle, but now I needed to know if her deviousness stopped at stealing clients or extended to her sister. I'd come to the conclusion that I needed to do a little research, ask a few questions, before I asked Gabrielle anything. She was slippery and I wanted facts when I talked to her. Thus, this road trip.

It was frightening how easy it had been to find information on Gabrielle's ex-husband. I checked Jean's obit in the local paper for his name, Dennis Matheson of Stockbridge, Georgia. Stockbridge wasn't far from Atlanta and it was small enough that I was able to find Matheson Builders listed in a local business directory. A few phone calls and I had Dennis's current job location, a warehouse under construction in an industrial district on the southeast side of Atlanta.

When the traffic snarled and slowed, I knew I was getting close to Atlanta. I exited the interstate for a state highway that took me directly to the industrial district. As I pulled into an unpaved parking area, kicking up dust, I called Mitch at the squadron. "I'm here," I said.

"You made good time."

"I should be back before the kids are out of school. You won't even have to leave work early. Did you find out anything?" Mitch had asked a few discreet questions at the squadron about Simon . . . if there was anything unusual going on in his life.

"Not a thing. He's a pretty boring guy, aside from his Hula-Hoop fetish."

So the word had gotten out on that. "Umm. I may have heard something about that," I said evasively.

Mitch's gusty sigh came over the line. "Of course you have, and did you share this with me? No."

"Come on, it wasn't my secret to share. I only knew about it because Waraday told me when he was questioning me. He specifically told me not to repeat it. Besides, would you have been able to keep quiet about it? Honestly?"

"Not for a minute," he said, and I could hear the smile in his voice.

"But that's it? Nothing else? No fights, arguments, disagreements . . . or, I don't know . . . secret assignations?"

"No, the word in the squadron is he was a loyal husband and a really good golfer."

"Okay," I said. "Well, let me see what I can find out about Gabrielle. I'll check in with you before I drive back."

I walked up to the cavernous building, scanning the people in hard hats. I'd had a fleeting look at Gabrielle's ex-husband at the funeral and I didn't see anyone who looked like him. I hoped I hadn't driven nearly two hours only to miss him. It didn't seem like a good idea to call ahead this morning. It was easy to say no on the phone—harder to do it face to face. But if he wasn't here . . .

I stopped a guy in his early twenties and asked for Dennis Matheson. He waved me toward a backhoe that was grinding around the corner of the building. I made my way over the uneven ground toward it. When I was close enough, I waved and the man driving it braked. Brown hair curled from under the edges of the hard hat and his worn face was sunburnt below his sunglasses. "I'm Ellie Avery. I live in North Dawkins. I'd like to ask you a few questions about your ex-wife," I called over the rumble of the engine.

A disgusted look passed over his face and he shook his head, waving me out of the way.

"She's asked me to work with her," I shouted, then suddenly thought of my mental jabs at Gabrielle for her dishonesty. But it was true, she had asked me to work with her. Okay, it was a half-truth, but I needed to get him out of the backhoe. Maybe Gabrielle and I had a few more things in common than I realized. Of course, I knew what my motives were. I wasn't sure what hers were.

He contemplated me for a second. I tried to look as if I was willing to stand in the sun all day and wait for him. He pulled some levers and the backhoe lumbered off to one side. I thought how thrilled Nathan would have been to see it up close. We'd read every picture book the library owned about construction equipment many, many times.

Dennis came walking back to me, moving quickly over the distance. He took off his hard hat and removed his sunglasses. "Over here," he called, leading the way to the gaping hole that would be a large rolling door when the warehouse was finished. Once we were in the shade, he turned to me as he tucked the stem of his glasses into the neckband of his dusty T-shirt.

"Working with Gabrielle, uh?" he said. "Now, you look like a nice, reasonable sort—except for showing up without an appointment." He said it with a flash of a playful smile. "Why would you want to get mixed up with Gabrielle?" He didn't really want an answer because he barely paused before pouncing. "Can't say I'd recommend it. There's only one thing I can tell you about her. She's as stubborn as she is beautiful," he said as he squinted over my shoulder, his dark lashes crinkling around vivid blue eyes.

"Is that why you got divorced?" I asked.

"We got divorced because of money." He put the hard hat down on a pile of steel beams and crossed his arms. "Or lack thereof."

"Oh. Sorry to hear that." He shrugged and broke eye contact again.

"I think she might be having a hard time . . . financially," I added.

"So she's trying to bring you on . . . bring in some capital? Everyone's got it tough right now. This is the first job I've had in six months, so there's no way I can send anything to her. I've still got four months of missed mortgage payments to clear off my house note and two kids in college. If she's asking you for money to keep her organizing business afloat, you'd better think long and hard on it. I won't be sending any cash her way."

"No, that's not what I meant," I said, deciding I better clear things up quickly. "She asked me to help her find out who murdered Jean and I'd like to help her—"

He snorted. "Thinks she can do better than the police, uh? That's classic Gabby, right there. Always knows better than everyone else. She should just stay out of it."

Since I'd heard the mind-your-own-business line quite a bit, I felt a little affinity with Gabrielle. "Actually, the police aren't making any progress." I didn't mention why they weren't making progress. No need to bring myself into this discussion.

He looked skeptical, then tossed his hands up. "You know what—I don't care. She can play Nancy Drew all she wants. Not my concern. Not anymore." He moved to pick up his hard hat.

"Look, I'm just concerned about one thing—if you'll tell me if it's true or not, I'll get out of your way. I've heard about something—something from her past that makes me wonder if I can trust her. I figured you were the person to ask about her past. There's no one in North Dawkins who's known her for more than a few months, well, except for Simon and he's not someone I want to bother right now."

"Okay," he said, looking resigned. "Shoot."

"Did Gabrielle and Jean ever argue about a house? An inheritance?"

Dennis wiped the film of dust off the hard hat as he said, "Yes, ma'am, they fought like two cats, squalling and clawing each other."

"Why?"

"I answered your question," he said as he put his hard hat back on.

"But it's related. Please." I sidestepped along beside him as he walked toward the open doorway. "Can you just tell me what happened?"

He stopped walking and braced one hand on his hip. "They inherited the house from their mom. Their mom's will left it to Jean with the provision that if she sold it or rented it, Jean got sixty percent and Gabby got forty. That lit up Gabby pretty good, that it wasn't divided fifty-fifty, but her mom reasoned that Jean was the executor of the will and would handle the estate. She figured Jean should get more. And Gabrielle isn't what you'd call farsighted. Their mom probably figured Gabby would put it on the market and sell it dirt cheap." Dennis grinned, his cheeks pushing his eyes into slits. "Of course, that's exactly what Gabby wanted to do. There was a buyer and all, but Jean said they should wait until the housing market came back. Even if it was in Buckhead, they'd get more for it if they rented it out now, then sold it later."

"Buckhead?" I asked, because Buckhead meant big bucks. It was one of the most affluent neighborhoods in Atlanta.

"Yes, ma'am, Buckhead. The neighbor was hot to buy it and expand his house over the two lots, but Jean wouldn't hear of it."

"So Gabrielle didn't take it well?"

"No. She was furious the day the rental contract was

signed. So furious that she called me to complain—old habits die hard, I guess."

"But they were talking and getting along when I saw them together at the party," I said.

His face softened and he said, "Gabby was still upset, but there was nothing she could do about it. Probably figured she should let bygones be bygones. Gabby has a quick temper, but it does die down fast."

"So they split the rental income sixty-forty?"

He nodded. "As far as I know."

Then why had Gabrielle needed food from the food bank? A house in Buckhead should rent for quite a bit.

". . . 'Course, they had just signed the rental agreement, so now with Jean's death, I don't know what happens to the house. It's probably tied up in probate. Doesn't really matter, I suppose, since the rental agreement is for two years. There's no way Gabrielle can kick them out now and sell the house."

"Thanks, you've been really helpful . . . I think," I said. Dennis touched the brim of his hard hat and strode away.

"Oh, wait!" I called out as I pulled a paper from my pocket. "I almost forgot. Do these numbers mean anything to you?" Gabrielle had sent me all the photos she'd taken and I'd printed the page with the jumble of numbers to bring with me today.

He shook his head after a quick glance. "No idea." He handed the paper back and resumed his fast pace.

I followed him more slowly. So Cecilia was right about the argument, but apparently Jean and Gabrielle had made up by the time the Christmas party rolled around, enough that Jean had brought Gabrielle along to help her find clients. Gabrielle must have reconciled herself to the situation. Maybe she decided the idea of some monthly rental income, even forty percent, was a good thing.

Or, did she still want it all, I wondered, thinking about those five to ten minutes that were unaccounted for before she arrived at Jean's house and found me over Jean's body. If she caught a few red lights, that could account for the delay, but still . . . Perhaps Gabrielle had already been to the house. If Jean was out of the picture, wouldn't Gabrielle control all the income from the house? What if Gabrielle left for a few minutes while I found the body, then returned?

Suddenly, it seemed very important to find out if Jean had a will.

Tips for a Sane and Happy Holiday Season

Make Your Decorating Easy

Wrap the end of each strand of holiday lights with a piece of tape, noting whether they are indoor or outdoor lights and where you used them. This simple step will speed up decorating next year.

If you use the same decorations in the same room each year, consider storing items that are displayed together in the same box or bin. Label the box with the name of the room where the decorations will be used and you'll save yourself many trips back and forth across your house.

Chapter
Fourteen

The traffic wasn't as light on the way back to North Dawkins, but I still arrived back in town well before school let out. I called Gabrielle. She answered on the first ring, sounding harried.

"Gabrielle, it's Ellie. I'd like—"

"Ellie!" she said, interrupting me. "Just the person I wanted to talk to. The book club was a total bust—they didn't know anything, but I found a handwritten list in the pocket of another jacket that Jean borrowed from me. We traded clothes all the time and I got to thinking that she was always leaving bits of paper in the pockets, so I went through the last few things she borrowed from me and found a list."

"What kind of list?" I asked as I took the exit for North Dawkins.

"The date is at the top—last Thursday," Gabrielle said, her excitement quickening her normally languid speech patterns.

"Yes, I know." The day Jean was murdered, I thought with a little shiver.

"The list says," Gabrielle continued, "borrow G's red suit, printouts, and an address."

"So this list wasn't in the pocket of the suit she was wearing that day she died?"

"No. The sheriff's department still has that suit. This one was from another jacket. I haven't worn this jacket since Gabrielle returned it to me. I bet she made this list a day or two before to help her remember what she needed for that day."

"Where's the address?"

"I don't know. I'm on my way there now. You should meet me," she said, and rattled off a number and street so quickly that I didn't catch it.

"Whoa, slow down. You didn't just look it up online?"

"No, I just found the note a few minutes ago. I'm between appointments. I don't have anything until two, so I just punched it in the GPS. It said I was only a few miles away."

"Where is it again?"

"2717 Sweetgum Way."

I heard the sophisticated voice of her GPS instructing her to turn left. I had enough time to meet her before school let out. Mitch had gone by the house at lunch to let Rex out, so I didn't have to head home right away. But I wasn't sure I wanted to meet with Gabrielle alone, especially since I'd wondered if she'd been in the garage wielding the paperweight.

"You have arrived at your destination," said the clipped British voice through the phone.

"Oh," Gabrielle said, her voice deflating like a popped balloon. "It's a restaurant. The Red Dragon."

"I'm not far from there," I said, thinking quickly. "I can be there in a few minutes. Have you had lunch?"

"No." She didn't sound enthusiastic about a lunch

meeting, but I wanted to find out if she knew anything about Jean's will. For instance, if Jean had one. I wasn't going anywhere near Waraday until I had all the details and I certainly didn't want to be alone with Gabrielle. What better place to ask my questions than a crowded restaurant? I'd been there a few times with Mitch and the lunch clientele was mostly business types and local government employees from the smattering of office parks and county offices located nearby.

"See if you can get us a table. I'll be there in a few minutes," I said.

Since it was after one o'clock, the Red Dragon wasn't packed, but there were enough full tables that I felt comfortable as I slid into the high-backed red leather booth across from Gabrielle. She wouldn't make a scene in here or do anything . . . outrageous. At least, I didn't think she would. I'd waved to the mayor and two county counsel members on my way to the table.

Gabrielle slapped the plastic menu on the table, causing a small square of yellow paper on the table to jump. "The hostess doesn't remember anything."

"It has been a week. Let me check something," I said as I found a number on my phone and dialed. When the receptionist at the food bank answered, I asked to be transferred to Diane. After I said hello, I asked, "Where were you and Jean meeting for lunch the day she died?"

"The Red Dragon," Diane said, her tone immediately infused with sadness. "I still can't believe I was sitting there waiting for her while . . . ," her voice trailed off.

"I know," I said quickly, because I could tell she was getting choked up. "Look, I'm sorry to dwell on this—I know it upsets you—but did Jean usually dress up for your lunches?"

"Dress up? No," Diane said, her voice sounding more normal. "She always wore the same thing . . . jeans, sweatshirts, that sort of thing. Why?"

"Just wondering. Gabrielle and I were talking and we were trying to figure out if Jean had some other appointment that day. She was wearing a really nice suit when she died."

"She never mentioned anything to me," Diane said.

I ended the call and said, "You got most of that, right? Jean was supposed to meet Diane here and she didn't mention another appointment."

"Yeah, I heard," Gabrielle said, almost sulkily, reminding me of Livvy when she was in a bad mood. She rotated the square of paper one quarter of a turn and said, "I'd hoped that there would be something else . . . some sort of breakthrough."

"Is that the note?" I asked.

She pushed it across the table and I examined it. It was just as she described. "Well, at least you found the restaurant," I said. "Any clue on what the printouts are?"

Gabrielle shook her head and the waitress arrived to take our order. Gabrielle carefully put the note back in the pocket of a fitted caramel-colored blazer while I ordered cashew chicken and a Diet Coke. Gabrielle ordered sweet and sour pork. "You probably should give that to Waraday. It could be important."

"I might give him a copy," she said.

I didn't think Waraday would be satisfied with that, but she clearly didn't want any more advice on the note. I picked up my silverware bundle and folded back the napkin. "Gabrielle, I heard that you and Jean had a disagreement about your mom's house."

She raised an eyebrow a fraction. "So?"

"I heard it was a pretty vehement disagreement."

She leaned over the table. "Who did you hear this from?"

I didn't think I should rat out Cecilia, so I said, "Someone in the squadron overheard you arguing, but does that really matter? Why did you say there were no conflicts or disagreements in the family, when you and Jean were fighting over the house?"

"We weren't fighting over it when she died," Gabrielle said, adjusting the collar of the creamy white shirt she wore under the blazer. "We'd worked it out. And it was nothing, anyway. Sisters argue all the time. It's like a natural law or something."

"So you were okay with not getting your way? Not selling the house?" I said as I carefully laid out my silverware on the table.

Her eyes narrowed. "What is this? Some sort of inquisition? Checking up on me wasn't the deal between us."

"No, the deal was that we'd find out who killed Jean. You were straight with me. Now, I'm going to be straight with you. You told me you didn't suspect me, but the more I hear about this fight, the more I wonder about you. Did Jean have a will? Are you going to get your way now that she's gone?"

Neither of us heard the waitress approach and I was startled when she set our steaming plates in front of us. "Watch those plates. They're hot." She placed my drink on the table, refilled Gabrielle's iced tea, and glanced from one to the other of us uncertainly. Gabrielle was staring at me with a hard, cold glare. The waitress asked tentatively, "Y'all need anything else?"

I raised my eyebrows at Gabrielle. She drew in a deep breath and I braced myself. I wasn't sure if she was about to launch into a screaming fit or stand up and stalk away.

She said, "No. We're fine. Thank you."

The waitress gave us an extra long look and backed away. I bet she wouldn't be back to check on us anytime soon. She was probably going to give our table a wide berth.

The intensity of Gabrielle's gaze dropped from a glower down to merely a frown as she busied herself flipping open the napkin vigorously and then aligning her silverware. I ate a few bites to give her time to decompress a bit more. Tangy and sweet, the food was wonderful.

Finally, she said, "Okay. While I think what you've done is underhanded, I appreciate you considering every possibility, but suspecting me is absurd." She dug into her pork and after a few bites, she said, "We disagreed about the house, but I wouldn't murder her over it." Her tone was earnest. I studied her face and thought she was probably telling the truth. Probably. "And in the end maybe Jean was right," Gabrielle said slowly as if it was painful to say the words. "The monthly income will be a good thing. As far as the will, Jean had one, leaving everything to Simon. She told me she was going to have a new one drawn up that left the house to me, but I don't know if she did that before she died. So you see," she waved her empty fork in a circle, "killing her would be the absolute worst thing I could do. Now her estate will be tied up until Simon figures out if she made a new will."

"But wouldn't that be something he'd know about?"

"She mentioned using one of those online legal services, so she could have done it all herself, had someone sign it—you'd think it would be Simon—but he *says* he didn't sign anything."

Was there a hint of disbelief in her words? "You don't believe him?"

"I don't know what to believe," she said with a sigh.

"Simon is a good guy, but he's been so unpredictable these last few days. I asked him about Kurt's birthday, which is coming up in three weeks, and Simon had completely forgotten about it. I know he's dealing with a lot right now, but to forget your son's birthday? Especially now. I just don't understand it. I wonder if the stress and the grief is messing with him . . . mentally. Does grief do that to you? Mess up the way you think?"

"I don't know," I said, thinking of how normal he'd acted at Helping Hands. Was he putting on a good front there or was Gabrielle exaggerating things?

"Anyway," she continued, "Jean might have run over to the neighbor's house or asked some friends to witness her signing a new will. So I don't know. I have all her files and paperwork back at my apartment. I'm going through them as quickly as I can."

"*You've* got them?" I asked, chasing a renegade cashew across my plate with my fork.

"Simon had them in the recycling bin! I found them by the curb this morning when I went by to check on him. See what I mean? Who throws out all their wife's papers the week after she dies?"

"It does seem a little hasty, but you never know how people will handle grief. Maybe he took your advice about cleaning out her things."

She shrugged and changed the subject. "I told him you're helping me."

"What did he say to that?"

"Nothing. He just nodded and went back to watching the morning show. I hope he goes to Helping Hands today. He seems to be able to function better away from the house."

"So he doesn't mind that you're asking questions?"

"No. He couldn't seem to care less."

"Did you ask Waraday about the break-ins . . . any connection between them and Jean?"

"He doesn't think there is any link. He mentioned all those same things you mentioned, about how it doesn't fit the pattern, but," she thinned her lips in disapproval, "I think there could be something there."

I was about to mention my having possibly seen Abby's stolen purse, when Gabrielle glanced at her watch and visibly started. "My two o'clock! I have to go." She dabbed at her lips with the napkin, then reached for her purse. "I'll leave you some cash for the check."

"No, that's okay," I said, remembering her trip to the food bank last night. And here I'd insisted we eat lunch out. No wonder she'd seemed reluctant to join me. She opened her mouth to argue, but I said, "Really, let me get it this time. Your turn next time. Besides, you need to go. It's ten till two."

I caught a flash of relief on her face, which she quickly hid by calling the waitress over for a to-go container. She scraped every last bit of her pork into the box before saying good-bye. I think every male in the place watched her hurry through the restaurant, hips swaying as she threaded through the gaps between tables. I swear, she even hurried seductively, I thought, shaking my head, half amused, as I cracked open a fortune cookie. *Happiness is your friend.* That's not a fortune—that's a statement, I thought.

The waitress dropped off the bill and I was reaching for a twenty when I felt someone loom at the edge of the table. It was Waraday. He was dressed in casual civilian clothes—a polo shirt embroidered with the name of the county sheriff's office and khaki chinos—but there was no mistaking the badge attached to his belt.

"Well, wasn't that cozy?" he said, glancing through

the window at the front of the restaurant, where I could see Gabrielle's dark head, hair shifting in the light breeze, as she walked to her car. "Mind if I join you?"

I was so surprised to see him that it took me a second to respond. How long had he been in the restaurant? He certainly hadn't been here when I arrived. I would have noticed him. He must have arrived while Gabrielle and I were talking, probably when I was wondering if she was about to turn the butter knife into a weapon. I put the money with the bill and hoisted my purse onto my shoulder. "I was just leaving," I said, scooting to the edge of the booth.

Waraday sat down across from me. "This will only take a minute. I hear you took a little drive today."

Did he know I'd gone on a short road trip? "I usually drive every day. Comes with the whole mom-slash-organizer thing. School, clients, store," I said.

He pushed Gabrielle's plate aside and rested his forearms on the table. "To Atlanta?"

How did he know about that? Was he following me around? I discarded that idea as soon as it popped into my mind. He had better things to do than tail me, but I wouldn't put it past him to assign someone else to keep an eye on me. I hadn't noticed anyone following me—to Atlanta or anywhere else—but I hadn't been looking for anyone. Thank goodness I'd put the cruise control on and hadn't broken any speed limits. He was still locked on to me as a suspect, I thought, and that faint drumbeat of fear that I'd managed to almost silence began to grow again, pounding along with my heartbeat.

"Yes, I went to Atlanta today," I said, careful to keep my tone even, bland almost. What was I thinking with that snappy retort about driving every day? I did not need to get cocky. And where had that quick reply come from? I usually wasn't fast off the mark. It would be awful if the one time I did manage to blurt out a smart comeback, it irritated an officer of the law. Did I have T. Randall Hitchens's phone number on me? Was I about to be taken into custody, I wondered, my gaze sweeping the restaurant. I didn't see any other uniformed law officers or anyone who looked like they were waiting for Waraday's signal to slap cuffs on me. I tried to take a deep breath without sounding like I was in a yoga class doing a cleansing breath. This was a free country. I could drive to Atlanta if I wanted to.

I used my most polite voice to ask, "Is there some problem?"

Waraday arranged his smooth baby-faced features into a scowl. "It's fortunate you came back. I wouldn't want to lose track of your whereabouts . . . that could be problematic."

My palms felt slick on my purse strap. "I didn't realize there was a limit on my activities."

"Just need to know you're still around, Mrs. Avery." He angled his head toward the front window. "Of course, I wonder why you felt the need to drive to Atlanta this morning, then turn right around and come back. And why would you and Ms. Matheson meet for lunch?"

Under the table, I pressed one of my palms down on my jeans. "Gabrielle doesn't think I killed her sister," I said, gazing steadily at him.

"So all that animosity between you two is gone?" he asked, his tone skeptical.

"I still don't know her very well," I said carefully. Nerves made my heart pound and I knew my voice sounded a bit breathless and uneven, but I continued, "We got off on the wrong foot, but we're both mature adults and can get past that."

There was a small part of me that wasn't totally convinced Gabrielle was one hundred percent innocent, but until I had more than a suspicion, I wasn't about to say anything to Waraday. No matter how badly Gabrielle had treated me, I wouldn't do that to her. And it couldn't hurt for him to see us getting along, either. That situation had to irritate him.

"Uh-hun," he said, clearly not believing a word I said about Gabrielle and me. "All right, Mrs. Avery." Waraday slid out of the booth. He adjusted his badge as he stood. "Just so you know . . . it wouldn't be a good idea to leave town again."

Chapter Fifteen

Thursday

I woke Thursday morning after a restless night of crazy dreams. I dreamt I was wrapping presents; well, more accurately, I was trying to wrap presents, but kept getting waylaid. I couldn't find the wrapping paper, then the ribbon, or even the presents themselves. Then Waraday popped up with a gift that he insisted I open, but I couldn't get the ribbon untied. In the way of dreams, it was all twisty and mixed up with lots of tangents and double-backs that seemed to make perfect sense in the dream, but in the clear light of morning were garbled and odd. However, the main underlying meaning was clear—I was stressed.

It was going to be a busy day and I plunged into it, glad to have activities to keep me busy. I had an appointment with Marie and I absolutely had to finish my Christmas shopping. The kids would be out of school soon and it was measurably harder to sneak gifts into the house and hide them when the kids were home. The squadron Christmas party was coming up, too. Had

I picked up my dress from the cleaners? I didn't think so. Another item to add to my list. And, I had masses of cupcakes to bake for school parties, I suddenly remembered.

I spent the morning in the toy aisles, then I baked and frosted cupcakes until the whole house smelled like chocolate. I left a few out on the counter for the kids and hid the rest in the laundry room. Absolutely no chance of anyone disturbing them in there.

I arrived at Marie's house at one o'clock and rang the doorbell. Above me, the wind whispered through the ancient branches of the pecan trees. I glanced around, feeling as if someone was watching me. There was probably one of Waraday's guys lurking somewhere nearby, but I couldn't see anyone. And there certainly hadn't been a sheriff's car following me this morning. Maybe Waraday had called off the surveillance. I shifted my feet and pressed the bell again, looking over my shoulder as the hairs on the back of my neck prickled. I twisted around toward a movement I'd seen out the corner of my eye, then relaxed. It was Marie's neighbor. He was again in his black-and-red flannel jacket, but this time the outfit was topped off with a red Santa hat. He was hauling several inflatable yard decorations out of his garage. His house was becoming quite Griswold-like. Lights rimmed every window and dripped from the eaves. I could see wires engulfing the trees and—I squinted—yes, those were strings of lights laid out in a grid pattern across the lawn. He was carefully stepping through the checkerboard pattern as he carried a sagging Rudolph made of lightweight nylon.

I returned my attention to Marie's house. I stepped back and looked at the windows. No movement. I'd stopped by yesterday for a short appointment last night after dinner. Marie was making great progress. We'd managed to clear her hallway and she was doing well on her own, too. I wouldn't have thought she'd have forgotten about our appointment today since I'd mentioned it last night as I was leaving.

Maybe she was around back. She'd never cancelled before. I dialed her number on my cell phone as I crunched through the dry yellow grass to her backyard and climbed the flight of steps to her raised deck. Her backyard sloped away from the house rather steeply, ending at a thicket of longleaf pines dripping with vines. The deck wasn't large but it was high. The sharply descending angle of the ground meant the edge of the deck farthest away from the house was about six feet off the ground. Panels of lattice stained the same dark brown as the deck enclosed the lower portion. It was quite a climb, but I was sure the view was terrific. I bet she could see beyond the copse of trees that enclosed her neighborhood to the gently undulating countryside in the distance.

I forgot all about checking out the view once I cleared the top step. *What was this?* One side of the deck was stacked waist high with bulging white trash bags. A potent smell of decaying things engulfed me. I crinkled my nose and made my way through the trash bags and knocked on the back door. "Marie," I called uncertainly.

I banged harder. "Marie," I yelled. "Are you all right?" She hadn't answered the phone and the putrid smell worried me.

The door inched open and Marie's eye appeared in the slit between the door and the door frame. "Hi, Ellie." She sounded miserable.

"Hi, Marie," I said, striving for a natural-sounding voice, even though I was surrounded by mounds of stinky trash bags. The last time I was here, she'd done really well—selecting items to throw away without her usual hesitation. I thought we might have turned a corner, but . . . maybe not. I glanced at the trash bags. Some of them were full of fabric—clothes pressing against the thin plastic. Other bags seemed to be filled with food. "What's going on?"

"Oh, Ellie," she said, her voice only slightly above a whisper. "I've messed up . . . really bad."

"Okay . . . what did you mess up?"

"Everything."

The door wavered an inch. "Can I come inside?" I asked. "It's cold out."

She took a sniffling, deep breath and said, "I guess so . . . you've already seen what I was trying to hide." She looked as if she were about to face a firing squad as she opened the door.

As I stepped into the kitchen, I pointed over my shoulder at the trash bags. "You didn't want me to see those?"

She nodded. Head drooping and shoulders hunched, she looked miserable. "I didn't mean to leave them there . . . it just sort of happened."

"That's the trash and charity donations from our last few appointments?" I guessed.

She grimaced. "Yes."

"Okay. That's not so terrible," I said, unwinding my scarf from around my neck. I unbuttoned my coat and placed it over the back of a chair, taking in a quick inventory of the kitchen. It wasn't organized and there were plenty of piles of accumulated stuff to deal with, but it was livable, a functioning kitchen. It wasn't in any worse shape than it had been the first day I'd looked around. The oven, microwave, and refrigerator were accessible and there was a tiny bit of counter space for food prep. Not ideal, but workable. I pulled out a chair and said, "Tell me what happened."

Marie sank into the chair across from me. The china teacups and tiny commemorative spoons were still there and looked like they hadn't been moved since Marie and I first sat here. Marie pushed her fiery hair behind her ears and said, "I was going to give the charity stuff away, but then the donation truck got rescheduled and the trash . . . well, I was going to throw the trash away." She tilted her head toward the door to the deck. "All of it. But when trash day came, I didn't want to do it." She looked down at her tightly clenched hands. "I told myself it was because I didn't want to haul everything to the curb, but truthfully . . ." She sighed. "I started thinking about all those things . . . how I might need them someday or that I could find a way to use them—like the cardigan with the tear . . ."

"And the glove with the hole that needed to be mended. And how you don't knit," I said gently.

"I was thinking about that. I might take a class."

I stifled a sigh of my own. I wished I could put this conversation on hold and make a quick call to Dr. Harper for advice, but that wouldn't be very effective and I had a feeling the advice would be the same—be patient and nonjudgmental, but remain firm. "Marie, it doesn't make sense to keep an item because you might one day take a class and learn to mend it. If anything, you'll take a class and knit a whole new sweater and then you'll need a place for it."

She stared at me for a moment, then blinked and looked away.

"What's going on with the bags of food out there?"

"Oh." She sat up a bit straighter. "Kitchen scraps— I'm going to start composting. It's so good for the environment and I'll save money because I won't have as much trash."

"That's a great idea," I said, "but shouldn't the scraps be in the composter, not on your deck?"

"Yes . . . I don't have one yet. I can buy one, or you can build them. I thought that Cole might want to build one when he gets back. He likes home improvement projects."

"It's not a good idea to keep food in trash bags on your deck. It will attract raccoons and other animals."

She stared at her hands, her face slightly mulish. She'd been so contrite a few minutes ago, but now she looked determined. "Look, it's up to you," I said, backing off. "You hired me to help you organize your house, not your backyard, but I'm seeing a pattern. You have great ideas and plans," I said, touching one of the commemorative spoons, "but you don't seem to follow through on them . . . that's one reason you have so much stuff. I think you might want to really think about what you enjoy and where you want to focus your time . . . otherwise, we'll get your house all sorted and organized, but then you'll fill it up again with more stuff related to new plans you have, plans that you don't get around to because you've moved on to a newer idea."

She moved the spoon I'd touched back into line, staring hard at it, her jaw working. *Oh no, she's about to burst into tears. I'd made a client cry.* I had to be the worst organizer in the world.

"You're right," she said flatly.

"Marie, I'm sorry—wait. What did you say?"

She sniffed and blinked a few times. "You're right. I don't follow through. All these grand plans are just excuses to hold onto things. I can talk myself into keeping these things . . . I really don't want to throw all that stuff away. Throwing it away bothers me, worries me."

"I know. I can tell," I said, trying to think of some way to encourage her to keep going. Despite the fact that my professional life would be easier if she wasn't my client, I didn't want her to give up. I wanted her to change the way she thought and the way she lived. I didn't want her to spend her time feeling guilty and worrying that she was messing up.

"Have you brought any of those things back into the house?"

"No."

"Well, that right there is progress, an accomplishment." Another thought struck me. "Do you like the way your entryway looks now?" I asked.

"Yes."

"Let's go look at it," I said, grabbing her arm and pulling her with me down the still-cluttered hallway. Once we reached her entry, I could feel myself relax in the open space. There was nothing on the floor, no piles of things, so there was room to stand without stepping on something. You could even turn around. "This looks great. You've done so good not filling it up again." Marie grinned faintly at my praise. "And look, you can open your front door and your hall closet door, too," I said, demonstrating. I sure hoped the closet was still in good shape after our last session, otherwise my little pep talk would backfire. I swung the door open and smiled. "See . . . you can get your coats now, all of them."

I'd been slightly afraid to open the hall closet when we'd first uncovered it, but it wasn't as bad as I thought it would be. It was almost as if the hall closet had been sealed off like a long-lost tomb as Marie's piles grew in the hall. Once we'd opened the closet door, she'd discovered forgotten jackets and several framed prints. I was relieved to see that she'd only added a few things to the closet since our last session. Gloves and hats were stacked on the shelf, coats hung neatly on the rod, and an umbrella was propped in the corner. There was a half-open box of toys, blocks, puzzles, dolls, and cars in one corner. A few scarves were woven through a hanger designed to hold several pairs of pants.

"Those toys are for my nieces," she said quickly, almost defensively.

"Great place for them," I said. "And I love the way you've stored the scarves. Very clever."

"Oh, thanks," she said. "It seemed like a good idea. They don't get as tangled and I can see what I have."

"I may have to borrow that idea for my newsletter."

"Great," Marie said with a big smile.

"Now," I turned serious. "What about the bags on the deck?"

She shook her hair away from her face. "I'll throw the food scraps away. Garbage pickup is tomorrow. You're right about composting. I shouldn't save kitchen scraps . . . what was I thinking?" she asked, and I could see she was in danger of slipping back into a bleak mood. I wanted her to stay positive, so I said briskly, "Good idea. You can decide later if you really want to compost. Now, if you're ready to get rid of the charity bags, I can make that happen, probably today." I had several local charities on my speed dial. I was willing to bet that one of them could make it to Wiregrass Plantation to pick up a significant-size donation.

Marie looked around the clear entryway and scanned the neat closet. She nodded. "Okay. Let's do it."

We bundled into our coats and carried the bags of trash to the curb for the morning trash pickup and then met the Goodwill truck and directed the two men to the back deck. They had a truck in the area and were happy to work in a stop at Marie's house. Even though I would be cutting it close for the carpool line, I stayed, partly for moral support and partly to make sure Marie followed through with the donation. I watched her for signs of anxiety, but she handed over the bags and watched the two men load them without any obvious distress, except for a tightness between her eyebrows. "So . . . how are you doing?" I asked as we climbed the steps to the deck and the truck lumbered away.

She nodded. "Okay," she said as if she was slightly surprised. At the top of the stairs, she paused and looked around. "The deck looks huge now . . . all this space. I'd forgotten how nice it is."

I ran my hand along the back of a patio chair we'd uncovered as the bags were removed. "It would be a nice place to drink a cup of coffee in the morning," I said, "once it gets a little warmer."

"But before the 'no-see-um' season," she said.

"Very true." The tiny bugs descended on middle Georgia every spring, making all outdoor activities from lawn-mowing to soccer practice into some level of miserable, depending on whether or not you remembered the bug spray. There was a good reason so many people had screened porches around here. "I've got to get my purse and run," I said, heading inside.

Marie was adjusting the position of the chair and made a move to follow me, but I waved her back. "Go ahead. It'll only take me a minute."

I retrieved my purse and wound my scarf around my neck, then checked my calendar. Marie came in and I confirmed that we were still on for our next appointment on Saturday, then I said good-bye. I dug in my purse for my car keys as I trotted down the deck stairs.

Halfway down, my foot caught, throwing off my quick cadence. I pitched forward and grabbed for the railing, but missed. I had a second of clear thought as the wooden stairs rushed toward my face: *I'm going to be mangled.*

I twisted and a flash of pain exploded as my arm hit the wood, then the world wheeled around me. Fleeting images of sky, wood, ground, and tree branches flicked by. I tumbled down the stairs, each thudding blow jolting through me.

Then it stopped.

I blinked a few times as I lay on the cold, hard slab of cement at the foot of the stairs, my heart thundering.

"Ellie? Are you okay?" Marie called. She paused at the top of the steps, spotted me sprawled at the bottom, and hurried down to bend over me. "What happened?"

"I tripped," I said, slowly pulling myself up into a sitting position. "I feel like I've been run through the dryer."

"Are you sure you should sit up? Maybe you should lie back down. I heard this awful thumping sound."

"That would have been me," I said as I flexed my feet, which still seemed to be in working order. I wiggled my fingers experimentally. They were functioning, too. My whole body was trembling slightly and I felt a little dazed, but, apparently, I was more embarrassed than seriously injured. "I'm okay," I said, pulling my purse toward me and refilling it. I scooted around on my knees—oh, they'd taken a beating. I gritted my teeth. I would be sore tomorrow, I thought as I picked up my phone, lipstick, and sunglasses, which were scattered around like they'd rained down from the sky.

"Do you want some water? Are you bleeding? Do you need a Band-Aid?"

"Only scratches," I said, examining the back of my left hand where a thin layer of skin had been scoured away in my tumble. It was pink, but there were no splinters. I gripped the stair rail and levered myself up. It seemed my coat had provided quite a bit of padding and protection during my unexpected somersault. "I'll be fine," I said, thinking I really should be more sympathetic to the kids when they fall down. Little searing stabs of pain were still echoing through my arms, legs, and back. I took a few experimental steps, probably looking like Livvy and Nathan did when they learned to walk.

"What happened?" Marie asked, and we both looked back up the stairs. "The stairs seemed fine when I came down them. Nothing broke or gave way?"

"No, I tripped. I wasn't watching the steps . . ." My words trailed off as I spotted something wedged into the base of the railing about halfway up the stairs.

Marie saw it, too, and climbed back up to retrieve it. It was a stick almost the same color of dark brown as the deck stairs. It was stuck between the balusters. She had to tug on it to get it out. I followed her cautiously up a few steps. I could see a scrape on the opposite baluster slightly above the stair tread. "You must have tripped on this. It looks like it got stuck right above the step. She glanced up at the pecan tree that towered above us. "I love these trees, but at the same time, they worry me. We always have branches on the deck and all over our yard when it's windy."

Cranking my head back, I studied the gnarled branches, dark against the sky. There was a light breeze, but it was barely moving the thick branches. "That seems kind of odd—that it would get stuck on both sides of the stairs, don't you think?" I said, pointing to the scrape. I remembered the feeling of being watched when I'd arrived. I quickly scanned the neighborhood, but I could only see the house with the Christmas light extravaganza from Marie's backyard, and their yard looked empty. They didn't have a fence enclosing their backyard, so I could see part of the street and it was quiet, not even a car passing.

"I don't know . . . that scrape has probably been there for years. The deck needed to be refinished when we bought the house. It's a little beat up," she said, pointing to some scratches on the handrail.

A faint ringing sound came from the house. "Oh, there's the phone. I better go," she said, backing up the stairs. "Cole's supposed to call me today and I don't want to miss him—" She stopped. "Unless you need me to stay with you. Maybe drive you home? You should be careful. You might have a head injury," she said, looking distraught.

"No, I think my head is the only thing that didn't hit something on the way down. You go on." I waved her away and she sprinted up the steps, but I noticed that she was gripping the handrail tightly.

Before I left, I looked at the scrape again. It was different from the rest, a thick white line, while all the other marks were darker, more weathered.

Tips for a Sane and Happy Holiday Season

Plan Ahead for Mailing

Don't forget to factor mailing time for packages going to family and friends who live far away. Check the post office for exact dates on deadlines for mailing packages and cards so they arrive at their destinations by Christmas. A good rule of thumb for overseas packages is to have them in the mail before Thanksgiving.

Chapter Sixteen

Later, that evening, I came out of the dry cleaners and tossed my little black dress encased in plastic over my shoulder—perfect for the squadron Christmas party—and felt a ripple of pain cascade through my arm. Obviously two ibuprofen were not enough to counteract the aftermath of falling down a flight of stairs. I winced and slowed down, which is not an easy thing for me.

I still wasn't sure about Marie's explanation. We had sticks and limbs fall out of trees, too, but to have one wedge into both sides of the stair railing? That seemed a little too curious. On the other hand, thinking that someone had intentionally placed it there to trip me seemed far-fetched as well. Who would do something like that? I had zero solid suspects for Waraday to check out. Had someone heard that Gabrielle and I were trying to figure out who killed Jean? Had it made someone nervous enough to track me down and try to waylay me with . . . with a tree branch? No, it was all too crazy, I told myself for about the fiftieth time. It was an accident. A strange accident to be sure, but wasn't the news full of stories of bizarre occurrences where nature was concerned? A Bible that stayed open to the same page while the rest of a house was destroyed in a tornado was one I remembered hearing about when I was a kid in Texas. Or was that just an urban legend?

I'd run my thoughts by Mitch when he got home from the squadron. He'd been concerned about how stiffly I was moving—I'd downplayed the whole thing on the phone earlier that afternoon—but I couldn't hide how gingerly I was moving to protect my sore body. I'd floated the thought that had been at the back of my mind all day by him: "Do you think it could have been . . . intentional?"

Never one to rush into anything, he'd studied me for a long moment, then said, "With anyone else, I'd say no, no way, but with you . . ." He sounded slightly exasperated as he said, "I don't know. You do have a tendency to, let's say, *attract* bad luck." I opened my mouth to defend myself, but he went on. "Even with that factored in, I'd say it probably wasn't on purpose . . . or, if it was, it may not have been directed at you. Since we don't know for sure, I think you ought to avoid staircases in the near future . . . and anything else that could be dangerous." His dark gaze was intent and worried.

I swallowed the sharp comeback that I'd been forming in response to his saying I attract bad luck, because of the genuine concern on his face. "Sure," I said. "No running down stairs without looking where I'm going—"

He drew a breath and I amended, "Okay, no stairs at all. Good thing we don't live in a two-story house or a city with lots of tall buildings," I said to lighten the mood.

"You probably should stay home from book club tonight. Soak in a hot tub, go to bed early," he said, and I saw the little glint in his eye and the slight raise of his eyebrows; since we were an "old married couple," I knew exactly what he was saying.

I grinned. "Unfortunately, I have to be there. I'm bringing the snacks." I kissed him, then said, "But I won't stay late."

Now, as I walked at my abbreviated pace, each step reminded me that muscles I didn't even know I had were bruised. I hobbled along the sidewalk that connected the string of businesses and restaurants in the small shopping center, glancing automatically in one of my favorite stores, New To You, a consignment shop where I'd found some terrific deals on designer handbags. I stopped and stared. I wasn't looking at a purse. There was a necklace displayed in the window. Suspended along several silver chains were a mix of pendants—a butterfly, a heart, a miniature high heel, a peace sign, and a star. It was beautiful and eclectic, a perfect present for Abby. She wasn't fond of mass-produced items. "Why buy something that's in every fifth house across America?" she'd ask. "Where's the fun in that?" The very act of duplicating something on a grand scale made it less interesting, she argued. She had very strong feelings about Restoration Hardware. Since I'd never seen a necklace like this one, I knew she'd love it. I shoved the door open and hurried inside.

Rita, the owner, was at the back counter. "Hi, Ellie. We just got in some new purses."

"For once, I'm not here for a purse. I want that necklace in the window, the silver one."

"Oh, that's lovely," Rita said, and while she bustled to the front to retrieve the jewelry, I admired the purses.

Rita hung the purses like works of art. Suspended on hooks or perched on little platforms, they were spaced from about waist high all the way to the ceiling across the back wall of the store behind the checkout counter. She kept a long hook in the corner to retrieve the highest bags. My Christmas budget was blown, but a girl could look. I scanned the rows of purses, then stepped back for a better look at one near the ceiling. It looked like Abby's missing gray snakeskin bag.

"Do you want a box?"

"What? Oh—yes," I said. "It's a gift."

Rita nodded. "I have just the thing."

"That purse up high, the gray one. Can I see it?"

"Sure," she said. "I knew you couldn't do it—resist the lure of the handbags."

"Well, you do have the best ones in town," I said as she lowered the bag to the glass counter.

I unzipped the tote, checked inside, then turned it around. "This looks like a purse that was stolen from my friend."

Rita had been curling ribbon she'd just tied onto the handle of a small red bag, but she stopped, her scissors open halfway down the taut length of ribbon. "Stolen?"

"Yes. I mean, I'm not sure this is the exact same bag. She didn't have her name in it or anything, but I loved it and I've been looking for one and couldn't find anything like it."

Rita pulled the scissors across the rest of the ribbon thoughtfully. "That came in yesterday. I took the consignment."

"Do you remember the person who brought it in?"

"Of course." She fluffed the ribbon curls, then tapped a few keys on the computer terminal of her cash register. "It was Cheryl Brown." Rita tapped her lips with one finger as she said, "She's young—probably early twenties. Blond hair, glasses."

The name was wrong, but the description sounded a

lot like Cecilia. Of course, it was a pretty general description—there were loads of blond twentysomethings who wore glasses.

"Was she pregnant?" I asked, and Rita raised her eyebrows.

"No . . . not that I could see. She was wearing a full-length coat."

It could have been Cecilia. The rest of the description fit and a long coat would easily cover her small baby bump.

"Do you know this Cheryl?" Rita asked.

"Maybe. The person I'm thinking of goes by a different name. Did you see any ID?"

Rita laughed. "No, this is a consignment shop. Anyone can set up an account. We just take them at their word that they're telling the truth when we ask for their name."

I carefully put the purse back on the counter, aligning the handles. "My friend's house was broken into. Her purse—a gray snakeskin tote—was taken along with a GPS and a cell phone. I thought I saw her purse in the trunk of a friend's car the other day, but I wasn't sure—that's why I wondered who dropped this off."

"Does it sound like the same person?"

"Different name, same description, but this woman is pregnant. Not very far along, so it could be hidden." The door chimed and two women entered the store.

Rita scowled. "Looks like I'll be making a call to the police tonight. The absolute last thing I want to happen to my business is to get involved in anything shady."

"It happened on base. I suppose you'd call the local police and they'd get in touch with the security police at the base."

"Wonderful! Now I'm involved in a crime that occurred on federal property," she said in a low voice as she punched the keys for the sale of the necklace with quite a bit of force.

"Maybe not." I handed over my debit card. "It could be a completely different bag."

Rita stowed the purse under the counter as the door chimed again and more people flowed into the store. "They're going to want to talk to you, too."

"Yes, I know," I said with that familiar gloomy feeling. At least Rita's store was in the city of North Dawkins. With any luck, it would take awhile for the word to get back to Waraday that my name was connected to a possible robbery report. "I can stay here while you call," I said reluctantly.

She waved her hand. "Oh, go on. I can't call now—I have customers—and I know where you live. I've got your number, too. I'll tell them to contact you. You know they're not going to show up right away. It might even be tomorrow before they get around to me."

Rita rounded the counter and greeted some of the customers. I gathered up Abby's gift and my purse. On my way out of the store, I stopped her and said, "Why don't you hold off on calling the police?" I didn't want my name to come up in connection with any more investigations unless it was a last resort and Rita was upset. I could tell I was quickly slipping out of the favorite customer category. And why should Rita call the police unless I was sure that purse was Abby's missing one? "I'll see if I can get a look in my friend's trunk—I'm on my way to a book club meeting at her house." I had the whole drive over there to come up with a way to do that. "If I find the purse, or the bit of gray snakeskin that I saw earlier in her trunk, it means the purse you have here isn't the one I saw and you won't have to contact the police."

"That sounds good," she said, eyeing a woman who was flicking through a dress rack.

"Okay, then. I'll call you if I find the purse. If you don't hear from me by nine, then go ahead and contact the police."

"Do you want to do it?" I asked Abby.

"No way. I'd be too nervous," Abby said as we watched Cecilia welcome three more book club members who were toting their copies of *Skipping Christmas*. I'd told Abby about the glimpse of gray snakeskin I'd spotted in Cecilia's car, the purse I'd seen at the consignment shop, and my idea for finding out if they were one and the same. Since every possible reason I came up with to look in Cecilia's car was extremely lame, I decided the best way to go was subterfuge. I'd slip away during the prediscussion mingling time and take a quick peek in her car. I thought it was only fair to offer to let Abby take a look. It was her purse. She'd be able to identify it better than I could.

"You go. I'll distract Cecilia." She wrinkled her nose in puzzlement. "Cecilia? Could it really be her? Why would she break into my house?"

"I don't know. Maybe she found the purse somewhere or someone gave it to her—if she has it. That's what we've got to find out, first—if it's here."

The doorbell chimed again and Cecilia's living room and kitchen filled quickly. Abby nodded and made her way through the crowd. I eased toward the door to the garage, which was down a short hallway from the kitchen. I made eye contact with Abby. She nodded and engaged Cecilia in conversation, then shifted around so that Cecilia's back was toward me. I slunk away down the hall, hoping that no one noticed me. I could always claim I was looking for a bathroom. I suddenly thought, what if Cecilia's husband—what was his name? George? Greg?—what if he was around? Or what if he'd taken the white Kia?

This spur-of-the-moment plan wasn't a very good one, but it was all I could think of, so I turned the knob and eased the door open. I was relieved to see the white car filling half the garage directly in front of me. The other side of the double garage was empty except for an oil stain and a row of makeshift shelves. It looked as if Giles?—Gavin? Yes, that was it. Gavin. It looked like he was gone.

I waited for my eyes to adjust to the dimness of the garage. I didn't want to turn on the overhead light because the top fourth of the rolling garage doors were windows. If the lights were on, a late arriver might mention it to Cecilia. The glow of the street lights filtered through the windows, providing some light. I waited until the items on the shelves resolved into the miscellany that accumulates in garages—cardboard boxes, tools, and plastic bins of who-knows-what.

The white Kia was parked close to the wall and I edged along it to the driver's door. I'd upped my ibuprofen dosage, which dulled the soreness from my tumble down the stairs and allowed me to move fairly easily along the tight space. The door opened when I pulled the handle—thank goodness. My pulse was already pounding. I wasn't up to the challenge of going back inside and trying to locate Cecilia's keys.

The interior light came on and an artificial pine smell mixed with the scent of Armor All wafted toward me. She must have just had the car cleaned. I could see the vacuum tracks in the carpet on the passenger side. The fresh coat of oily protectant on the dashboard glistened in the low light like sunscreen on a sunbather. There was nothing on the front seat.

I patted around until I found the trunk release. It sprang open with a pop that seemed unnaturally loud. I cringed, gently closed the door, and made my way to the back of the car. I tried to ease by the rolling trash bin positioned in the corner near the garage door. Black trash bags were piled so high that the lid couldn't close.

As I shuffled by, I hit the trash bin with my foot. It tottered and one of the black trash bags slid off the stack. I snatched a handful of black bag and steadied the rolling bin with my other hand. That was the last thing I needed—to set off a resounding crash. I gathered up the bag, which only had a few heavy things in it that strained at the plastic. Metal and plastic clunked against each other inside the bag as I hauled it back onto the top of the rolling bin. It began a slow slide to the side. I braced my hands on the plastic, repositioned it, and eased back, then waited a second with my hands poised in the air, but the bag didn't move. I blew out a breath. I hadn't even opened the trunk and I was a nervous wreck. Maybe Abby should have been the one to do this, after all.

I didn't even have to search the trunk. There was absolutely nothing there. Totally empty. I patted the sides to be sure there wasn't a storage compartment, but other than the spare tire, there was nothing. I pressed the trunk down until the latch caught, then I moved to the passenger side and checked the front and back seats. Nothing there, either. I turned, slowly looking around the garage.

There were too many places to look. If Cecilia had Abby's purse, it could be anywhere. I retraced my steps and opened the door to the house just a crack. The light seemed glaringly bright after the gloom of the garage. A flicker of a shadow darkened the slit of light and I drew back, but it was someone moving quickly down the short hall. I quickly stepped through the door.

Did I have a scarlet letter on my shirt, maybe an *S*, for *Snoop?* It sure felt like it. I took a hesitant step into the kitchen. Abby handed me a small plate with a cupcake, a few cheese straws, and a deviled egg on it. "Anything?" She was clutching her plastic red cup so tightly that it was indented. She looked more nervous than I felt.

"No. If it was in there, it's gone now. It could be anywhere out there . . . or in here, for that matter. I guess I will be talking to the police again." And all I'd be able to say was that I *thought* I saw it in Cecilia's trunk. I was dreading it already. However, on the plus side, no one seemed to have noticed my absence. I didn't feel quite so conspicuous as when I first emerged from the garage. The murmur of chitchat filled the room. I spotted Cecilia in the living room, seated with her hand poised on her barely rounded belly. She threw back her head and laughed at a comment from Hannah.

"Eat," Abby said. "Look natural."

"That's one way to guarantee I'll look anything but natural. There's nothing to worry about now," I added before licking a dollop of green frosting off my finger.

"Yes, there is," Abby said, turning so that her back was to the room. Quietly she said, "Well, there might be. What if Cecilia did take my purse? Then that means she broke into my house to get it and took the other things, too, the GPS and my cell phone. What if it wasn't the first time she did it?"

I kept peeling back the paper liner around the cupcake as I said, "You mean Cecilia could be the person who's been breaking into houses?"

Abby looked slightly uncomfortable, but continued. "It would fit. She's part of the squadron. She knows the schedule. She would know when certain spouses were going to be gone. We thought it had to be someone in the squadron, right?"

"Well, yes, we did, and the same thoughts have crossed my mind . . . but she's pregnant!"

"Ellie, I'm surprised at you. You're usually the first person to point out that pregnancy doesn't incapacitate women. You hated it when people treated you like you couldn't do anything when you were pregnant."

"You're right," I admitted. That whole delicate-condition-thing drove me crazy. "Okay. So, pregnant or not, she could have done it. She's certainly in good enough shape to climb in and out of windows. She can lap me when it comes to the stroller brigade workouts. But why would she do it?"

"I don't know," Abby said. "I'm completely mystified on that. Does she need money? The thrill?"

"Neither one of those things seem to fit," I said, glancing around the house. It wasn't extravagant, but it was a nice three-bedroom house in a great neighborhood. The furniture was basic, but not shabby. Framed posters hung on the walls interspersed with wedding and other family photos. It looked like the house of a young couple who were just starting out. "Their house looks perfectly normal. They both drive nice cars. And Cecilia doesn't seem to be the type of person who thrives on excitement or danger."

"Well, maybe it's Gavin," Abby said.

I thought about it a moment, then said, "But wasn't he deployed when most of the break-ins happened?"

"He was gone when some of them happened, the more recent ones, I think. He came back around the same time as Jeff," Abby said, then returned to her thoughts on Cecilia. "I know that she doesn't seem like a . . . thief, but once I started thinking about it, it made more sense. Even the break-in at Amy's house." I popped the last bite of the cupcake into my mouth as Abby said, "Remember how Hannah called the whole squadron spouse club to let us know that Amy was with her mom in Atlanta and that the meeting would be at your house?"

That cupcake suddenly tasted too sweet. "That's true," I said. "But even if Hannah only called the squadron spouses about Amy being out of town, I'm sure other people probably knew, too. I told Mitch about it. The whole squadron probably knew by the end of the day."

"Right, but it does explain why Amy was targeted. It was common knowledge, in the squadron spouse club especially, that she was out of town. And then I started wondering if there was a connection between the robberies and Jean's death." Abby watched my face as I shot a quick look around the room. No one was paying any attention to us. Before I could say anything, she sucked in a breath and said, "You thought the same thing! Why didn't you say something to me?"

"Because I didn't know for sure. I wasn't even positive it was your purse I'd seen in the trunk of her car. I couldn't go around insinuating that she'd committed murder."

Abby looked slightly mollified. "Well, we still have to be careful—"

"Let's get started, ladies," Hannah called, and we moved to seats in the living room. I couldn't concentrate. My gaze kept resting on Cecilia's bright, rather plain face. Could she have broken into Abby's house? And done all those other things we were speculating about? It was all guesswork, I reminded myself. I didn't contribute much to the discussion, but Abby made up for my lack of participation, throwing out ideas and thoughts with a little too much sparkle and energy. And if she glanced at Cecilia a little too often, I think I was the only one who noticed. Suddenly everyone was standing, picking up purses and pulling on coats. I'd completely missed the choice for the next book but wasn't concerned. As I belatedly stood up, I noticed Nadia's cell phone was still on the end table in the living room and she was almost out the door. "Nadia, wait!" I called, and held it up. "Your phone."

I responded to her thanks automatically, thinking about the feeling of her phone in my hand . . . the shape of it in my palm. I'd felt something just like that earlier . . . in the garage, I realized. When I'd pressed my hands down on the black trash bag to keep it from slipping, I'd felt the same flat, rectangular shape. I could be wrong, but if I wasn't . . . I was sick of all the endless speculation constantly circling in my head.

I looked around. There were still about eight or nine women in the room. Plenty of people to distract while I made a detour. If I made it quick . . . before I could mentally talk myself out of it. I swept up the plastic cups and a few lingering paper plates off the coffee table. I hurried into the kitchen and dumped the trash into the tall kitchen trash can. I pulled the plastic trash bag out, quickly yanked the handles into a knot, and scurried into the garage.

Chapter
Seventeen

I slithered down the space between the car and the wall of the garage to the rolling trash bin in the corner. I set down the bag of kitchen trash at my feet and patted the black trash bag on the top of the stack. The rectangular pieces that felt exactly like Nadia's phone were there. The ties at the top of the bag were cinched so tightly I couldn't pick them apart. I gave up and dug my thumbnail into the black plastic of the bag and pulled the opening wide, angling it toward the small amount of light filtering through the row of windows at the top of the garage door.

Opaque screens of cell phones, a GPS, and a few iPods reflected back the dull light. It looked like a clearance bin at Best Buy. There had to be about fifteen items in the bag. I swished my hand over the ones on the surface, revealing two small notebook computers at the bottom of the bag. In the cascade of metal, plastic, and glass, one phone caught my eye. The striped navy, green, and pink phone cover looked familiar. I fished it out and held it up for a better look. A group of women clattered by outside the garage, their boots clicking on the driveway as they called good night to each other. I barely noticed as I searched for the power button on the phone. A chime sounded, then the screen filled with a picture of Charlie.

"Ellie!" a voice hissed, and I spun around, nearly dropping the bag and the phone. "What are you doing out here? I thought I saw you disappear through this door, but then I thought, no way would Ellie be so silly and go *back* into the garage. Come on, almost everyone's left."

I held up the phone. "Look what I found."

"That's my phone." Abby stepped into the garage, quickly shut the door behind her, and burrowed down the aisle between the car and the wall toward me.

"I know. I found it in here." I handed her the phone, then held the ripped opening of the bag so she could see inside. "Along with all this other stuff."

"Oh. My. God," Abby said as she stared at me, her mouth literally hanging open. "Then that means . . ."

"I know."

Abby was pawing through the stuff in the bag with one hand. "I think that's our GPS . . . and, I don't believe it!" She pulled out the duck decoy. "She took the white elephant gift, too?"

"I don't think that's the biggest issue we have to deal with right now. We've got to get out of here—" I broke off as the overhead fluorescent lights flickered to life. Abby and I both spun toward the door. Cecilia had a baffled look on her face. "Abby, I saw you come out here . . . what's going on? Ellie, is that you, too?"

I grabbed the bag of kitchen trash which was listing against my foot. "Just taking out the trash," I said, trying to use the bag of kitchen trash to cover the ripped bag I held in my hands.

"Oh, thanks," Cecilia said, then her gaze fell on the phone Abby had clutched in her hand.

And the duck decoy in her other hand.

My heart did that plunging, lunging thing that made me feel like I'd just taken the express elevator from the top of a high-rise to the basement. Cecilia stared at the phone Abby held clutched against the decoy for a long moment. Then Cecilia's face went an unhealthy chalk-white shade that I'd only seen on my kids' faces seconds before they threw up on my shoes. Cecilia gripped the door frame and swayed.

Abby lunged for her. "Cecilia, are you okay?" Abby steadied her and helped lower her to the floor. "Put your head between your knees, if you feel like you're going to faint. Should we call your doctor?"

Cecilia shook her head emphatically back and forth, then moaned and gripped her head. She took a few deep breaths before slowly sitting up. She leaned her head against the door frame. "You know, don't you?" She touched the phone that Abby still held in her hand. "You found them." Her eyes were glassy with tears and her complexion had a pale, washed-out tone. "Please, let me explain. I can explain everything."

A few minutes later, we were seated around her oak kitchen table. The ripped black trash bag was the center-piece. Cecilia took a sip of the glass of water Abby had brought her. "Thanks," she said.

"I'm not sure this is a good idea." I leveled a look at Abby, who'd gone into nurturing mode as she'd helped Cecilia into the kitchen, then had brought her the glass of water and a damp paper towel to press to her fore-head. "We should call the police. Right now," I said.

Abby shot a look right back at me. "We need to make sure she's all right." She turned to Cecilia. "Just take your time. Tell us all about it."

Cecilia ignored me. "I didn't want to do it. It was Gavin's idea."

"Stealing?" I asked. "Breaking into homes and stealing electronics?"

Abby raised her eyebrows at me and, after a quick, scared glance at me, Cecilia shifted so that her blond hair fell forward, hiding most of her face.

How did I become the bad cop in this scenario?

"It was Gavin's idea," she repeated. "We needed money. We tried to sell our house in Nevada before we moved here. We'd bought a house there. Everyone said property was a good investment," she said bitterly. "Anyway, we did everything so that it would sell. We knew it was a tough market so we painted, landscaped, even hired one of those staging consultants, but it didn't work. We needed a house here. We're having a baby. We could swing two house payments for a couple of months, right?" she said as she closed her eyes and shook her head, conveying that she thought the idea was absurd now. "Now, after a year, we're stretched to the breaking point. We couldn't do it anymore. We'd used up all our savings and when I saw that Gavin had used our credit card for the house payment, I lost it. We had to do something."

"And what did you do?" Abby asked, speaking softly, coaxing the information from Cecilia.

Cecilia shrugged. "You know . . . took stuff. Gavin checked the schedule for the deployments and figured out which houses to go to. He'd wait until it was late, really late, then get inside and take a few things. Nothing big— just small stuff that wasn't hard to replace." I could tell Abby was doing her best to keep her face blank and nonjudgmental, but I knew she was thinking of the invasion of her privacy, the threat and fear she'd felt when she was alone with Charlie, and the hassle of fil-

ing a police report and an insurance claim. Cecilia must
have seen the flicker of disapproval on Abby's face because she said, "It's not like we were stealing cars or
hugely valuable things . . . just little stuff . . . it was nothing."

She seemed to realize that it wasn't exactly the right
tone to take with us. She brushed her hair out of her
face, pushed her glasses up on her nose, and leaned
forward. "Look, I feel terrible about all this." She ap-
pealed directly to Abby. "I realize now that I shouldn't
have taken anything—it was wrong. Let's just forget the
whole thing. I promise I'll return all these," she said,
pointing to the black bag. "Anonymously, of course. You
see what a horrible position we were in. You can understand, can't you?"

I could see Abby was about to lose it, so I said, "Isn't
there a program, a federal grant or something to help
military families who can't sell their houses?"

"Gavin checked into that. We don't qualify. We
bought our house before some arbitrary date, so we
don't get anything. We're on our own. We had to do it."

Abby's eyes narrowed as she asked, "Hasn't Gavin
been gone? I know he was deployed with Jeff. So how
could Gavin have broken into my house?"

Cecilia readjusted her glasses. "Oh, that. Well . . .
Gavin had to deploy, but we still had bills to pay and
once I saw how easy it was, I . . . ah . . . I got a kid who
lives around the corner to . . . do a few things for me."

"How?" Abby barked, completely abandoning the
good-cop role.

Cecilia scrunched back in her chair at Abby's sharp
tone. "I told him we were playing a prank on my
friends. Look, you don't understand. It's not like anyone missed anything I took. You could go right out and
buy a new phone. I wasn't hurting anyone."

"Anything *you* took?" I asked, tilting my head. "I thought you said it was only Gavin and this neighborhood kid who took stuff."

"It was," she said quickly. This was sounding a lot like the rambling, not quite consistent explanation that I got from Livvy a few days ago when I found the stash of candy-cane wrappers under her bed. I didn't believe Cecilia was a bystander. Was there even a kid? Probably not. I bet that Cecilia took over the stealing when Gavin deployed. That would explain the differences between the earlier break-ins and the slightly sloppier later ones.

"Why don't you sell this house?" Abby asked. She was obviously still trying to work out why Cecilia had resorted to breaking and entering.

"And live where? In an apartment? We can't even afford a studio in a crummy part of town. No, I won't live in a place that's dangerous. We have our baby to think of."

There was a huge hole in her logic, but I figured pointing out that breaking the law wasn't an ideal way to prepare for parenthood would be lost on her.

I wasn't sure what the end game was for Abby and me. We were getting our questions answered, but what would happen after that? Did we want to try and talk her into calling the police to confess? Were we going to leave, then call the police? Would she let us leave? There were two of us against one of her, if it came down to that, so I figured Abby and I could get out, barring something that tipped the scale in her favor. I quickly scanned the kitchen, but didn't see anything that could be used as a weapon—no visible knives or . . . heavy pans. Not even a rolling pin in sight. Since we were barreling along this road like a car without brakes, we might as well ride it out and get all the information out of her that we could, so I asked, "How did you make any

money . . . pawn shops?" Unlike Abby who was interested in the why, I wanted to know the how.

"No, that would be stupid. The police check pawn
shops."

"But not consignment shops?" I asked conversation-
ally. "I saw a purse today at a shop that looks exactly like
the one stolen from Abby's house."

Cecilia closed her eyes briefly, then said, "Okay, look.
Yes, I took the purse to the consignment shop, I had to.
Gavin had a . . . system. He found this guy—Jerry—who
bought the stuff from us. God, I could kill him," she
said, her tone exasperated. "If he'd just showed up yesterday like he was supposed to, you never would have
found this stuff."

"You don't mean that, do you?" Abby asked, a horrified look on her face. "That you'd . . . kill someone?"

"No," Cecilia said, confused. "Of course not." Cecilia
stared at her, confusion and then shock chasing across
her face. "You think I—you think I killed Jean? No. No
way. I would never, *never* do something like that. Taking
a few things is one thing, but killing someone? No.
That's not me."

She said it so vehemently and looked so frightened
that I almost believed her. Cecilia had lied about so
many things. And she was a good liar. I'd bought her
breezy line about not having anything made of gray
snakeskin that night outside the food bank.

Her head swiveled between Abby and me, her eyes
wide with fear behind her glasses. "I know you don't
have a reason to believe me, but it's true. I promise. I'd
never hurt Jean. Oh, wait," she said, tension flowing out
of her body. "Last Thursday, I was at the bank during
lunchtime. We had an overdraft and it took forever to
get it straightened out," she smiled triumphantly. "Nothing to do with it." When neither Abby nor I responded,

she sighed. "I can prove it. I got to know Debbie, the branch manager, quite well while I was there. Look, I'm sure we can figure this out, but right now I really have to pee."

She stood up, then quickly grabbed the back of the chair to steady herself. Abby jumped up, but Cecilia held up her hand. "I'm okay. Just a bit of a head rush. Must be everything that's going on. I might be a bit dehydrated."

"I'll get you more water," Abby said. Cecilia nodded and walked down the short hallway that ran by the garage to the guest bathroom and spare bedroom.

I grabbed my cell phone and moved to the opposite corner, in the living room, searching for a signal.

"What are you doing?" Abby asked.

"I'm already a suspect in a murder investigation. I can't risk Waraday thinking I'm a party to this, too," I said, holding up the phone near the window.

"Don't you think it would be better for Cecilia to call?" Abby said.

"Yes, of course, but will she do it?" I asked. Abby didn't have an answer. I moved back into the kitchen. "What if she comes out of the bathroom and refuses to call? Then what? Aha!" I said as several bars appeared on my phone.

A crash sounded from down the hall. Abby and I both looked at each other, then I replaced my phone in my pocket and we walked down the hallway.

The bathroom door was closed. "Cecilia? Are you okay?" I called.

Silence.

Abby knocked. "Cecilia, we heard a crash. What happened?"

After a few more seconds, I tried the door handle. It was locked.

Abby knocked harder. "Cecilia, open up. We're getting worried."

It was a simple push-button lock like the ones at our house. I tried to pop it with my fingernail, but that didn't work because my nail was too short.

"Cecilia, please say something to let us know you're okay. I'm sure everything will work out. We'll figure out something," Abby called, then whispered. "We need a nail file—or a knife. Something long and slender."

I nodded, about to scurry away, then remembered that our house in Washington State had tiny narrow keys stowed on the trim surrounding the door frames. I patted the thin edge of wood above the door and touched metal. I pulled the key down and called, "Hang on, Cecilia, we're coming in."

A twist popped the lock. Abby turned the handle and the door swung open, revealing an empty bathroom.

Tips for a Sane and Happy Holiday Season

Crafty Kid Ornaments

If you have kids, more than likely you have an over-abundance of crafty ornaments that your kids made in school or church. What to do with all these Popsicle stick snowmen, clothespin reindeer, and macaroni-wearing angels?

A couple of options: Some families create a separate children's tree solely to display their children's ornaments, which can be a good solution if you have the space and the funds for a second tree. Another idea is to rotate the handmade ornaments each year, since many are delicate and tend to lose parts and pieces as the years go by. Only display a few at a time, including the crop from the current year. Keep the rest for your kids when they leave home. You can pass them on to your kids so they'll have a few special ornaments for their own first Christmas tree.

Chapter
Eighteen

The shower curtain had fallen. It lay across the tub at an angle. The window blind cords trailed over the floor. The blinds were gathered into a tight packet near the top of the window, thudding rhythmically against the glass. A cool breeze filtered through the open window, curling around us as we stood there staring, our motionless image in the mirror reflecting back our surprised faces.

Abby moved first and in two short strides she was leaning out the window. "I can't believe it—she went out the window." She pulled her head back inside and turned to face me, hands braced on her hips. "The screen is down there on top of the hedge that runs along the house."

I walked over for my own look. The window was wider than my shoulders and with the pane pushed all the way to the top, the opening was at least three feet high. Cecilia could have made it through the window easily. The drop to the ground was only about five feet. Several branches of the hedge with thick, waxy evergreen leaves were flattened. I scanned the backyard. I couldn't see the farthest corners of the backyard, and Cecilia wasn't lurking anywhere in the faint circle of the glowing back-porch light.

"If the police are quick, she won't be able to get very far," I said, turning from the window. Abby was already dialing on her newly recovered cell phone.

I heard a car engine turn over. It sounded odd, as if the noise was coming from two directions. I could hear the distinct rev of an engine through the open window, but the sound was muted, too, and coming from somewhere else—somewhere inside the house? I tilted my head and listened. Abby heard it, too. She moved the phone away from her ear.

I pushed by her as I dashed down the hall to the garage. I yanked open the door that led to the garage in time to see Cecilia's white Kia surge backwards down the driveway, bounce over the gutter, and jerk to a stop inches from the bumper of my van, which was parked on the street. I could see Cecilia in the driver's seat. She threw the car into drive and then sped away with a screech of the tires after giving us a jaunty wave. Then all I could see were diminishing red taillights.

For just a second, I thought of trying to follow her, but then I remembered that Cecilia's house was one block away from the entrance to the neighborhood. She'd be on the busy state highway before I could even get my keys.

I went back in the house and looked around. A row of hooks inside the kitchen held a single key, probably a spare house key. Cecilia must have picked up the set of keys on her way to the bathroom. I hadn't been watching her. I was too busy trying to find a signal on my phone and Abby had been refilling her glass of water.

"Well, this is going to be fun," I said to Abby. "The police already don't believe me."

Abby asked, "We're staying until they get here?"

"Afraid so."

She tilted her head toward the garage. "Did not see that coming. Or the escape out the bathroom window, for that matter."

"Me, either. I guess I do have some latent bias toward pregnant women, after all. I never would have thought—" I broke off suddenly as my gaze swept the kitchen. The bag of electronics was still on the kitchen table. The only thing missing was . . . I hurried into the living room to check. Nope, not there, either.

"What is it?" Abby asked.

"The duck decoy. It's gone."

"And how would you describe this missing duck decoy?" One of North Dawkins's finest waited for Abby's answer. Another officer was in the kitchen cataloging the electronics on the table.

Abby raised her eyebrows and her shoulders. "I don't know much about decoys. It was wooden with its head turned backwards. I'm not sure what kind of duck it was—not a mallard. No greens or anything like that. It was all dark neutrals, browns, and cream. Really pretty. The painted feathers were very detailed."

As he nodded and took down the description, I said, "You know, Nadia took a lot of pictures at the Christmas party. There might be one of the duck decoy."

"That would be helpful," Officer Fawkes said, but I got the feeling it was more of an automatic reply. "So, you're saying that Cecilia Cedrick and her husband Gavin were part of a theft ring?"

"Yes," I said. "That's what she told us."

"And after she told you this, she went to the bathroom, palming her keys and the wooden decoy on the way. Then she climbed out the window, entered the garage, and drove off in a white four-door Kia?"

"Yes," I said in a small voice. It did sound odd when stated so baldly.

"And she just told you all this . . . admitted it freely?"

"Well, when I found the phones and stuff in the trash bag, she wanted to explain. I think she was hoping that she could talk us into keeping quiet."

Abby nodded. "She did ask if we could just forget everything. She promised to return the stolen items, but then she realized that we suspected she might have killed Jean. That must have been what spooked her."

I cringed. This was going to take a lot longer now. Officer Fawkes said, "Killed?"

"Yes, Jean Williams," Abby said, her words slowing down as she realized how she'd just complicated things. "She died last week."

"She was murdered," I said, resigned to a long night. "You'll want to contact Detective Dave Waraday at the sheriff's office. "Cecilia denied having anything to do with Jean's death."

"But she sure got out of here fast. How did she get in the garage?" Abby wondered, obviously not worried about how strange our story sounded.

The other officer walked into the living room, carrying the electronics in an evidence bag. "There's a coded entry pad outside the garage."

"I guess we didn't hear it because we were at the back of the house, trying to get into the bathroom," I said.

"Where is Mr. Cedrick?" Officer Fawkes asked.

Abby and I exchanged looks, then I said, "We don't know. Cecilia didn't say where he was. Most of the time, the guys leave the house to the girls on book club night."

"Have a seat," Officer Fawkes said, "and I'll be back with you in a moment." He and the other officer stepped into the kitchen to confer. I pulled out my phone and dialed our house. When Mitch picked up, I said, "Sorry, honey, but I'm going to be a little late."

Friday

The next morning, I cleared Mitch's spreadsheets off the island and replaced them with rolls of wrapping paper, gift bags, and ribbon. It was the kids' last day of school before Christmas break and my best chance to get all the gift wrapping done without locking myself in my bedroom, an action which immediately drew the kids' attention. Last year, the situation had brought up the is-there-a-Santa-Claus question. Livvy had already guessed the truth about Santa, but I figured this was probably the last year before Nathan figured it out, too, and I wanted him to enjoy the Santa legend to the hilt before the imaginary bubble burst.

It hadn't taken quite as long as I thought it would last night at Cecilia's house. Waraday hadn't shown up, but I expected his path would cross mine today. When I'd arrived home, the kids were in bed and Mitch was dozing in our bed, too. He was propped up against the headboard with the light on, surrounded with his spreadsheets. I'd gently removed the layer of paper, switched off the lamp, and crawled into bed. He'd come awake enough to wrap his arm around me, and pull me to his chest. I'd filled him in on everything that had happened with Cecilia over the phone earlier in the evening. "Did they find Cecilia or Gavin?" he'd asked, his voice thick with sleep.

"No," I said in a near whisper. Gavin hadn't come

home while we were there. I'd heard one of the cops report to Officer Fawkes that Gavin had been at the nearby Applebee's watching Thursday Night Football during the book club meeting. The bartender reported that Gavin got a phone call and left abruptly. "Do you think we should be . . . worried? Do you think they'd come around here?"

Groggily, Mitch had shook his head. "I doubt it. They're probably long gone. Headed for Florida or something." His last word got lost in a yawn and we had both drifted to sleep.

Rex rubbed against my leg, and after cutting a huge swath of wrapping paper decked with wreaths, I reached down to pet him. "Good thing I've got you, isn't it, boy," I said to him. "I don't need to worry about anyone bothering me with you around, right?"

His ears pricked up and he wagged his tail. He bounded away and returned with his tennis ball gripped on one side of his mouth. The only threatening thing he would do to someone would be lick them to death, but at least he looked tough. I tossed the ball for him a few times, then focused on wrapping again. Soon I was stuffing the last items into gift bags and fluffing tissue paper. I grabbed a roll of red ribbon and set to work making bows and tendrils of curlicues. Working with the gift wrap made me think of the white elephant gifts . . . the duck decoy and all the other presents that had been exchanged at the party. Could they be the key to everything that was happening? To Jean's death? Something was definitely up with the duck decoy.

I set the last bag under the tree, then retrieved the file on my computer with the photos that Nadia had e-mailed to everyone after the party. I found one of Abby holding the decoy up to the side, like a prizefighter hoisting a trophy. It took me awhile but I clicked, zoomed, and cropped until I had a close-up. Solid items, things that could be sorted and shifted, were what I felt most comfortable with, but I was getting better at this digital stuff. I minimized the decoy photo and did a Web search for duck decoys. After sifting through several pages of links and trying different descriptions, I found a link to a news article about the growing popularity of duck decoys as collector's items. I scrolled down to a picture of a decoy that looked almost exactly like Abby's white elephant gift. I nearly fell out of my chair when I read the tag line. "Preening pintail drake decoy by A. Elmer Crowell. Sold at auction for over a million dollars."

"A million-dollar duck," I said, stunned, and patted blindly around on the desk for my phone as I skimmed the text. I dialed and it was only when Abby's voice mail picked up that I remembered she was teaching. "Abby. Call me. I found the match to your duck decoy online. It wasn't exactly a white elephant—not by a long shot. Call me and I'll tell you how much the twin to your decoy went for at auction."

No wonder Cecilia had taken the duck decoy and left the electronics. Reluctantly, I decided that this was big enough news that it warranted a call to law enforcement. Instead of calling Waraday, I dialed the police department and asked for Officer Fawkes. "Oh, hello," I said, surprised when he answered on the first ring. "I thought I'd get your voice mail."

His voice sounded rougher than I remembered from last night as he said, "Long shift. Just going off duty. How can I help you, ma'am?"

"I think I know why Cecilia took the duck decoy. I found a picture of one almost exactly like it online. It sold at auction for over a million dollars." I clicked between the two pictures as I spoke, still amazed at the similarity of the two decoys. Abby's had a few scratches and a couple of nicks, but it looked remarkably like the one that was auctioned.

There was a long pause, then he cleared his throat. "A million?"

"Over a million, actually."

"Better send me that link," he said, and gave me his e-mail address. "I'll forward this to the detective who has been assigned to the case."

Before he could hang up, I quickly asked, "Any news about Cecilia?"

"We are pursuing all leads at this time," he said, sounding as if he was reading off a press release.

"Oh. Well. Just wanted to check. With all the strange things that have been going on . . . the robberies and then Jean's murder. It makes me a little . . . worried."

His voice lost its formality as he said, "I can't go into detail, but let's just say that it appears you only need to worry about Mrs. Cedrick if you own a priceless duck decoy."

That must mean Cecilia's alibi had checked out. We'd told the police officers about Cecilia's claim that she was at the bank during the time Jean was killed. "Thank you, Officer Fawkes. That's good to know," I said, and hung up. I felt slightly better. Cecilia had apparently confined her illegal activities to theft, but that still left the question of who killed Jean.

My phone rang and I answered it when I saw it was Abby. "I've got five minutes and then I have to be on the playground. What's this about an auction?"

"A duck decoy like yours went for over a million dollars in an auction." I waited a moment. "Abby?"

"Yes, I'm here. Did you say a million?"

"*Over* a million."

"I think I need to sit down." Abby said faintly. "Are you sure?"

"No. I'm not sure, but the pictures online are extremely similar. Even if what you have isn't the same thing, Cecilia must think it is."

"But how did she know?"

"I don't know, but she did grow up on a farm. Maybe her dad or someone in the family was into hunting and she recognized it from that. Or, maybe she knows someone who collects them. Maybe *she* collects them." I hadn't seen any in her house, but you never knew . . . "Duck decoys are a hot item right now."

"I think that's an understatement." Abby sounded numb. "Do you think that if they find Cecilia and Gavin, I'll get the decoy back?"

"I would think so . . . eventually. It is evidence. Who gave it away at the party? Do you remember?"

"No, I don't know who brought it. Whoever it was couldn't have known . . . I should give it back."

I smiled. "I think that would fall in the category of generous to a fault. Besides, you have to get it back before you can do anything with it. And I wouldn't be too quick to hand it over . . . finder's keepers and all that."

"Says the woman who didn't keep valuable letters from one of America's most famous literary recluses," Abby said tartly, referring to an incident that Mitch and I were involved in last summer when we visited his family in Alabama.

"Point taken," I said. Obviously, the shock was wearing off. "All I'm saying is that you might not want to be impulsive, if you get it back. Still no sign of Cecilia and Gavin, according to the police—I passed along the info about the decoy to them."

"Do you think they're still here? Cecilia and Gavin, I mean. Hiding out somewhere?" Abby asked.

"Why would they stay here—especially since they have this valuable collector's item? Wouldn't they try to sell it before anyone here realized what it was worth?"

"I suppose so," Abby said. "I have to run, but I'll ask Nadia if she knows who brought it to the party."

"Good idea. I won't tell anyone else about the auction. Probably better to keep quiet on that."

"Sounds good. Possible millionaire off to playground duty—that's a new one."

I hung up, still smiling. Abby could take pretty much anything in stride.

I clicked on the photo of the duck decoy again thoughtfully. Those white elephant gifts Jean took home . . . were they the key to her murder? Absurd to even think along those lines . . . but, then again, who would have thought one of the supposedly worthless gifts would be extremely valuable?

I found the photos that Gabrielle had e-mailed to me of Jean's garage. I'd seen several of the white elephant gifts in the garage. I enlarged the photos of the box that had been sitting on the floor. I could see the larger items easily—the sewing machine, the bat house, and the picture in the ugly frame. The smaller objects were a little blurry, but I could still make out the Hot Wheels cars at the bottom of the box. That was everything except—I closed my eyes, searching my memory. Someone else had added an item to the stack that Jean was going to take home—what was it? My eyes popped open. The jigsaw puzzle with a picture of butterflies, the one that was too hard for Nadia's kids. She'd handed the butterfly puzzle to Jean at the end of the party. Where was it?

Chapter Nineteen

"So where do you think the missing puzzle is?" I said to Mitch as I stepped into my heels.

No answer from the bedroom. "It's the missing piece," I said, twisting my arm around to zip up my dress as I prepared for the squadron Christmas party. The hasty move reminded me that I still had a sore arm, which was beginning to show some nasty bruises.

More silence. I'd searched every photo Gabrielle had taken of the garage and house—and totally reversed my thoughts on her crime scene pictures. A complete set of photographs had been an excellent idea. And I was going to tell her that just as soon as she called me back. Thanks to her exhaustive pictures, I knew that the puzzle was missing. I gave up on the zipper and stepped out of the closet to see Mitch fully dressed in a sport jacket and tie and sitting on the edge of the bed with spreadsheets fanned out around him. Those spreadsheets, some special project from work, were his constant companion lately.

"Did you get it? The missing puzzle is the missing

piece," I repeated as I walked over and stood beside him. "Pun intended."

"Hmm," he said as he highlighted a row on the paper.

I pulled my hair to one side and looked over my shoulder at him. "Zip me up?"

"What? Oh, sure." He whipped the zipper up, murmured, "You look nice," and went back to highlighting.

I turned around and stared. This was not the normal reaction to the help-me-with-my-zipper request, not by a long shot. The zipper thing had made us quite late several times. I picked up a spreadsheet and looked at the columns of numbers. I immediately had his attention.

"Ah, so this is what I have to do to get you to notice me?"

He stood up. "Sorry," he said as he dropped a kiss on my mouth. "Just wrapped up in work."

"I can see that," I said, not missing that he'd deftly removed the paper from my hands. "What is that, anyway?"

"Special project." He stacked the pages, then turned back and gathered me into his arms. "When I figure it out—*if* I figure it out—I'll tell you about it," he said, his gaze locked on mine. "Now, you were insinuating I'm not paying enough attention to you?"

"Yes. You weren't listening to a word I said."

"I am now. How's that zipper? Need any more help with it? I should probably check to make sure it's still working."

"My zipper is fine," I said. "What I need help with is the puzzle." He looked blank for a minute, then his face cleared. "The jigsaw puzzle."

"Yes. I know I saw it somewhere, but I can't remember where."

"You're sure you're not remembering it from the party?"

"No, I've thought about it all afternoon and I know it wasn't here at our house that I'm thinking of. It was somewhere else . . ." I shook my head. "I'll think of it later. The bigger question is—does it matter?"

Mitch shrugged. "Hey, it might. I wouldn't have thought a duck decoy would matter, but it did."

The missing puzzle kept nagging at me even after we arrived at the party. The wide wooden floorboards creaked as I moved down the central hall that ran the length of the Peach Blossom Inn from its double front doors to the large French doors that opened onto the wide veranda that encircled the building, which had once been a rather modest plantation home. Now a thriving restaurant and bed-and-breakfast, it was one of my favorite places for a night out. I'd read the paragraph on the back of the menu and learned that the Peach Blossom Inn was built in the Tidewater style of architecture. Narrow, square pillars supported the two-story structure and enclosed the wide verandas on both floors. Instead of ornate moldings, the trim around the doorways, windows, and fireplaces had simple, clean lines. The owner of the B-and-B, Kate Navan, had maintained the traditional elements when she remodeled and only changed the floor plan to add bathrooms and a full kitchen.

I smiled to myself, thinking that she would contradict me on that statement about not changing much. I'd gotten to know her pretty well shortly after we moved to North Dawkins. The history of the Peach Blossom Inn came up when I was researching the area's local history. Kate would have pointed out that practically everything—from the walls to the outdated electrical system—had been refurbished. With the restaurant bustling and the squadron Christmas party going on, I'd only caught a glimpse of Kate as she hurried back and forth to the rooms on the left side of the central hallway. These served as the restaurant where her guests dined at linen-covered tables positioned so they had a view of the peach orchards and the massive live oak that shaded the B-and-B.

The low murmur of conversation interspersed with occasional laughter drifted from the rooms on the right-hand side of the central hall where the pocket doors that had once divided the front parlor from the formal dining room had been pushed open. Tables with centerpieces of mistletoe, holly, and poinsettias were scattered around the room.

The gift baskets for the Helping Hands fundraiser were set up on long tables in the main hallway. I put bids in for a spa-themed basket (for me), a sports-themed basket (for Mitch), and a science-themed basket (for the kids). The heavenly smell of fresh bread and barbeque sauce permeated the air. I hoped dinner would be served soon because I was starving. I meandered back down the central hallway, threading through the knots of people looking at the baskets and overhearing snippets of their conversation.

". . . our fourth party this week!"

". . . and the police have no idea where they are. Just drove away and disappeared . . ."

I wasn't surprised that Cecilia and Gavin's disappearance was a topic of conversation, but I didn't hear the words "duck decoy," which was a good sign. At least, that detail was still under wraps. I was a bit surprised to see Simon standing with Hannah at the end of the long hallway, but then I realized he must be here in his capacity as a Helping Hands board member. His dark suit seemed to hang loosely on his shoulders as if it were a size too big. The green-and-red-striped tie showed that he'd made an effort to join in the festivities, but his face looked gaunt and more lined than I remembered. While his face seemed slightly drained and his eyes tired, I didn't see any evidence of the moodiness and emotional swings that Gabrielle had remarked on. He seemed to be handling everything okay right now, nodding at Hannah as she said, "Such a shame that you had to cancel the home construction for the low-income families."

I smiled at them both as I moved past them. "It's a heartbreaker for us," he replied. "We hated to do it, but the donations this year have dried up . . . that's one reason I wanted to be here in person tonight. We appreciate—"

He broke off abruptly to stare at me. "Sorry," I said as I all but screeched to a halt and practically snatched up one of the baskets that had been shoved behind another larger one. "I missed this basket before," I said. It was a puzzle-themed basket and the second I saw the jigsaw puzzle of a medieval castle nestled in its corner, I thought of the missing butterfly jigsaw puzzle. Maybe I couldn't find it because someone had packed it in the basket and donated it to the auction. I twisted the auction basket around and examined it from all sides. There were Sudoku books, crossword puzzle books, a 3-D puzzle of a globe, and a book of brain teasers, but no butterfly jigsaw puzzle.

Both Hannah and Simon were staring at me with perplexed looks. I repositioned the other baskets to make room for the puzzle basket. As I shoved it back into line with the others, I said, "Sorry to pounce like that. It's just that I thought it might have a puzzle I was looking for. Remember the butterfly puzzle Nadia won at the white elephant gift exchange?" I asked Hannah, and she nodded. "She gave it to Jean to put in the on-line auction, but I realized it wasn't in the garage with the other auction items. I thought it might be in here, but it's not."

Hannah shook her head. "I do remember Nadia gave it to Jean when I gave her the framed painting. Why are you looking for it?"

I shrugged. I couldn't tell them about the duck decoy, so I simply said, "It seemed . . . odd. It bothered me that it wasn't in the garage." I shifted my attention to Simon, hoping that the topic of his garage and Jean's auction-item box hadn't upset him, but he didn't look distressed. He was discreetly checking the time on his watch.

"Maybe Jean took it inside the house for some reason," I said, almost to myself.

"No, I don't think she did. I haven't seen anything like that in the house," Simon said, his gaze shifting to someone standing behind me. I turned and saw Marie hovering behind my shoulder. "Hi, Marie," I said, turning toward her. To include her in the conversation, I said, "We were talking about the jigsaw puzzle that Nadia won in the white elephant gift exchange. Do you remember it? The one with the butterflies. Monarch butterflies, I think."

Her face flooded with color and she said, "No. No, I don't." She looked inordinately relieved a second later when a loud buzz came from her purse. "That might be Cole. Excuse me."

She hurried away and I was left wondering why she would blush such a fiery red color at the mention of the puzzle, especially if she didn't know anything about it.

Saturday

I gripped the handrail firmly and moved like an old lady as I climbed the small set of porch steps to Marie's front door. I felt every one of the bangs and bumps I'd sustained in my tumble down the back deck stairs. My bruises, which had been pale yellow yesterday and fairly easy to camouflage with dark hose and a crimson pashmina shawl at the Christmas party, had turned an ugly mauve shade. I pushed the doorbell and then realized I probably should have taken a quick look at the back deck to make sure Marie hadn't stashed more bags of stuff out there, but it was too late now.

Marie's Christmas-crazy neighbor was outside again, this time hanging garland across the front porch. He spotted me and gave a wave. I raised my hand in return, then glanced up at the pecan tree above me as the wind seeped through its branches. Unlike the last time I was here, when there had been little wind, today the branches were bobbing as the wind buffeted them. The late afternoon sun hung just above the tree line in the west and, with the wind slithering through the branches, it was chilly. It would be dark when I left. I checked my watch and rang the bell again. Maybe Marie had forgotten, which would actually be nice. There was something about the gathering darkness of a winter afternoon that made me want to hide away at home. If she didn't answer the door, I could head home, curl up on the couch, and read a good book or find an old movie to watch until Mitch returned from the mall with the kids. They were on a shopping trip, picking out a Christmas present for me. The daylight seeped away as the shadows lengthened and a dimness coated the yard. I dug my chin into the collar of my turtleneck and glanced over my shoulder. I again had the funny feeling that someone was watching me. Except for the neighbor and a jogger with a Yorkie on a leash, the neighborhood was quiet.

Maybe Marie hadn't forgotten. Maybe she was avoiding me. She'd certainly steered clear of me at the party after I'd asked her about the puzzle. Of course, dinner had been served shortly after our conversation and she'd been seated at a table on the other side of the room from us, so we didn't have a chance to talk then. After all the toasts were made and the baskets were presented to the winners, I'd headed across the room toward her. Abby had stopped me to show off the basket she'd won and by the time I'd turned around, Marie had slipped out.

My phone buzzed and I saw it was Gabrielle.

"I found it," she said when I answered.

I leaned sideways, trying to catch a glimmer of movement through one of Marie's windows as I said, "Found what?"

"Jean's will," Gabrielle said, excitement lacing her voice. "She did make a new one, with one of those online services. It was in her papers, the ones that Simon put out to be recycled."

"What happens with the house?" I asked.

"She left it to me, free and clear."

I paused, then said uncertainly, "That's great."

"What? Don't you see? It means she trusted me . . . in the end she knew she could count on me to make a good decision."

"Ah—that's good," I said, glad that Gabrielle felt better about her relationship with her sister, but it did bring up a few new issues.

"Have to go," Gabrielle said before I could bring up the fact that being the sole beneficiary of the will had a downside. Inheriting the house added her to the suspect list. And I hadn't even been able to bring up the missing puzzle. I was about to dial her number back when the door swung open and Marie said hello. There was a guardedness about her.

I put my phone away. Talking with Gabrielle would have to wait. "Hi, Marie," I said, and tried to keep my tone as normal as possible. "Chilly out here. Ready for our session?" Instead of a normal tone, the words came out in that fake cheery tone that teachers use to jolly along a recalcitrant student, but Marie matched it and said, "I've been working in the living room."

I followed her down the short entry hall and looked around the living room in disbelief. "Marie . . . this is spectacular."

"There's still a lot to do," she said, the stiffness dropping away from her.

"I know, but you've made excellent progress. You did all this on your own?" I gestured to the front fourth of the room, which had been covered with teetering mounds of papers, books, magazines, and other miscellany. "You can sit on your couch now!" I said, excited for her and for the progress she'd made.

She nodded and a happy smile curved up the corners of her lips. "Surprised?"

"Yes. And look—you've uncovered a chair. I didn't even know you had that chair."

"I know. There was so much stuff on it you couldn't even see it." She grinned widely now. "Try it out," she said, motioning to the club chair.

I plunked down in the soft cushions and surveyed the room. It was looking better. I ran my hands over the fabric of the chair arms as I said, "You know, Marie, I think you're on your way. You may not need me much longer."

She'd gathered a stack of clothes in her arms and was

turning away from me when I spoke, but she quickly spun to face me. "Not need you! Of course, I need you. I still have all this," she said, nodding at the rest of the room. She spoke quickly, "And I need your help with those piles over there. I've sorted them, but there are some things that I'm not sure about . . . You're not quitting, are you?"

"No. Not until you feel comfortable. I only meant that you're doing so well on your own that you probably don't need me to come over as often. Maybe once a week or every other week."

"Once a week. Definitely once a week. Knowing you'll be here keeps me going on all this."

I stood up and unbuttoned my coat. "Okay, then. Let's get started."

We worked steadily for about an hour, talking about Marie's upcoming job interview at the local hospital while finding places for the things in Marie's "keep" pile.

"I'm really hopeful about this interview," Marie said as she sorted through a stack of books. "I managed the medical records department in a hospital before I was downsized . . . before I started," she waved her hand toward the remaining stacks of stuff, "doing *this.*"

"Is that what triggered it? Being downsized?" I asked. We hadn't talked about why she had hoarding issues, but she had brought the subject up and seemed to want to talk about it.

"I think that's part of it. I had a busy, productive job and then almost overnight it was gone. I could have searched for another job, but we knew we were moving, so I threw myself into searching for a job here. When I didn't get anything after a few months, I started looking for bargains, thinking since I wasn't working, I'd go to yard sales and outlet stores and at least save us money

that way." She shook her head. "I can see now that I wasn't
saving money, especially as it got out of control. I was
buying more and more and keeping everything. And
then with Cole's deployment coming up . . . well, Dr.
Harper says that probably contributed to it, too."

"I can see that. Deployments are incredibly stressful,"
I said as I placed a stack of books she'd handed me in
the donate bin. I picked up a flower-pressing kit. She
obviously found it at a yard sale, because a sticker with
the handwritten price of one dollar was still on the un-
opened box. "This was a good deal, but are you sure
you want to take up flower pressing?"

"That's not for me. It's for my nieces. They're coming to visit in the summer."

"Right," I said, remembering she'd mentioned them
before. "Then we can put this with the other toys in the
hall closet."

She snatched the box from my hand. "Don't get up,"
she said. I was kneeling on the floor so that I could
reach the bottom of the pile. "I'll do it," she said as she
placed it on a tower of items that needed to be put away
in other rooms. "I'll put these away now. This stack is
about to fall over."

I rocked back on my heels, suddenly remembering
where I'd seen the missing jigsaw puzzle.

Chapter
Twenty

Marie tossed the flower-pressing kit into the box in the hall closet and closed the door quickly. She avoided my gaze as she hurried into the kitchen with two cookbooks, three clean tea towels, several pairs of work gloves, and an extension cord that would go to the garage.

I sat for a moment, listening to her moving around the kitchen, opening and closing drawers. The door to the garage creaked. I hopped up and rushed to the hall closet door, gimping as my sore muscles slowed me down. I only had a few seconds before she'd be back, but that was all I needed. I scooped the flower-pressing kit off the top of the box in the closet with the toys and there it was—the jigsaw puzzle. I frowned at it. Why did Marie have it? And why did she lie about it? Thoughts whirred through my mind, but nothing made sense. The only thing I was completely clear on was that Marie didn't want me to see that puzzle. She'd intentionally kept me out of the closet and I knew I shouldn't let her see me poking around in here now.

I replaced the other toys on top of the puzzle, closed

the closet door, and skidded back into place on my knees in the living room, poised over the last few items in the "keep" pile, just as the garage door squeaked open.

Surely Marie didn't have anything to hide . . . she had nothing to do with Jean's death. But there was that branch placed so strategically across the steps of her deck. A thought whispered through my mind. *That had happened here, at Marie's house.* She had been outside alone before I left that day, supposedly arranging her deck furniture. She hadn't been out there long, but certainly long enough to put the stick in place to trip me. But why? Why would she do that?

"Ellie?" I jumped at Marie's voice behind me and glanced over my shoulder at her. "Are you okay?"

"Yes, fine." I directed my attention to the object I held in my hand. It was a picture frame. I realized I'd been turning it over and over in my hands. Hurriedly, I said, "What about this frame? It's nice. Do you have a picture to go in it?"

Marie's gaze traveled from the remnants of the "keep" pile to the frame in my hand. "Ah—yes, on the fridge. I've got a snapshot," she said, but didn't move to get it. Marie had a funny look on her face—dread mixed with . . . what? Fear? I wasn't sure, but suddenly I wanted to get out of the house. I scrambled to my feet, pressed the picture frame into her hand, and said, "About time for me to get going." My voice sounded falsely jolly and artificial.

"Already?" Marie asked.

I cleared my throat. "Yes." I had no idea if it was time to go, but I was heading out. Now. I swept up my coat from where I'd dropped it on the end of the couch, slung my purse onto my shoulder, and hurried toward the front door. "I'll have to call you to schedule our next meeting," I said over my shoulder as I speed-walked to the door.

"Wait—"

"I forgot my calendar," I improvised. "I'll need to check the dates and give you a call later," I said as I turned the knob on the front door and wrenched it open. Marie's hand closed around my arm, just above my elbow. "Ellie, wait. I can explain."

I twisted away, breaking her grip, but her tall, gangly form was right behind me as my nervous fingers fumbled and slipped over the lock on the glass storm door.

"Please, Ellie, don't tell them."

The lock finally clicked open and I pushed out into the cool night air. It was almost dark now, but the multitude of lights on the neighbor's house glowed, brightening that yard as well as Marie's yard. Several cars crept slowly past the neighbor's house, faces pressed to the windows to take in every blinking light, nodding reindeer head, and spinning snow flurry in the inflated snow globe.

"They'll never understand," she said, and there was something about her tone, a pleading, a hopelessness, that made me pause on the first porch step and look back at her. I didn't see the anger or the aggression that I'd expected after her viselike grip on my arm. Instead, there was an expression of such misery and fear that it stopped me in my tracks. "Ellie, please. Let me explain what happened. I know you figured it out."

"Figured it out?"

"That I have the jigsaw puzzle. That I took it from Jean's garage," Marie said, speaking in such a rush of words that I wasn't sure I'd heard her correctly.

"You took it from the garage?"

"Yes. On the day she died. Late that morning," Marie said, misery and remorse shading her face. She threw her gaze up to the inky sky and her shoulders sagged.

I'd pulled my car keys from my coat pocket. I jiggled them in my hand, thinking that meant Marie was in the garage shortly before Jean died.

Marie blinked rapidly and shook her head to the side a little, tossing the thatch of her orangy-red bangs out of her eyes. "I couldn't help it. Surely, you understand . . . about me . . . why I do—did—things like that."

"I'm not sure I understand," I said slowly. A blast of music from next door startled us both and I recognized the opening notes of the energetic, almost frantic, Trans-Siberian Orchestra's "Wizards in Winter." Christmas lights synchronized with the music flashed on and off.

Marie rubbed her hand across her forehead under her heavy bangs. "Please, will you come back inside and let me explain?"

The tempo of the music increased and a car driving down the street honked along enthusiastically. I hesitated a moment, then put my keys back in my pocket. Marie was frightened, but she wasn't a danger to me. "Sure. Let me give Mitch a quick call and let him know I'm running late." I didn't have a clue about the time—I hadn't checked my watch—but despite my feeling that I'd been off base in my momentary fear of Marie a few minutes earlier, I didn't want to be stupid, either.

After leaving a message on his voice mail, I stepped back inside Marie's house and even I was relieved when she closed the front door on the increasing traffic, the frantically blinking lights, and the pounding music.

"I used to like that song," Marie said with a half smile.

"I can see how it would get old." I could still hear the faint pulse of the music. The lights flickered against the windows at the front of the house like a faraway lightning storm.

"The lights and music are causing problems in the neighborhood. Some people are threatening to take him to court. Someone threw eggs at his Santa sleigh yesterday," she said as she opened the closet door and retrieved the puzzle.

She ran her hand over the bright orange and black butterflies pictured on the box, then she pushed it roughly at me. "Here. You take it. I don't want it anymore."

She'd shoved it at me so fast, I almost dropped it. I steadied the box in my hands as she walked away from me into the living room.

I quickly peeked in the box while she was busy clicking on a table lamp. Nothing but jigsaw pieces. She collapsed into the chair. "You know how I am about things," she said, and shot me a quick glance out from under her bangs, which had fallen back over her forehead.

"Yes," I said as I perched on the end of the couch, the puzzle centered on my lap.

Marie focused on a loose thread on the arm of her chair. "Having you here, helping me organize and meeting with Dr. Harper . . . I'm beginning to see things differently, but back at the party, it was different. I was different." She pulled the thread taut. "It was one of the hardest things I'd ever done. Picking out a white elephant gift from something I owned. I didn't want to give anything away and I wasn't even going to go, but I'd had a horrible job interview that morning and decided at the last minute to go. I thought it would take my mind off things. And I knew Cole would like it if I went, so, after agonizing for half an hour, I finally decided the jigsaw puzzle would be my gift."

She smoothed down the thread, running her fingertip over it.

"Nadia won it," I prompted, cringing inwardly as I remembered Nadia's nonchalant attitude toward the gift—it was too hard for her girls and it was missing pieces—and the quick way she'd handed it off to Jean to auction online.

Marie continued, "At the end of the party, I saw Nadia put it in the auction pile." She pulled at the thread again. "I couldn't handle it. I can see now that it would seem absurd to worry, to obsess, about a puzzle, but . . ." She shrugged and clasped her hands together in her lap. "I couldn't help it. I wanted it back. If Nadia wasn't going to keep the puzzle, I wanted it back. I should have just grabbed the puzzle and made some lighthearted comment about keeping it myself, but it was like I was paralyzed—I was afraid to make a move to pick it up and afraid that everyone would think I was weird for wanting it back."

"So you didn't get it back that night?" I asked, amazed at what had been going on under the surface. I hadn't picked up on Marie's distress, but I did remember thinking it was strange that she was so adamant about keeping her white elephant gift, the rather worse-for-wear elf figurine.

"No, I made myself walk away. I kept telling myself it was okay. It was only a puzzle." Marie's forehead wrinkled and she shifted uncomfortably in the chair. "But I couldn't stop thinking about it. I know it's idiotic to obsess about a puzzle—an incomplete one at that—" She flashed a quick, self-deprecating smile at me, then went on. "But I was obsessed with it. I tossed and turned all night and the next morning I went online to search the auction sites to see if it was up. When I couldn't find it online, I decided to go by Jean's house and just ask for it back. I had an elaborate story about how I'd just found out a friend collected butterflies." She shook her head slightly. "Looking back, I realize I was . . . a little messed up. Anyway, I went over to her house and the garage was open."

"What time was it?"

"Noon, straight up. The news was on the radio and they always do that at the top of the hour."

"Okay, so the garage was open?"

"Yes. I'd planned to go to the front door and ring the doorbell, but when I saw the open garage door, I thought Jean or Simon might be in there. Since I'd parked a little back from the house on the street, I had to walk up the driveway anyway, so I went in the garage."

She paused and I said, "What happened? What did you see?"

"Nothing." She spread her hands, palms open to me, emphasizing her words. "No one. I think I called Jean's name, but there wasn't anyone in there and no one came out of the house."

"Are you sure?"

"I'm sure no one was in there," Marie said. She tilted her head to the side and pulled at the loose thread again, twisting it around her finger. "I saw the box of white elephant gifts on the far side of the garage. And I suddenly realized that if I moved fast, I could take the puzzle and get out of there. I wouldn't have to explain myself to anyone or tell my butterfly collector story."

She jerked on the thread and it popped loose from the seam as she said, "So I did it. I ran over there, grabbed the puzzle—it was on the bottom of the box, I had to move some stuff to find it—and the whole time I was terrified that Jean would appear and see me taking it." Marie wound the thread around her finger.

"But you didn't see her?"

"No. I got out of there, practically running. I was only there a few minutes."

I gripped the puzzle box in my lap as I asked, "So all the white elephant gifts were still in the box?"

"Oh, yes," Marie said, and I could tell she was glad to focus on the gifts, not on her movements. "All of them were there. The bat house, the sewing machine, the picture, the paperweight. And there were some toy cars at the bottom of the box."

I fell back against the cushions of the couch. The murder weapon, the paperweight, was still in the box when Marie was there.

"Do you realize you were in the garage shortly before Jean died? Probably only a few minutes. I got there about twelve-fifteen. That means Jean was killed between about five after twelve and twelve-fifteen. You've got to talk to Detective Waraday. I have his number in my phone," I said as I reached for my purse.

"No," Marie said, her voice soft—but she was adamantly shaking her head from side to side.

"But he needs to know."

"No," she said even more firmly. "I'm not talking to the police."

"He's actually with the sheriff's department, and it's so critical. Narrowing down the time of death is really important."

"I thought you'd understand," Marie said, and I looked up from scrolling through the contact list on my phone to see Marie's disappointed expression aimed at me. "Do you really expect the police to understand why I'd go back for a worthless jigsaw puzzle the next day?"

"I suppose that might take some explaining—" I wasn't completely focused on what Marie was saying. There was something else significant in this conversation. It was right there, just out of reach, but I couldn't quite make it out. It was like a fuzzy cell phone connection where a word or two came through, but the larger meaning was lost.

Marie leaned forward, drawing my attention back to her. "And even if we could get over that hurdle, do you think they'd understand why I snuck into the garage and left again? My embarrassment? My," she swallowed, "my fixation on a box of puzzle pieces?"

"I'd vouch for you and help you explain how you've changed."

"Thanks, but I don't think the police would put much weight behind your words. I know that sounds awful and I know you didn't hurt Jean, but they think you're a suspect. If they find out we were both there moments apart, they're likely to think we worked together."

Her words stung, but I had to admit she was right. I wasn't exactly the person you'd want for a character witness, but Marie's information was important, so I tried another tack. "I'm sure Dr. Harper would speak to them and could explain everything."

"Ellie." Impatience made her voice sharp and brought me to an abrupt halt. "My fingerprints are all over the box of white elephant gifts. I had to dig through there. I've heard the rumors about the paperweight—that it was the murder weapon. My fingerprints are on it. I know I picked it up to get to the things at the bottom of the box." She combed her fingers through her bangs, moving them out of her eyes, then she ticked her points off on her fingers. "I snuck into the garage shortly before Jean was killed. I touched the murder weapon. I left, almost at a run. I didn't come forward after her death. Don't you see? They'd suspect me." She finished and leaned back, crossing her arms over her chest.

I carefully set my phone down on the bright butterflies. "I heard the murder weapon was wiped clean." Her expression didn't change. "You're not going to say anything? Just let it go? What if some small thing you saw or heard could make a difference? You might know something that would lead to catching Jean's murderer."

Marie jumped up and paced over to a stack of items we'd put aside to be donated. A large lamp with an ornately painted base balanced on top of several plastic bins. She ran her hand lightly down the lampshade. "Don't you think I haven't thought about that? I didn't see anything. Anything," she emphasized, and I recognized frustration in her tone. She paced back to the chair, then turned again for another short circuit of the room. "Now I can't sleep, but it's because I haven't said anything. I've gone over every second from the time I drove into her neighborhood to the time I left and I can't remember one thing that would make a difference. I can't help them. Going to the police will only cause trouble for me—and for you, too. I'm surprised you can't see that."

"I can see that you're scared and that you don't want to get involved, but, some day, some how, they'll find out you were there. And then they'll be even more suspicious. It will be much better if you talk to them now."

"I'm not going to. You're not going to convince me." Her chin stuck out a fraction of an inch and, despite her tall, gangly body, she reminded me of Nathan when he got his mulish face on and didn't want to leave the playground when I called him.

I put my phone away and stood up. "I can see that. I'll go now. What do you want me to do with the puzzle?"

"I don't care. I can truly say that I don't want it anymore. Keep it. Throw it away. Donate it," Marie said, and there was a hint of sarcasm in her words as she repeated the mantra I'd often said to her as we went through her things.

"Right. I'll let myself out," I said. It looked like I'd lost another organizing client and Gabrielle had nothing to do with it.

On the front porch, I blew out a breath of air, calming down from the tension-charged scene. The same music throbbed through the air, a slow parade of cars moved down the street, and the lights flickered, but I hardly noticed. I took a few steps, watching a woman in a heavy coat and red muffler walking her basset hound along the sidewalk as she paused to watch the light show. Something had caught my attention while Marie and I were talking. Something that might make a difference . . . a half-formed thought had flitted away in the heat of the discussion. What had it been?

Tips for a Sane and Happy Holiday Season

Common Sense Celebrating

The holidays can be a crazy time of year. Besides coordinating gifts, decorating, sending holiday cards, and baking special foods, there are also more parties and events to attend during the holiday season. To reduce holiday stress, keep your schedule as simple as possible. Don't overload your calendar with parties and events. Some events, like the office Christmas party, are mandatory, but for those that aren't required, pick and choose the celebrations you really want to attend.

Chapter
Twenty-one

I moved slowly down the short flight of steps, carefully gripping the balustrade, mentally reviewing our conversation. At the bottom of the steps, it hit me. *Time.* That was it. I hurried forward, then remembered I didn't have to go anywhere to check out my hunch. I tucked the puzzle under my arm and opened my purse. I'd kept the flyer, hadn't I? I shoved my wallet, sunglasses, and package of tissues around until I found the green paper folded in the side pocket with my lipstick.

I smoothed the creases in the pages and studied the flyer Paige had handed me. There it was: Hula-Hoop class from eleven-fifteen to noon. I pulled my phone out.

"Excuse me, ma'am." I looked up and saw a man with a black newsboy cap pulled low over his eyes moving down the sidewalk. A wool scarf encircled his neck and lower face. He pointed with his gloved hands over his shoulder as he drew closer. "My car broke down. Can I borrow your phone?"

His words were innocuous but there was something . . .

off. Something wrong. I didn't have time to analyze what it was. I just had the impression that he was moving too quickly toward me. It flashed through my mind that most strangers would approach tentatively, slowly. I backed away, but he trotted the last few steps and closed the distance between us. He plucked the phone from my hand. "Thank you very much, Ellie," he said as he dropped it into his pocket. Then, in one fluid motion, he grasped my wrist and twisted it behind my back, swinging me around so that I faced Marie's house.

In that split second before he swiveled me around, I was close enough to see his face. "Simon, what are you doing?" I gasped as he wrenched my wrist higher and an arrow of pain shot to my shoulder. *Not good. This is not good.*

"No talking. Up those steps," he said, and I stumbled. Instinctively, I swung the puzzle box, which I now held in my left hand. I aimed the corner at his face, but he threw up his free hand. The sleeve of his coat absorbed the blow. I lost my grip on the box and he swatted it away into the yard where it burst open. As puzzle pieces showered through the dry grass, I shifted half a step forward and tried to twist and wrench my arm away, but his grip on my wrist tightened and he yanked me back to his chest.

"Oh, no you don't," he admonished as if I were a toddler who'd thrown a toy across the room in defiance. He propelled me to the top of the steps and pressed his mouth behind my ear, his voice almost singsong. "You don't want a broken arm, do you?" He rotated my wrist farther up my back than I thought possible, then yanked on it. My eyes stung with tears at the surge of pain.

I whimpered and shook my head.

"Good. Now. You're going to press that doorbell with your left hand. I'm going to stay over here, out of sight," he moved slightly to my side so that he couldn't be seen from the door. "When Marie opens the door, you tell her you forgot something and step inside. Got it?" He cinched up his grip on my wrist.

"Got it," I said before he went to work on my arm again. I pressed the doorbell. *Don't open the door. Don't open the door.* I prayed that Marie was so upset with me that she'd refuse to open the door. The seconds stretched and I snuck a glance out the corner of my eye at Simon. He nervously surveyed the over-the-top holiday scene in the next yard. The line of cars was bumper-to-bumper now, a slow parade winding through the neighborhood to take in the light show. Red and green lights flashed, alternately tinting his cold, set features a flushed red, then a sickly green. His eyes narrowed as he watched the cars. He wanted to get inside the house, away from the attention. It was the last place I wanted to go. At least out here there were witnesses, plenty of people to see what happened.

The heavy wooden door whipped open, startling me. The glass storm door pressed into its frame, pulled by the suction of the opening door. It must not have been completely latched because it bounced back a little, creating a small opening as the latch missed and didn't click into place. Before I could do anything to warn Marie, Simon slipped his hand into the opening and pushed his way inside, dragging me with him.

"What is—?" Marie faltered backwards. "Simon? Ellie?"

Simon released my wrist and roughly shoved me into Marie. We both crashed to the floor in a tangle. Blood rushed back into my arm, sending pins-and-needles sensations tingling from my elbow to my fingertips. I rolled away from Marie, gingerly cradling my arm.

"That's far enough. Stay on the floor," Simon said as I collapsed back against the wall. During our fall, Simon had closed and locked the front door. My arm ached and I realized that my legs were shaking, so I was glad to stay where I was. I glanced at Marie. Simon's shove and our fall had carried us into the living room. Marie was huddled up against the "donate" bins, her face slack with amazement and her eyes wide as she stared at Simon. "That's a Glock," she whispered.

I whipped my head around. Simon did indeed have a gun. It must have been in his pocket and he hadn't wanted to pull it out when we were outside with all the holiday-light sightseers within view.

"Very attentive," Simon said, rummaging in the pocket of his coat with his free hand.

"What is going on?" Marie asked, her voice very quiet, barely above a whisper.

"You are going to help me solve a very tricky problem," he said in a conversational tone.

The stinging sensation in my arm had died down a bit and the sheer unbelievability of the situation hit me. Up until that moment, things had been moving so fast that I hadn't had time to do anything but react—and react badly. I hadn't been able to get away from Simon or keep us out of Marie's house. I shook my hair out of my face and scooted up a little higher on the wall. "Simon, I'm sure that this isn't what you want to do—"

"Yes, it is. It's exactly what I want to do." He extracted a large zip-top plastic bag from an inner pocket of his coat. He raised the bag. "Jean's scarf," he said, and I remembered she'd worn it on the night of the white elephant Christmas party. The brown-and-tan plaid scarf had been loosely draped around her neck when she and Gabrielle arrived. Through the plastic, I could see several irregular dark splotches on the fabric. About half the fringe was matted together and covered with the same dark stain.

"Is that . . . ," Marie swallowed, steadied herself, and said, "blood?"

I poked Marie with my sore elbow, a warning. I didn't want to talk about blood or about Jean. Right now, we only needed to focus on getting out of here, but Marie was fixated on the plastic bag and seemed not to feel the jab in the ribs.

"Yes. Jean's. Fortunately for me, she was wearing it that day. When the police find it in that puzzle box that you took from the garage and hear about your rather odd obsession with—" he glanced beyond us to the piles mounded along the living room "—keeping things, it will tie you directly to the murder—opportunity and motive."

"But . . . no one was there. No one saw me," Marie said.

"Oh, I saw you," Simon assured her.

"Were you in the house? Your car wasn't there. And there wasn't anyone on the street. I checked," Marie said, showing more animation.

"That would be stupid, to come directly into the neighborhood, in plain view—like you did," he said sarcastically. "No, I took the back way, shall we say, but I am glad you made your little visit. You arrived, saw the puzzle, and when you thought Jean was going to prevent you from taking it, you struck her, and left."

"But that's not what happened," Marie sputtered.

Simon didn't seem to hear her. He turned his attention to me. "Of course, Ellie figured it out and came here to confront you. You lost your head—again—and killed her. Then, full of remorse, you killed yourself. A sad little story, but it wraps everything up neatly."

A ringing sound came from his pocket. He stuffed the plastic bag with the scarf under his arm, transferred the gun to his left hand, and pulled my phone out of his pocket. He glanced at the display. "Your ever-attentive husband," he said. "Don't worry. I'll send him a reassuring text. Let him know you're fine and you will be late. Extremely late," he said.

He pulled off his thick winter gloves, revealing blue latex gloves underneath. The sight of the bright blue gloves already stretched tight over his hands made me queasy. He had carefully prepared for this encounter. The winter gloves were to hide the latex gloves while he was outside the house. But, now that he was inside, he needed full movement of his hands and he didn't want to leave any fingerprints. He stuffed the winter gloves in an interior pocket, then switched the gun to his right hand and began tapping at the screen of my phone with the thumb of his left hand.

"But that's not what happened," Marie said, turning to me. "I didn't kill Jean."

"Of course not," I said soothingly, because Marie was all but bouncing up and down in earnest self-defense. "I know you had nothing to do with Jean's death." The scenario he'd laid out wasn't what had happened. It was a convenient explanation with facts twisted to make sure his name was clear. Marie still looked slightly dazed. I wanted to be sure she understood exactly what we were dealing with, so I said, "It was Simon. He killed Jean."

He didn't look up. Marie gave a warning shake of her head and made a shushing sound in an undertone. Her eyes widened as she glanced from me to Simon, who was painstakingly tapping away with his thumb.

"Don't upset him," she breathed.

In my normal voice—or what I hoped was close to my normal voice, except for a few fear-induced breathy pauses—I said, "I don't think he's upset. He looks quite rational and calm, in fact."

Marie's eyes widened in disbelief. I shrugged. "It's not going to do us any good to pretend he's made some awful mistake or that he can be talked out of this." As I spoke, I scanned the living room. I knew her home phone was in the kitchen, but her cell phone had to be here somewhere . . . or there had to be something else that would help us. Marie seemed to catch on to what I was doing and she began edging slightly sideways toward the donation pile where the heavy lamp perched.

Quickly, I said, "I'm sure he had another way of arriving." *The back way*, had been his exact words. "The cul-de-sac," I said, remembering the other neighborhood that backed up to Simon's house. "If he parked in there, he could have walked to his neighborhood and watched you, then entered and left through the back door with no one in his own neighborhood spotting him. I wonder if the police asked any questions in the other neighborhood?" He didn't pause or look away from the phone. Marie scooted another inch closer to the lamp. Texting with the thumb on your left hand was quite laborious, it seemed. Simon didn't even look up.

"But that wasn't the only clever thing you did, was it?" I said, wanting him to look first toward me, not Marie, but his attention remained focused on the phone. Marie dug her heel into the carpet and rotated slightly toward the lamp. "It wasn't just about how you got in and out. It was about time, too."

Marie tilted her head to the lamp, then pressed her palms down on her jeans. Her lips moved and it took me a moment to comprehend that she'd mouthed, "On three."

I gave a nod. I had to keep talking. What had I been saying? Oh, time. "It was all about having an alibi, wasn't it? Your faithful attendance at the Hula-Hoop classes established a normal pattern of behavior." Marie shot me an incredulous look. Simon didn't seem to be paying the slightest bit of attention to me. He murmured something about the OFF button, but I wasn't about to tell him where it was. He swiveled the phone side to side, frowning.

I kept blabbering on, my heartbeat picking up pace. "On the day you killed Jean, you set the clock in the workout room ahead by five minutes. I spoke to Paige at noon. She thought she was running late, but she was actually on time for our noon appointment and she mentioned that they didn't get through the whole workout . . . that it had seemed a shorter workout than normal. That was because you'd changed the clock. Class runs from eleven-fifteen to twelve, but you were actually able to leave at eleven fifty-five."

One, she mouthed.

"Because the gym, your house, and Helping Hands are all so close together, that would give you just enough time to drive to the adjoining neighborhood, watch Marie retrieve the puzzle and leave, walk in the garage," I swallowed hard before I said, "kill Jean, and then get back to your office by twelve-fifteen or so, all well within your typical routine. What I can't figure out is why? Why did you kill her? An affair?" I asked. It was a shot in the dark, but I had to say something.

Two.

He tapped at the phone, quickly thumbing through screens. "Hardly. This had nothing to do with emotion." A chime sounded from my phone. It was powering down. I didn't dare look at Marie because Simon was studying me now. "It was about cold hard cash." He put the phone back in his pocket, but before he could remove his hand, Marie twisted and the lamp sailed through the air. I scrambled to my knees. He threw his left arm to block the lamp. In a split second, I realized it was falling toward me. I ducked, but before I could raise my arms, pain exploded in my head.

Chapter
Twenty-two

Why did my pillow feel so scratchy? Searching for my plush memory-foam pillow, I shifted my chin up and down in a burrowing motion—mistake. A wave of nausea coursed through me. I held myself still and swallowed the bile in my throat. After a second, I felt better and opened my eyes, but didn't move my head.

Nothing but blackness. I blinked rapidly, but the darkness still engulfed me.

I wasn't in bed at all. The surface under me was carpet, I realized.

The memory of what had happened hit me like a physical blow. Simon. And Marie. Where were they? Cautiously, I moved my head and felt okay—a bit like I'd just had a serious bout with the flu—shaky and tender. So, no sudden moves. I touched my temple, then winced. A lump was already forming. I reached out, my fingers exploring the prickly carpet. Before I could extend my arms fully, my hands hit solidness, a wall. My legs, folded at the knees, bumped against another wall when I tried to extend them. I carefully rolled from my side to my back and rotated my head. Now that I was on my back, I could see a strip of light cutting through the black, just above the carpet. I remained still, listening, straining to hear something. No sounds at all.

I inched up onto my elbows. My head felt okay, so I shifted into a sitting position and a swath of heavy cloth fell over my face, blotting out the strip of light as effectively as a blackout curtain. I swatted the fabric away with probably more force than was necessary and then had to pause while my stomach settled down. I ran my hands over the fabric and encountered buttons and more fabric suspended in the air. I was in a closet, Marie's hall closet, I thought. I patted the air until my hands connected with the door frame. Lightly, I traced along it until I found the light switch I remembered was inside the closet. The light clicked on, dimly filtering down through the coats and scarves above me. I recognized the coats, Marie's special scarf rack, and the box of toys for her nieces.

I sat, listening. The complete silence unnerved me. Hearing Simon moving around on the other side of the door would have been frightening, but at least I would know where he was. Was he still in the house? Did he have Marie with him? Was she okay? Was she out there, maybe on the other side of the door, unconscious like I had been? I shook my head. It was no use, sitting here making up scenarios in my head. He and Marie could be out there, but he could be long gone, too, and that would mean I could walk out of here. I stood up cautiously, alert for any dizziness, but I felt okay, so I turned the door handle gently, pressing against the door, prepared to open it just a sliver.

The door didn't move. I put my hand against it and shoved. Nothing. I braced my feet and leaned into it with my shoulder. It didn't budge. I dropped back, became entangled with the coats, and bumped my shoulder against the coat rack. I grabbed the hangers, stilling the clattering they were making. I paused. If Simon was near the closet, he'd know I wasn't unconscious anymore, but I didn't hear anything from outside the door. No creaking floor, no slamming door, no voices. Nothing.

I released the coats and hangers and dropped back to the floor since it was easier to sit than to stand hunched over below the coat rod, and I suddenly felt a bit woozy from all that exertion. I rubbed my head and studied the doorknob. It didn't have a lock on it, so Simon must have put something against the door—a chair?—to make sure it stayed closed.

I shifted my feet around, stretching my legs out as far as they could go, thinking it was rather absurd that I was locked in this closet. A few weeks ago, it had been hidden by piles of stuff. If I hadn't helped Marie organize and clear out her hall, Simon would have never known the closet was even there.

The quote about being hoist by your own petard was echoing in my mind as I gave the door another go, using the shoulder that Simon hadn't twisted like a pretzel, but it was clear that because of whatever he'd put in front of it, it wasn't budging. In my mind, I upgraded the blocking item from a chair to the heavy tallboy from Marie's living room.

I sat back against the wall, catching my breath. *I'm trapped.* How long would it be before Simon came back? I was pretty sure he'd come back. And he had a gun. What would I do then? How long would it be before Mitch questioned the text Simon sent him from my phone?

The nausea was fading and with it the rather hazy pain-laced view of my situation was dispersing. Everything was coming sharply into focus and I was scared.

I checked my watch, almost unable to believe that it was barely past six. I wasn't sure what time Simon had arrived, but the whole scene from him marching me back into the house to Marie throwing the lamp couldn't have taken that long. It had felt like it went on forever, but it was probably only ten minutes or so. I'd told Mitch not to expect me until six-thirty or seven, figuring on my normal three-hour session with Marie, so it would probably be at least an hour, probably longer, before Mitch began to worry.

Trying to get out the door had been instinctual. That wasn't going to happen. A sense of hopelessness filled me. I'd never thought I was claustrophobic, but I felt like an animal trapped in a crate. There was nothing I could do to get out. I had no phone or purse. My phone was probably still turned off in Simon's pocket and I'd dropped my purse when Simon shoved me into Marie. My purse was either out there in the hall or he'd taken it . . . somewhere. Not that the purse itself would do me any good, but there might have been something I could use . . .

I took a few deep breaths, lecturing myself about staying calm. Throwing a fit, or dissolving into tears—which actually sounded pretty good—wouldn't help things. Better to assess the situation and keep trying things.

I squished down until my eye was level with the opening below the door, but it wasn't wide enough for me to see anything or work my fingers more than a few inches through the carpet. I sat back on my heels and felt through the pockets of my coat, but all I came up with were my car keys, one chocolate kiss, and a wrinkled grocery list. Not exactly the mother lode.

I ate the chocolate, which made me feel a tad better—chocolate always has that effect on me—and switched to going through the pockets of the coats hanging in the closet. I found enough spare change to buy a Diet Coke, but nothing else. I went through the box of toys. No help there, not even a toy gun. Next, I checked the shelf above the coats. "Now we're talking," I said, pulling out a large golf umbrella. I remembered it. It had been one of the first things Marie and I had sorted through. She'd put it away in the hall closet, just as we'd discussed. It wasn't much, but it was better than the mittens and boots I'd found so far.

When I was absolutely sure there was nothing else useful either to get me out of the closet or to possibly use as a weapon against Simon, I dropped back to my knees and looked at my pitifully small pile of potentially useful items. I picked up the keys and considered the door speculatively. Only two screws held the doorknob in place.

Maybe I could remove the knob and then use the umbrella to push away or tip over whatever was in front of the door. Not much of a plan, but it was all I could come up with. Using the keys and my fingernails, I set to work, trying to loosen the screws. I scratched and scraped, scarring the wood as the large car key repeatedly skittered out of the small grooves of the screw head. Had Simon taken Marie away from the house? Why would he do that? It didn't fit with the plan he'd outlined. Unless he intended to stage some sort of suicide scene away from the house . . . a car crash? But how would you guarantee someone would die in a car accident? What if she survived? He'd have to kill her first, then stage the accident. I grimaced as the key slipped and I forced myself to cut off those thoughts. I had to focus on something else. Something that didn't get me any more worked up and scared than I already was.

I stripped off my coat. The air was stuffy and smelled

of wool and leather. I switched to using my fingernail and millimeter by millimeter I made progress. Okay . . . something else to think about besides what will happen when Simon comes back and what could now be happening with Marie. Mitch and the kids might be finished shopping by now. Never one to linger in stores, I bet Mitch had guided the kids in and out of the mall as quickly as he could, especially since it would be crowded with holiday shoppers. They were probably having pizza or ice cream right now, completely unaware I was locked in a closet. I sniffed. This was no time to go maudlin. That train of thought was no good, either.

My hand was cramping up, so I switched to my other hand, but I wasn't nearly as agile with my left hand and it was slower going. *Don't think about the kids and Mitch. Or Marie.* I smiled, thinking of how brave she'd been, throwing that lamp. What had Simon said right before that? It was something important. He'd killed Jean because of money. But what money? Was he talking about the house that Jean inherited? Surely he wouldn't have killed her over that. And, Jean made the new will with Gabrielle as the beneficiary, so he wouldn't have control of the house or the income unless he killed Gabrielle, too, and wouldn't that look just a tad suspicious?

I breathed out, a sigh of satisfaction as the tiny screw head rose above the housing. Quickly, I twisted it the rest of the way out and it fell into my palm. I felt like I'd won the lottery. I shifted to the second screw. What other money could there be that Simon would kill for? He would be receiving retirement income and had control of how it was invested.

This second screw was set tight in the housing and my fingernail broke off as I tried to turn it, but I barely noticed. "Helping Hands," I murmured to myself, falling back on my knees. He was on the board of the charity. Hadn't Jean told me he was the financial advisor? I chewed at my broken nail, thinking back. I'd talked to Jean after the white elephant gift exchange. Yes, I was sure she'd said he handled the finances. And she'd mentioned a big donation. A donation so large that they would be able to build two new houses.

I returned to trying to loosen the second screw, but my thoughts were racing. At the squadron Christmas party last night, I'd overheard Hannah and Simon talking about the cancellation of the home construction. At the time, I'd thought their big donation must have fallen through. Simon had said something about contributions being down, but what if they'd received the donation and Simon was skimming money from the charity? If that was true, it would have to be a significant amount to force the cancellation of two scheduled home builds. If Jean had figured it out and she threatened to expose him . . .

I paused, sucking in my breath as I remembered the list of numbers Jean had in her date book, the two columns of numbers. They were financial figures. Jean must have found them . . . the real financial figures for Helping Hands and the set of fake numbers. She must have written down the main figures, just enough to show what Simon was doing. She'd written "printouts" on her list of things for that day. Maybe she also had hard copies of the financial figures.

Jean wasn't meeting with someone else after she had lunch with Diane. Diane *was* her business meeting. Jean and Diane did meet occasionally for lunch, but Diane was the food bank manager and she was on the board of Helping Hands. Jean was going to reveal to Diane what Simon had been doing. Jean didn't wear her normal casual clothes because it wasn't a relaxed meal between friends. In her mind, at least, the lunch was a business meeting and Jean wore a power suit, probably thinking that if she dressed seriously it would help her be taken seriously. And it was quite a charge she was laying out against Simon—embezzling from the charity. Jean had probably figured she needed all the ammunition she could get and a serious suit might help. Had she told Simon what she was going to do? Given him an ultimatum? Had she demanded he turn himself in, or else she would tell everyone what he'd done? I shivered in the stuffy closet. Gabrielle had said that Jean was a rule follower and from what I knew of Jean, she didn't seem like a person who'd turn a blind eye to her husband's embezzling money. I thought back to those lists of numbers in her date book, then my hands stilled as I remembered what else had been tucked into the back of her date book . . . brochures for apartments.

Gabrielle thought they were left over from when Jean helped her search for an apartment, but one of those flyers had a border of holly—those flyers were current. And there was the gap I'd seen in the closet where a rolling suitcase would fit. What if it wasn't Kurt who'd packed the suitcase, but Jean? Had Jean planned to leave Simon? Maybe spend a few nights with Gabrielle after her meeting with Diane, and then look for an apartment for herself? But if Jean had packed the suitcase, where was it?

I returned to working on the screw, thinking that whether or not Jean was leaving Simon, he couldn't let her tell anyone—that was why he engineered his alibi at the gym. He had to make it home and kill her before her lunch meeting, when she was going to reveal what he was doing. It only took a few minutes to drive from the gym to his house. By changing the clock in the gym, he gained about five extra minutes. I thought back, trying to remember the group of people I'd seen leaving their class when I went to talk to Paige. They had been in workout clothes, but weren't toweling sweat off their faces, so the Hula-Hoop class was a low impact workout and Simon could leave without showering. He would take a minute or two to change clothes, but he could still be in the neighborhood behind his house to see Marie leave the garage by five after noon. Then, he would have been in and out as quickly as he could so he could make the short drive back to Helping Hands and be at his desk around twelve-fifteen.

I attacked the doorknob with renewed vigor. I worked fruitlessly for ten minutes, breaking and snagging every fingernail. The screw was set too tightly. It wouldn't budge. I went back to using the keys, but they kept slipping away, gouging deep scars in the housing and the door.

Frustrated, I threw the keys on the floor and sat back on my heels, blinking away tears. I couldn't stay in here. I had to get out. The well of panic that I'd tamped down earlier began to rise. I dropped my face down into my hands, wanting to give up and have a good cry.

But I couldn't. I couldn't lose it now. I wiped my nose on the back of my hand, then reached out for the keys, which had bounced behind me to the closet's back wall. The key fob had settled into a slight groove between the carpet and the trim board at the base of the wall. I pulled the keys out and ran my fingers along the groove. The furrow ran almost the length of the wall, then made a sharp right angle and continued to the front of the closet. I quickly traced my fingers along the line that turned two more right angles to form a square. I hadn't noticed it at the front of the closet because the carpet had been flattened and pushed down, covering the shallow indention, but at the back of the closet where there wasn't any activity, it was more noticeable.

Eagerly, I clawed at the edge. I thought I knew what it was. I couldn't get any purchase because I didn't have any fingernails left. I worked one of the keys into the furrow, then angled the square of carpet up, exposing a patch of dirt a few feet below the surface of the floor.

"A crawlspace," I whispered to myself, smelling the earthy scent. I'd been sitting on an escape route the whole time. I hadn't seen one of these for years. We'd had one in the house where I grew up. They were handy if you lived in Tornado Alley. If you didn't have a basement—and only a smattering of houses in our area had basements—a crawlspace under your house was the last refuge if a severe storm was bearing down. A section of the subfloor was cut out so there was access to the crawlspace under the house. Carpet had been attached to this removable square so that it blended in with the rest of the floor. There had been many times when we had sat on the floor in my parents' closet on spring afternoons, the crawlspace open, listening for the shriek of the tornado sirens. Cut slightly wider than the opening, this piece of subfloor fit snuggly over it like the backing of a picture frame.

I dipped my head into the opening. It wasn't completely dark. I could see dirt about two feet directly below. The ground sloped steeply toward the backyard, dropping away to create a space under the portion of the house below the deck, which was enclosed on all sides with lattice. The floor of the deck was about five or six feet above the slight bumpy layer of earth. I'd be able to stand up over there. Backyard floodlights filtered through the lattice, throwing a grid pattern onto the soil. I pulled myself back up and worked my arms into my coat, making sure I had my car keys in my pocket. I shifted my feet around and dangled them over the edge.

I didn't really want to crawl through the dirt. I was trying not to think about what could be down there, but I couldn't quite block out thoughts of spiders and bugs. They had to be down there. I swung my feet and braced my hands, but still hesitated. The closet had seemed close and tight. The crawlspace would be even smaller. And dirtier. I steadied myself. *You wanted a way out. Here it is. Take it.*

A faint sound penetrated my mental pep talk, the creak of a door. It took a few seconds for it to register because it was such a normal, everyday sound. I strained to listen, slowing my breath. Yes, there it was again, the faint squeak of a door, the door from the garage to the house, I realized. I'd heard it only a few hours before when I snuck a look in this closet while Marie was in the garage. Was it Marie? Simon? But why would he come in the garage?

Undecided, I froze where I was, straining for some indication of who it was. My heart pounding, I suddenly decided I couldn't afford to stay and see. If it was Marie, she'd call out for me, wouldn't she? A pouf of dirt rose as I dropped through the opening. There was movement on the other side of the closet door, the sound of shifting and straining.

My eyes were level with the strip of light under the door and I saw shadows slowly move as something was pushed across the doorway. With a quivering hand, I grabbed the golf umbrella and dropped into the dirt on all fours. Like a crab scuttling through shallow water, I low-crawled, elbows out, belly and face to the ground, kicking up dirt.

Tasting earth, I paused, checked above me. There

was more space, so I struggled up and ran, doubled over in a low crouch, to the lattice. Why hadn't I put the subfloor back? That would have thrown him off. The ground dropped down and I was able to hit a full stride just before I came to the lattice, but it was fastened tight and only gave slightly when my left shoulder hit it.

I glanced behind me, hoping to see Marie's head or hear her voice.

A pair of men's dress shoes dropped through the crawlspace hole, then tan khakis.

I turned back to the lattice, gripped it with both hands. I shoved and pushed. I heard a rustle behind me as a body began furrowing through the dirt.

I wanted to sob in frustration. I couldn't have made it this far only to have him drag me back.

The umbrella was at my feet where I'd dropped it when I hit the lattice. I picked it up, prepared to turn toward Simon, but I saw a corner where the lattice was bowed slightly. A foundation planting had worked its way between the sturdy support post and the lattice.

I sprinted for the corner. I stuck the umbrella into the opening and cranked it back toward me.

There was a satisfying pop as the industrial-size staple that held the lattice in place gave way. I raised the umbrella point and popped the next staple. I had the hang of it now and was moving upwards, separating the lattice from the post like I was unsnapping one of Nathan's shirts. Out the corner of my eye, I saw Simon move into a crouch. The lattice wasn't completely disconnected, but I wiggled a leg through the opening. I was backing through, the heavy coat protecting me from the staples and splinters, when Simon stood and raced toward me. He was coated in dust. Good, I thought fleetingly. *So much for his neat little scenario.*

Almost out, I worked one shoulder through the opening.

His eyes were wild and angry as his latex-gloved hand reached for me. I grabbed a handful of dirt and threw it at his face. He fumbled to a stop, swiping at his eyes. I wiggled my other shoulder out of the opening and ran.

I didn't have a clear plan except to put as much distance between me and Simon as I could, so I circled the deck and sprinted into Marie's side yard. I saw the lights and heard the music of the holiday display in the neighbor's yard, which, up until this point, I'd completely blocked out. It was like someone had turned up the volume on the radio. *People.* There had been a steady parade of cars in front of the house and now that it was fully dark, I bet there were even more lookers. I had to get into that yard.

I looked back over my shoulder. Simon was emerging from the panel of lattice. The opening must have been too small for him and he'd had to make it bigger. I aimed for the center of the brightly lit yard next door and ran like there was a gold medal on the line.

I crossed into the illuminated yard, skipping over extension cords, the bright lights making me squint. It was like stepping to center stage with floodlights focused on me as I zigzagged through snowmen, reindeer, angels, and the life-size Nativity scene near the porch.

There were cars, plenty of them. Yes! I aimed for the one closest to me, a cream-colored oversized SUV. I leapt onto the running board. "Call the police," I said. The woman in the passenger seat looked horrified. I could hear the solid click as she hit the automatic lock button. "No, wait." I glanced over my shoulder at Simon. With his layer of dirt, blue latex gloves, and furious face, he was scary. He was trying to run and work something out of his pocket. His gun, I was sure. "Please help me. He's got a gun."

The man in the driver's seat shouted and waved me off. I was holding onto the side-view mirror. He reached for a switch and the mirror moved, causing me to lose my balance. I dropped back to the ground and he accelerated away. I looked to the next car in line, but they swerved away, too, looks of dismay on their faces. One little kid who'd had his face pressed against the window was crying. I realized I must look as weird and frightening as Simon.

Suddenly the music cut off in mid-song and I heard a heavy thud behind me as something solid hit the ground. The lights continued to flicker as Simon writhed on the ground, trying to untangle his feet from several extension cords. I changed course and dashed for the house.

"That's enough. I don't want any trouble. Now y'all best calm down or I'll call the police." I swiveled toward the porch where garlands were lighting up, then falling dark, at a frantic pace. Wreaths flashed on and off across the façade of the house. I finally spotted the source of the voice. It was Marie's neighbor. I'd spotted him on my mad dash through the yard, but, bundled in a plain blue coat, and with his beard, I'd mistaken him for one of the Nativity figures placed near the porch. I saw now that he'd been sitting in a rocking chair on the porch, not actually in the Nativity scene.

"Please do," I shouted, trying to sound as rational and calm as I could to counteract my appearance. "He's got a gun and he's trying to kill me."

"Is that so? Good thing I have one of my own," he said, and reached down to pick up a shotgun from near his feet. "Y'all stay just as you are, until we get this sorted out."

Simon stopped thrashing about. He'd finally managed to pull the gun from his pocket, but the neighbor saw it and barked, "Drop it." Simon slowly put the gun on the ground and I collapsed into a sleigh beside an enthusiastically waving Santa.

I'd forgotten about the cars on the street until I heard a shout behind me. A teenager leaned out of his window as he called, "Best light show ever. What time is the next show?"

Chapter
Twenty-three

My breathing was still ragged from my sprint when I stood up abruptly. "Marie! Where's Marie?" I said, advancing on Simon.

The neighbor moved quickly down the steps, gun poised in his arm and aimed mostly at Simon, whose feet were still hopelessly tangled in extension cords. The neighbor kept a wary eye on Simon as he asked me, "Are you talking about Marie? Next door?"

"Yes. Where is she? What did you do with her?" I said, addressing Simon.

Simon shook his head. "I'm not saying another word."

A short woman in a sweater and jeans opened the front door and stepped outside. She held a phone in her hand. "They're on the way . . . the police," she said, taking in the scene before her and the long line of cars at a standstill on the street. "I knew this would come to no good, Ed," she said, crossing her arms.

"I've got to find Marie," I said to Ed. He wife moved down the steps as I explained. "His name is Simon Williams. He killed his wife. You may have heard about her death in the news—struck on the head in her garage. He came here today to kill me, then frame Marie so that the police would think she killed his wife and me . . . Marie is probably still in the house." Ed and his wife exchanged a glance, but didn't move. "He separated us. He locked me in a closet and I don't know what happened to Marie. Please. She might be hurt."

His wife threw up her hands. "Fine. I'll check on her," she said, and stomped off, still carrying the phone. She crossed the lawn, giving Simon a wide berth, and climbed the steps to ring the doorbell at Marie's house.

"She's not going to answer the door," I called, yearning to run over to the house and explore myself. "She's probably unconscious somewhere inside."

She pressed the bell again. In the distance, I heard sirens. I couldn't stand it any longer. Once the police arrived it would take even longer to explain what had happened.

"I'll check the back door," I said as I broke into a run. "Please don't shoot me," I called back over my shoulder.

Ed's wife came back down the steps and was retracing her path back toward us when I skidded to a stop in front of the garage. "Do you hear that?" I asked. She took a step backward. "That low hum?"

"What is it, Vicki?" Ed called.

"Sounds almost like . . . a car running," his wife said slowly.

"We've got to get in there. Simon said he was going to make it look like Marie committed suicide." The garage door didn't have a handle, so I dropped to the ground and tried to work my fingers under it.

Out the corner of my eye, I saw that the woman—Vicki—wasn't moving. She was standing beside the remote entry keypad mounted outside the garage. I stood up and moved to her side. "Do you know the code?"

The sirens blared from the end of the street and cars were inching to the side of the road to let the police through.

She ran her hand over her forehead. "I did . . . Before Marie moved in, I watered the neighbor's plants when they were out of town . . . what was it? Not their address number . . . oh! The last four digits of their phone number." She quickly tapped through her contact list in her phone, then punched numbers on the keypad. "If Marie's changed it . . . ," her voice trailed off as the door clanked upward, releasing the pungent smell of exhaust.

With our hands over our mouths, we ran inside. Vicki opened the driver's side door and there was Marie, limply slumped on the seat. Somehow we pulled her out and carried her to the front lawn.

Vicki leaned over her, gripped her wrist, then said, "She's got a pulse."

A few hours later, I tapped on the door of the hospital room before gently pushing it open. If Marie was asleep, I wasn't going to wake her, but I had to stop by and check on her before I went home. She was sitting up in bed, clicking through the television channels with the remote control. "Ellie!" she said when she saw me, and turned the television off.

"Feel like a visitor?" I asked, still standing in the doorway.

"Yes, come in," she said, pointing to a chair as I handed her a bouquet of hydrangeas and a magazine that I'd picked up at the hospital gift shop. She thanked me for the flowers, then said, "You didn't have to do that."

"Oh, yes I did. I mean, considering what happened

to you simply because I was at your house . . . well, let's just say that flowers don't really cover it."

She waved me into a chair. "Don't be silly. It's not your fault. If anything, Simon is the one who's responsible for everything."

"But if I hadn't been at your house . . ." I still felt guilty for suspecting Marie. What had I been thinking?

"He would have attacked you somewhere else. Somewhere you didn't have me to throw a lamp at him," she said lightly. "Besides, I'm fine. The doctors are keeping me here overnight for observation, but I should be able to go home tomorrow."

"I'm so glad to hear that. You look good. Better than me, probably," I said, brushing at my dusty coat. I didn't want to look in a mirror. Layered in dirt, with my scraped and broken fingernails, and a growing lump on the side of my head, I knew I probably looked like a cross between a crazed, dust-encrusted Medusa and a bag lady. I'd gotten some weird looks in the gift shop and I was thankful that there were no small kids in the hospital lobby when I'd arrived. "They don't think there will be any problems later because of the carbon monoxide?"

"No," she said definitively. "Simon thought he was being very clever, setting up my 'suicide,'" she said, using air quotes to emphasize the word, "but he forgot to check what kind of car I drive."

"I don't understand."

She smiled. "It's a hybrid—very low emissions," Marie said. "Serves him right, for being so . . . evil. Anyway, the doctors told me that all cars now have very low carbon monoxide emissions and it's much more difficult to commit suicide that way than it was years ago before the cars had—what did he call it?—catalytic converters, that was it."

"But it smelled awful in the garage and you were out cold when we found you."

"Oh, I'm sure it's still dangerous—otherwise I wouldn't be spending the night here. Simon used chloroform to knock me out. That's why I was unconscious. It had nothing to do with fumes from the car."

"He had chloroform with him, too?" I said, amazed. "What a twisted person he was, remembering to bring the blood-soaked scarf with him *and* chloroform."

"And a gun, don't forget that one," Marie added.

"What did he do, pull out a bottle after I blacked out and douse a handkerchief?"

"No, he had another one of those sealed plastic bags with some wet fabric in it. As soon as you went down and he saw you were out . . . he came at me. I was scrambling away, but he caught me near the door to the garage. He pressed the fabric over my face as I tried to break away, but it was over my nose. It only took a few seconds and I was out, too." Her voice got quieter and she focused on running her fingers along the edge of the magazine, which she held in her lap. "I remember very distinctly thinking, I don't want to die. I don't know what happened after that."

"He must have dragged you to the car in the garage," I said.

"I should have tried to get out the front door. Running through the house made it easy for him. He only had to move me a few feet to get me to the garage."

I described how Simon must have put me in the closet and secured it with some furniture in front of the door before dealing with Marie. "The time he was gone and I was alone in the closet, he must have been putting you in the car."

"Yes, and I'm sure it took him longer than he thought it would. My car was outside. He had to bring it in, then drag me out there and get me into the car. I'm not exactly petite, so it wouldn't have been easy."

And he also needed to pick up the puzzle pieces from the front lawn, too, I thought, which brought up something that was nagging at me. "How did you know I'd seen the puzzle?" Her eyebrows wrinkled together. "Before Simon showed up. I said I had to go and you said you wanted to explain, then gave me the puzzle. How did you know I knew about it?"

She smiled faintly. "When I came back from the garage, you were staring at that picture frame with the strangest look on your face, like you'd never seen a picture frame before. I'd never seen you look at something like that, especially something we were organizing. You were usually so calm and competent. I knew something was wrong and then I saw the closet door wasn't completely closed and I just knew you'd figured out that I had the puzzle. I still can't believe he barricaded you in there." She strummed the edge of the magazine pages as she said, "It's probably a good thing I don't remember anything. I can't imagine what it was like for you in the closet."

"I did eventually find the crawlspace and got out that way." Marie had been through enough and I didn't want to detail how scared I'd been. I didn't really want to relive it myself, either. "Thank goodness you woke up and were able to answer Waraday's questions in the ambulance. He didn't believe anything I told him until you backed me up."

She tilted her head. "I only vaguely remember that conversation. That young guy was your detective? The one you wanted me to talk to?"

"Yes. And he's not *my* detective. I'm sure he'll be along either later tonight or tomorrow to ask you more questions."

"Oh, wait. It's coming back. It's all very hazy, but I do remember he kept asking me about whether or not you'd hit me . . . or hurt me. I told him Simon was the one who'd caused all the problems already. I got mad and told him to stop asking stupid questions. I think the paramedics kicked him out of the ambulance after that."

"I'm so glad you were there to vouch for me," I said with a smile. "Waraday did not want to believe that I was innocent. Simon worked the whole 'I am an upstanding citizen' angle, refusing to admit anything, and acting outraged. It was a mess, but Waraday finally worked out that I was telling the truth, especially when they found the bloody scarf."

"Those blue latex gloves and the gun didn't tip them off?"

"Amazingly, by the time the police arrived, they couldn't find the gun. I think he ditched it somewhere in your neighbor Ed's Christmas display while everyone was distracted getting you out of the garage. When I left, the police were doing a grid search of his yard."

"That could take awhile."

"I know. Thank goodness Ed was on the porch and that he had a gun. I don't know what would have happened if he hadn't been there."

"It doesn't surprise me that he was out there. Neighbors have been complaining for weeks and threatening lawsuits. He got egged yesterday and one night last week someone cut a couple of his power cords. He was livid. I'm sure he was trying to keep an eye on the light display. He's kind of obsessive about it."

There was a knock and Hannah inched open the door. "Marie? Are you up for a visitor?"

As Marie called for her to come in, Hannah caught

sight of me. "Good grief, Ellie. You look like you need a hospital room of your own." From someone else, the words would have sounded harsh, but coming from Hannah with her gentle tone and rolling southern accent, they only conveyed her concern.

"I'm fine. Nothing a shower won't cure," I said, standing up. Now that Hannah was here I knew Marie was in good hands. I was sure there would be many more flower arrangements and phone calls for Marie as the word spread through the spouse club that she was in the hospital—the upside of the squadron grapevine.

I rode the elevator down to the lobby and dropped into a seat beside Mitch. He closed a sports magazine and tossed it on the side table. "How is she?"

"Great. She looks better than me, that's for sure," I said, going for a light tone. Mitch threaded his fingers through mine. "You always look good to me."

"Liar," I said, but smiled.

"You do," he insisted. "In fact, you never looked better than when I saw you in the middle of all those Christmas lights."

I squeezed his hand. "So why did you show up? I know you told me, but in all the confusion . . ."

"It was the text. You spelled everything out—no abbreviations. Not like you at all. And you don't usually text me. You almost always call. I called you back, but it went straight to voice mail. It didn't feel right. Then when you didn't call back after a while . . . well, I thought it was odd, but I figured you were busy and would call later. It was only after we got home from the mall and I looked over the spreadsheets again that I was afraid something was wrong. You hadn't called back, so I called Dorthea and asked her to stay with the kids while I checked on you."

"I don't see the connection with the spreadsheets at all—you'd been looking at those for days and wouldn't talk about them."

"I was asked not to talk about them. They were the books for Helping Hands. I didn't know that when I first got them. Everything was blanked out—no names, no indication what kind of business it was, just the numbers."

"So who asked you to go over the books?"

"Another thing that had to remain confidential, but now it will all come out so I don't think it matters. It was Colonel Stanek."

"I don't recognize the name," I said.

"He was in the squadron a few years ago, but he's retired. I see him at the gym a lot. He was on the board at Helping Hands and suspected someone was embezzling money. He wanted someone completely disassociated with the charity to look at the books."

"But why pick you?" I asked.

"Thanks. Thanks a lot for that vote of confidence," Mitch said in a mocking tone.

"No, I know you're good with numbers. You're like a human calculator, but you don't have any accounting experience."

"That's what I told Colonel Stanek, but he said that was what he needed. 'Fresh eyes' is what he called it. I couldn't find anything until last night. That was when I found the first discrepancies. Tiny things, really. And very cleverly done. But there was enough there that it got me to thinking. By then, I was pretty sure the books belonged to Helping Hands because of some of the entries. I knew Simon was on the board. And when I realized it had been over an hour since you'd texted me . . . I just had a bad feeling."

"So Simon was embezzling money?" I thought I'd worked it what happened while I was trapped in the closet, but I didn't know for sure I'd gotten it right.

"I'm pretty sure. While you were with Marie, I called Colonel Stanek and he said he'd also hired an independent accountant from somewhere outside of North Dawkins to look over the books and they'd found discrepancies, too."

"Why would Simon do that? Didn't they have plenty of money?" I asked, but the last word got lost in a huge yawn. The adrenaline that had been fueling me had seeped away and I found I was incredibly tired.

"No idea," Mitch said. "Come on, let's go home."

Sunday

That steaming hot shower and a good night's sleep did help and twenty-four hours later, life was feeling almost normal as we herded the kids up the steps and into the church lobby for the single performance of the Christmas pageant. It was interesting how a building could take on a certain atmosphere. The whole place buzzed with energy. As we greeted people, Livvy and Nathan were vibrating like tuning forks, their excitement ratcheting up as they took in the dimmed lights in the auditorium, the bales of fresh hay around the manger scene, and the other kids already in costume dodging through the crowd.

Mitch saw Gary and headed over to say hello. I was sure he'd get the inside scoop on Simon, who had been arrested.

My phone buzzed and I saw it was Waraday. My stomach didn't do its usual nervous flip. I'd called him this morning and told him about the feeling I'd had at

Marie's house, that I was being watched, and the strange placement of the stick on the stairs that had caused my fall. There had been a marked change in his attitude toward me—he was actually nice and his voice had the same cordial tones now. "Mrs. Avery," he said, "I'm calling to let you know that we've put together a timeline of Simon's movements over the last few days, using his cell phone and data from his car navigation and emergency system. He was near Marie's house on the day you fell down the stairs. Unfortunately, even though he was in the neighborhood, we don't have any direct evidence linking him to the placement of the branch that caused your fall. No fingerprints or witnesses who saw him place it there."

"You sound disappointed," I said.

"I wouldn't have minded adding assault to the list of charges against Simon, but I suppose what we've got will do. Happy holidays, Mrs. Avery."

"Ellie!" someone cried as I hung up, and I was engulfed in a smothering lily-scented hug, my vision obliterated by masses of dark hair. Gabrielle pulled away, scarlet fingernails flashing, and pressed her hand to her chest. "I was so scared for you when I heard what happened. Simon with a gun!" Her eyes narrowed. "I never liked him. I always knew he didn't have Jean's best interests at heart. And poor Kurt, his family destroyed, and for what? So he can have a degree from some Ivy League school? Ridiculous."

Nathan pulled on my arm and I whispered it would be a minute. "This was about Kurt?"

Gabrielle nodded and I again saw the serious side of her. Beneath her gushy manner was a core of steel. "Yes. When Kurt got into Harvard, Simon decided he would go no matter what it cost the family. Jean didn't want him to go. Kurt was ambivalent about it because of the cost, but Simon insisted, said their investments were doing great and they could afford it."

She rolled her eyes. "And this while the economy was tanking. Jean was too sweet by half. She trusted him too much. And when she did find out what was going on, he murdered her so Kurt could get his precious degree. Fifty thousand dollars a year in tuition," Gabrielle said, outraged. "And no financial aid."

"Why was it so important to Simon?"

"Because he's warped," Gabrielle said, practically spitting her words. "He was ranting on today about how taking money from Helping Hands was really a good thing. He was going to insist that Kurt go to medical school and then practice in some rural area or third world country. Like that would ever have happened. It was all about prestige, first being able to say he had a son at Harvard and then later it was about his prestige in the community. He couldn't let Jean say anything or he'd lose his position on the board and Kurt would have had to come home. Not to mention whatever criminal charges there would have been."

"So he's talking? He confessed?" I asked as I gave Nathan another warning look for yanking on my arm again.

"No. He was only trying to get me on his side. That will be the last time I visit him in jail, let me tell you."

"Did the suitcase turn up?" I'd told her and Waraday about my assumption that Jean was planning to leave Simon. Her face infused with sadness as she said, "Yes. Apparently he took it when he left the garage and tossed it in a Dumpster on his way back to the food bank along with the printouts Jean had with the details on his embezzlement. I guess he didn't look inside, just assumed it was her clothes. He dropped it behind a business that had moved to a new location. The trash wasn't picked up. It was sitting there waiting for the police."

"So she really was leaving him."

Gabrielle nodded. "Just not fast enough."

"What will happen to Kurt?"

She sighed. "That poor boy. My heart goes out to him. I'm not sure what he'll do. He can't go to school at Harvard anymore. There's no money. And with his family in this state . . ." she shrugged. "I don't know. I'll try to convince him to go somewhere less expensive and finish his degree. He'll always have a home with me and I will *not* let Simon hurt him anymore," she said with that same steely glint in her eye.

"Sounds like he'll be in good hands," I said, thinking that having Gabrielle on your side could be a good thing.

"Now," Gabrielle said, squaring her shoulders and shaking her hair away from her face, "to work." She scanned the crowd and waved at someone over my shoulder.

"Work? Aren't you here for the pageant?"

"Of course, I'll watch it, but church is one of the best places to network. Got to keep those clients rolling in. Looks like I've got another college tuition to pay for now, too." She flitted away.

"Same old Gabrielle," I muttered to myself.

Mitch rejoined me. "Gary says the word is that Simon will be charged with Jean's murder. The bloody scarf was pretty incriminating."

I shivered, thinking of how he wanted to use it to implicate Marie. Before I could reply to Mitch, Nathan pulled on my hand again. I was ready to say some sharp words to him about how interrupting is bad manners, but the reprimand died on my lips as I took in his frightened face. His eyes were wide and his death grip on my hand tightened as he said, "Mom, I don't want to be in the pageant."

"Why not?"

His gaze swept the crowded room, then he shrugged and ducked his head. "Just don't want to," he muttered.

"But you love wearing your shepherd costume. If you want to wear it, you have to be in the pageant," I coaxed. "And your shepherd's crook. You want to hold that, too, don't you?"

He shrugged again.

Livvy, who'd been orbiting around me, talking to various friends, returned to my side. "Mom, it's time. We have to go get dressed."

"Just a minute," I said, trying to think of some other enticement to get Nathan into his costume and on stage. I wasn't going to force him to be in it, but I knew he'd be disappointed later if he sat out.

"Miss Molly is counting on you. You know all the words and she needs you to sing really loud."

No reply.

I exchanged a glance with Mitch, signaling *Your turn. I'm out of ideas,* but before Mitch could squat down and get on Nathan's level, Livvy grabbed Nathan's free hand and said, "Come on, it'll be okay. I'll be there the whole time." She wasn't using her usual bossy older sister tone. She sounded matter-of-fact and slightly comforting.

Nathan's gaze slid from me to Livvy, clearly undecided.

"Shepherd's crook," I cajoled. "It's back there with your costume."

He nodded once, then said, "Okay," and allowed Livvy to lead him away down the hall toward Molly, who was energetically waving the kids into the dressing room.

Mitch and I hurried into the auditorium and snagged two seats on the aisle near the front. We were lucky to get them. I'd forgotten what a crush kids' plays and pageants were. The enthusiasm of the families with parents angling for the best video position had to rival Hollywood red-carpet events.

Abby and Jeff were one row up from us and she twisted around to talk to me over the back of her chair, exclaiming that she was glad I was okay, then she leaned farther over and lowered her voice.

"I'm getting the duck back," she confided.

"They found it?" I asked.

"Yes. The police contacted that dealer you found online. He's the premier dealer in that type of collectible. They asked him to be on the lookout for it. He called them this afternoon. There was a couple in his gallery with a decoy just like the police were looking for."

"Cecilia and Gavin?" I asked.

"Yep. The police took them into custody. Apparently, it will take awhile to get them moved back down here— this was somewhere up northeast—but they will be charged. At least, Cecilia will be charged in North Dawkins. I suppose Gavin will have to face the military justice system."

"And the decoy?"

"I've been assured it will be returned to me after it's photographed and fingerprinted. The dealer even said he'd be interested in it. He said it's not quite as valuable as the record-breaking one because it's not in as good a shape, but it should still *generate significant interest.* Those were his exact words. And I figured out who brought it—Gabrielle."

"Really? What are you going to do?"

"Split the sale with her."

"Are you sure you want to do that?" I asked, wondering how the two women would get along. They were both very strong personalities.

"Yes, I'm sure. Jeff and I talked it over. I haven't mentioned it to her. As soon as I get the decoy back, we're going to have some legal papers drawn up describing exactly how I got it and how the proceeds of any sale will be split—fifty, fifty."

I smiled at her. "That's a very generous thing to do."

She waved her hand in dismissal. "She needs it, considering she's helping her daughters and her nephew with college tuition."

The lights dimmed and Abby twisted forward, camera at the ready as a shaky high-pitched voice read the verses from Luke about Caesar Augustus issuing a census decree. "Mary" and "Joseph" entered and settled down in the hay around the manger. The narrator described the shepherds. Mitch raised our video camera and hit the RECORD button as Nathan filed into place. I studied his face anxiously, but, except for one quick stolen glance at the audience, he kept his eyes on the angel. I breathed an inward sigh of relief.

An uncomfortably long silence stretched across the room as everyone waited for the angel to say her line, but she had the classic deer-in-the-headlights stare on her face as she took in the packed auditorium. There was a hissing from the wings, but the angel remained speechless.

"Don't be afraid," whispered one of the shepherds so loudly that it carried to the last row.

A look of relief flooded the girl's face and she rushed through her announcement of the birth of Jesus. Spotlights came on illuminating the angel choir and I found Livvy in the top row singing with gusto, her glittery halo sparkling. Mitch still had one hand raised as he recorded the pageant. He slid his other arm along the back of my chair and I snuggled into the curve of his arm, glad that he was here to see the pageant and not deployed. With his unpredictable schedule, we often had to celebrate holidays either before or after the actual date. But this year we were together, at least for a few more weeks before he left on his next deployment. I realized I'd hardly thought about the deployment. There had been too much going on lately—so many stressful things in my everyday existence that I'd completely forgotten to worry about it.

Mitch zoomed in on Nathan, who was singing along, looking completely comfortable. I shared a quick smile with Mitch, vowing to enjoy every minute of this holiday without worrying about the upcoming deployment. We'd get through the deployment. We always did. And now was the time to enjoy our family and the Christmas season. The wise men trooped in with their gifts and after a few more songs it was over. The applause was deafening.

Nathan scampered down the steps from the stage, brandishing his crook. "That was fun. I want to do it again."

Livvy joined us as I said, "Next year," and draped an arm around Nathan's shoulder to guide him to the room where snacks were waiting.

"I know. I told Miss Molly I want to be a wise man next year," Nathan said. He broke away from me, jumping along the aisle in his excitement. "I told Miss Molly you could make my wise man costume, too."

"Oh," I said weakly, thinking of all the velvet fabric, heavy braided trim, and my nonexistent sewing skills.

"There are cookies in that room," Mitch said, pointing around the corner, and Nathan and Livvy hurried ahead. Mitch wrapped his arm around my shoulder and pulled me close.

"Don't say anything about my sewing skills," I warned.

"Costume shop," he whispered in my ear, and I laughed. "That's all I was going to say."

"Great idea. I'll put it on reserve tomorrow," I said.

Acknowledgments

As always, a big thank you to Michaela and the team at Kensington. I'm thrilled to continue writing Ellie's adventures. Michaela, you always hit on exactly the details that need to be refined. Thanks to the Kensington team, who work so hard and make the books look amazing.

To Faith, thanks for your steady confidence.

To my writing friends, especially the Deadly Divas, Denise Swanson, Heather Webber, and Marcia Talley. Thanks for ideas and support—you're the best and make book tours so much fun.

To my parents, thanks for being my best cheerleaders.

To my kids, who have shown endless patience with Mom when she's typing on the computer, thanks for inspiring me.

And to Glenn, thanks for listening and telling me to go for it.

Turn the page for an exciting preview of Sara Rosett's
next intriguing Ellie Avery mystery,
coming from Kensington in Fall 2013!

"No, I don't have any messages for you." The desk clerk was a fiftyish woman with a deep southern drawl rolling through her words. "Sorry, darlin'," she said after I thanked her. My Florida Gulf Coast vacation was not turning out the way I'd expected. Mitch was grounded in Canada, awaiting a part for his broken plane. The kids and I had gone ahead without him because we had nonrefundable hotel reservations as well as plans to meet with relatives—my brother Ben and Mitch's sister Summer, who both lived in the general area.

I made my way to the breakfast area and sat down at the table with Ben. "Nothing. No word from Angela," I said as I set my cell phone on the table and nodded at the waiter that I'd like a glass of juice. "The cell phone reception in my room is terrible. I'd hoped I'd just missed Angela's call and would have a message from her."

My ideal vacation also hadn't included meeting with Angela Day, the owner of an Internet boutique. I have a weakness for designer handbags, especially bargains that come from thrift stores or online auctions. I'd been thrilled to find a genuine Leah Marshall summer tote at Angela's online boutique at a bargain basement price. I'd been perplexed when I'd opened the box and found a cheap knockoff. A few quick e-mails established that it was a mistake and Angela, who lived in the area, had offered to bring the authentic designer purse to my hotel, but she'd been a no-show last night. I thought the excellent customer service might be more due to the fact that she'd dated my brother than a desire to get a good online review.

Ben's mouth was full. He shrugged one shoulder, then concentrated on cutting his Belgian waffles. I'd had pancakes and a bowl of chopped fruit while he had an omelet as an appetizer. Apparently, the waffles were the main course. I watched him work through his food, slightly amazed. "It's so unfair you can still eat like a teenager," I said, noting that his long, lanky frame didn't show an ounce of flab.

He swirled more syrup on his waffle and grinned. "It's not every day that I get a free breakfast buffet. Got to take advantage. You should have one of these waffles. They've got something in them . . . cinnamon, maybe."

"No way. If I ate like you, I'd be wearing a mumu at the end of my vacation."

"Since when did you start counting calories?"

"Since I had two kids. And the big three-oh is coming up soon. So enjoy that food. You can't eat like that forever," I said, raising my glass in a mock toast.

Ben wiped his mouth with the cloth napkin and asked the waiter if he could have the recipe for the waffles. I blinked. "You're cooking? Not just microwaving leftovers? You're cooking with actual pots and pans?"

"Of course," Ben said, his forehead wrinkled. "You don't think I live on takeout, do you?"

"Ah—well, yes, I did. Do you even *have* a waffle iron?"

I asked. I'd never seen his small apartment near the base. I'd pictured it as spartan.

"Sure. The person who lived there before me was a foodie. Worked in one of the restaurants on the beach, but got a job in New York and couldn't take all his stuff. The landlord was going to send it to Goodwill, but I said I'd take it. I did the ramen noodle and pizza thing in college, but I like to eat, you know? There's nothing like a good steak or spaghetti Bolognese."

"*Bolognese?* You make spaghetti Bolognese?"

"Yeah," Ben said as the waiter returned with a printout of the recipe. Ben thanked him and tapped the page. "Cinnamon. I knew it. And vanilla sugar . . . interesting."

I sat back in my chair. "My brother, a foodie. Who knew? Aren't you the same kid who refused to eat roast because Mom cooked it with a bay leaf?"

"That was a long time ago," Ben said, but he was smiling.

"I know," I said, leaning forward. "It's for a girl, isn't it? You want to impress Angela, don't you?"

Ben folded the paper and tucked it away in his pocket. "Not especially for Angela, no."

"Really? I got the impression she was very interested in you."

Ben shrugged. "So, how are the kids?"

I noted the obvious conversational dodge, but went with it. I figured I'd already ribbed him enough over the cooking issue. If he didn't want to talk about Angela, I knew my brother well enough not to press him. "We've already talked about the kids and about Mitch. I want to hear about you. What's going on with you?"

"Flying. I had a TDY to Japan last month. That was cool. I got Mom a tea set."

"She'll like that. What else?"

"Not much. Just the same old thing."

I rolled my eyes and muttered, "Guys," in exasperation. "Would it kill you to give a few details?"

"There's not much to tell. I go to work, I go out with the guys, I go to the gym. You know, normal stuff."

"And people think the life of a pilot is so romantic."

Ben snorted. "Yeah. It's just like the movies. *Top Gun* all the time."

My phone chimed. It was the kids, but they didn't have long to talk. They were simply calling to check in because Aunt Summer made them. Summer had insisted the kids visit her for a sleepover, so she could have them all to herself. After a few hours at the beach yesterday, they'd gone with her, practically skipping away through the hotel lobby without a backward glance. Nathan informed me that Aunt Summer didn't have a night-light, but it was okay because she'd left the bathroom light on *all night.* Livvy's news involved a report on the status of the cookies they'd baked (delicious) and their plans for the day (beach, movies, and more cookies).

I hung up and clicked through the various screens on my phone. "Still nothing from Angela," I said.

"Really? No texts?" Ben asked.

"No. I think it's odd that I haven't heard from Angela at all." I had bought several handbags from her and she had always been prompt in her replies to any questions I had. Lately, she'd sent me an occasional e-mail, sometimes updating me if she had a new bag for sale, but more often than not, to share one of the funny stories or photos that make their way around the Internet. We'd gradually become what I thought of as "cyber" friends, people I knew online, but had never met. Recently, there had been an uptick in the cute puppy photos she e-mailed. She was seriously thinking of getting a dog and wanted my take on having a big dog since we owned a rottweiler. I'd advised her to get a smaller dog since she lived in an apartment, but she'd replied almost instantly, "Purse dogs are too cliché for words, Ellie. No itty-bitty outfits or jeweled collars . . . if anyone's wearing jewels, it's going to be me! What do you think about a Weimaraner?"

"Do you know if she got a dog?" I asked. Ben was checking his phone and murmured, "Hmm?"

"She was thinking of getting a dog and wanted to know what I thought about Weimaraners."

"A Weimaraner?" Ben asked, looking up from his phone, perplexed.

"The gray dogs with the blue eyes. Very distinctive. But that's all I know about them and that's what I told Angela."

Ben nodded in a distracted way, then said, "She hasn't replied to my text, either."

"Is that unusual?" I asked.

"Very." Ben checked his watch. "Want to go for a walk down the beach road? You're not getting the kids until later, are you?"

"No, they'd run at the sight of me. Livvy informed me I'm not to arrive a minute before noon so I don't cut into their time with Summer."

"Okay then," Ben said, standing up. "Angela works in a store about half a mile down the beach road. She usually works Saturdays. Why don't we walk by and see if she's there? She probably ran into friends or something and got distracted last night."

"Sure," I said. "Let me run upstairs and grab the purse she's going to exchange for me."

* * *

The sun was already hot when we emerged from the hotel. I slipped on my sunglasses. The crowds were light and we were able to walk side by side. Boogie boards, racks of T-shirts and postcards, along with all sorts of sea-related kitsch, like seashell wind chimes and plaques declaring MY OTHER HOUSE IS A BEACH HOUSE, spilled out of the stores onto the sidewalk. The smell of sunscreen permeated the air, except when we walked by the fudge shop. I breathed in deeply. "Got to come back here later," I said as the aroma enveloped us.

"You and your chocolate," Ben said, shaking his head.

"It makes me easy to buy for," I said, moving to the side as several kids trotted down the street, their flip-flops slapping the ground. Their parents followed at a slower pace, pulling a beach tote with cooler, toys, folding chairs, and a huge furled beach umbrella.

"They look like they're prepared for a siege."

"You just wait. Soon that will be you."

"God, I hope not," Ben said. "At least, not for a long time." Then he gestured to a small store called The Sea Cottage. "We're here," he said. "After you."

The store had wide wooden floor planks in a pale blond wood. White walls and images of the gulf made the small space feel bigger than it was. Stacks of clothes in taupe, pink, gray, and cream sat atop tables of weathered white wood. Gauzy scarves and long necklaces dangled from driftwood displays on a glass counter at the back of the store. A light airy soundtrack, mostly of flutes, played softly in the background. It was the kind of store that catered to wealthy middle-aged women, and it surprised me that Angela worked here.

A girl in her early twenties came around the counter. Her name tag identified her as Cara. She had a thick swath of bangs combed across her forehead that dipped into the crease of one eyelid and a faint trail of freckles along her cheekbones. She wore a white short-sleeved cotton shirt, tied at the waist, open over a pale pink tank with gray pants. Three inches' worth of thin gold bracelets jangled on both wrists as she moved across the wide plank floorboards. "Can I help you?"

I said, "We're looking for Angela. Is she here?"

Cara's lips pressed into a thin, disapproving line. "No. Are you friends of hers?" Now that she was close to us, I could see that she had a piercing near the corner of her mouth and several along her earlobes, all empty of jewelry.

Ben hesitated, so I said we were.

"Well, you can tell her she better call in or she's not going to have a job."

Ben asked, "So she was scheduled to work today?"

"Yes. And I'm not covering for her anymore." Her heavy bangs slipped over her eyelashes and she tossed her head, flicking them back in place. "And after I closed for her last night, too. Like I'll be doing that again for her."

"So what time did she leave last night?" I asked.

"After eight-thirty. We're not supposed to close up alone, but she got a phone call and said it was like super important, so I told her to go ahead." She sighed in exasperation and crossed her arms over her waist. Her short nails were painted a glossy black and stood out sharply against her pale skin.

"That was probably me," I said, glancing at Ben.

"So have you tried her phone?" Ben asked.

"No, I texted her," Cara said, and I wondered how many more years I had before Livvy began using that tone, which implied we were stupid for even asking the question. "No personal calls at work," she explained.

"Does she usually text you back?" I asked.

"Yeah. Right away. Her phone is like glued to her hand, you know," she said.

I exchanged a glance with Ben. "Maybe she's at home. She could have overslept or maybe she's sick."

Cara's forehead wrinkled into a frown. "You think she's okay, don't you? I mean, it *is* kind of weird that she didn't call or anything today. That's not like her." Her irritation had ebbed away, replaced with concern.

"She's probably just delayed," I said, going into soothing mom–mode. "Or her phone battery is dead."

"No, she would never let that happen," Cara said as she raked her dark fingernails through her bangs. "She might miss a call."

"So she had her phone with her when she left last night?" I asked, wanting to make sure Angela knew we were trying to reach her.

"Yeah, she was like texting as she walked out the door," Cara said. "Maybe she got her big payoff," Cara said in a quiet voice, more to herself than to us.

"Payoff?" Ben asked.

"Yeah, she was talking about getting some big find. She kept saying she'd have tons of money soon," Cara said.

"Was she listing something online, something exclusive?" I asked, wondering if Angela had found some rare designer outfit or bag, maybe a Birkin or something along those lines.

"I don't know, but I don't think so. She said it wouldn't be like her allowance from her dad, but *really* big money. Like enough to buy a house on the water or travel anywhere she wanted. She said when it came in, she was booking a flight to Paris for the fall shows."

Even the most expensive Birkin bag wouldn't pay for a house with a water view. "Was it an investment, something like that?" I asked.

"No idea," Cara said. "I didn't believe her. I thought it was all talk, but now that she's a no-show . . . well, maybe it wasn't all made up."

We left the store and retraced our steps toward the hotel. "That didn't seem like a place Angela would work," I said. "She seems more like the pulsing music and bright colors kind of girl."

"Yeah, that's what she likes when it comes to clubs," Ben said. "But Angela said she needed the money. Her dad works overseas. He does something in electronics or computers. He sends money to her and her brother every month. She's not that good at managing it and usually runs through it pretty fast. She'll get her money from him and buy some designer dress or purse, then a few weeks later, she's out of money."

"Does she go to college?"

"She took a couple of classes last semester, but she wasn't into campus life. I think she mostly hangs out on the beach and works in the store when she needs extra money to make it until the next check from her dad. Then she hits the clubs at night. If she runs through her money, which happens quite a bit, she sells some of her designer duds on eBay to tide her over until the next check arrives from her father."

"Designer duds?" I asked. "I would recommend not describing designer clothes as *duds*, especially around Angela."

"Yeah, I got the lecture. I guess you could say I view clothes as something to wear and she thinks of them as . . ."

"An art form?" I supplied.

Ben nodded. "That's one way to put it. We're not on the same wavelength." I looked at him out the corner of my eye, but didn't ask anything else. I could see from his face that he wouldn't have any more to say on the subject, but I had to wonder if Angela's rather carefree approach to life was why Ben seemed to be distancing himself from her. It had taken Ben a few years to find his niche. After high school, he'd worked in sales for a plastics company, then he'd found a job as a tour guide for a company that coordinated trips abroad for high school students. That ended when the economy shriveled and parents' disposable income dried up. He'd returned home with a host of useful phrases in five foreign languages and a list of the best restaurants to eat at in European capitals—so maybe his interest in food wasn't that unexpected, I thought tangentially. He'd enrolled in college when he returned from his tour guide stint. He'd graduated with honors and a degree in engineering, then secured a slot for pilot training through his participation in the Reserve Officer Training Corps. Ben was more focused than he appeared at first glance. It sounded like Angela was more of a party girl than I'd realized.

"Where's her mom?" I asked.

"South Beach. Divorced. Sounded like it was messy. Angela said she hadn't talked to her since her high school graduation."

"Wow," I said, trying to imagine a life without family connections. We might not live close to our families, but we talked on the phone and visited as much as we could.

"I know," Ben said.

We walked a few paces in silence, then I asked, "Do you think we should call her home phone—just to check? Or is that kind of weird, for us to check up on her? For all we know, she could have gotten an unexpected inheritance and jetted off to the French Riviera."

"Somehow I don't think that's where she is," Ben said, taking out his phone. "She doesn't have a home phone, just her cell. That's why it's odd that she's not answering or texting. She might go a few minutes without calling back, but, like Cara said, she's *always* texting. I'll try her cell phone again."

Ben walked a few more paces, then stopped and scanned the sidewalks. A bald man nearly bumped into him, but Ben didn't even notice the man's glare as he stepped around him. "Do you hear that?" Ben asked. "That music?"

I could faintly hear the notes of "Girls Just Want to Have Fun."

"Yes, I do," I said.

"That's her ringtone," Ben said, looking around. I scanned the people in our immediate area, but didn't see anyone reaching for their cell phone. The song cut off in midnote and Ben pulled his phone away from his ear. "It just went to voice mail. That's got to be her phone."

"Call it again," I said, but Ben had already hit redial.

The notes sounded again and we both moved down the street a few steps, then paused over one of the large flowerpots that lined the edge of the street. "It's louder here," I said, pushing begonias aside.

"Here," Ben said as he ended the call and simultaneously put his phone in his pocket and picked up a small phone with rich, dark soil almost obscuring a shiny gold case.

Ben flipped the phone open. I edged over to him and focused on trying to read the screen in the bright sunlight. I grabbed Ben's arm and lowered it, so that it was easier to see. "Thirty-six missed calls. Fifty-two text messages," I said in astonishment.

"I think that's normal for Angela."

"But Cara said she had her phone with her when she left the store. She got all those calls and texts overnight?"

My mind reeled. I was old, I realized. I couldn't imagine having that many missed calls, much less texts. I doubted I'd have that many calls when we returned from our vacation.

Ben punched some buttons and scrolled through the incoming calls. "There's mine," I said. "Eight thirty-seven."

"Lots of incoming calls after that. Several from you and me through this morning." He switched over to the list of SENT calls. "Nothing after eight-thirty last night."

I studied the street, looking toward my hotel. It wasn't in sight because the street curved gently back on itself and our hotel was hidden behind several other high-rise hotels. "How far do you think it is to the hotel?" I asked.

"Maybe a quarter mile."

"What are the chances that she dropped her phone by accident?"

"And she didn't realize it?" Ben said. "Zero." He shook his head. "If she'd dropped her phone or lost it, she'd go back and look for it. And if she couldn't find it, the first thing she'd do is go buy a new one today, even if it was a cheap disposable one." He punched some more buttons. "I'm calling her brother."

"I think that's a good idea," I said, leaning against the flowerpot as Ben pulled up the number from Angela's contact list. After a moment, he said, "Chase, this is Ben. We met a few weeks ago in June when I came to pick up your sister." He explained how Angela hadn't arrived at the hotel last night, her no-show at work, and how we'd found her phone with no outgoing calls or texts since last night.

I examined the strap on the fake Leah Marshall purse as he talked. This morning, I'd switched to a Fossil crossbody wallet bag in light tan so I'd been able to take the Leah Marshall purse out of the box and carry it on my shoulder.

I listened to Ben's one-sided conversation. "Right, but would she go off without her phone?" he asked.

His jaw tightened. "Without calling in to work or telling you?"

"Was she home last night? Oh, well, don't you think—"

He threw his head back, studied the sky, then paced away and back, murmuring, "Right. Okay, well, I don't agree with you . . . but you're her brother. Sure. You're on your way there now? I'll meet you."

Ben turned to me and said, "He doesn't get it. He says she's checked out before—just picked up and left without a word to anyone, so we should just 'chill.' He thinks she'll be back in a day or two."

"Did he see her last night?" I asked, fiddling with the zipper on the Leah Marshall purse, which was caught at the halfway point.

"Chase was out of town, so he doesn't know if she was there or not, but apparently that's nothing to worry about," Ben said.

I picked up on the edge of disdain in his words. "You don't like him?"

Ben shook his head. "I've only met him once, but he's . . . slick."

Interesting description. I processed that information silently, then said, "Well, like you said, he is her brother and if he thinks everything is fine, then . . ."

"I know," Ben said shortly.

"I wonder where her car is," I said, shading my eyes to look up and down the street, which was filled on each side with cars parked in parallel slots.

"That's a good question. I'll check at the apartment. I told Chase I'd meet him there and give him her phone. I know that sometimes she just leaves her car there and walks to work. It isn't that far and parking is a hassle on the beach road."

"If it's not at the apartment, it could be anywhere," I said, gesturing to the beach road. "There are several public lots all along the beach." I glanced at my watch. "Do you want to go over there now?"

He nodded. "It's not too far from here."

"Okay. While you do that, I'll go pick up the kids from Summer's condo. By the time I get there, it will be almost noon."

We walked back to the hotel. Before I climbed in the van, I called, "See you in a little while."

He waved and pulled out of the parking lot in his sporty blue Mazda and joined the traffic slowly creeping to the east, the direction we'd walked that morning. I turned the opposite way and inched along. It was late Saturday morning in a Florida beach town on July Fourth weekend. We weren't going anywhere fast. After a few blocks, I took a road that led north, away from the beach, and the congestion eased. My phone rang and I glanced at the screen—blocked number—before I answered the call with the speaker on.

"Ellie? Is that you?"

I didn't recognize the female voice, but I got calls at all times of the day and night about my organizing business. Being a professional organizer was a bit like being a Realtor. I wasn't ever really on vacation, even when I was out of town, and with the economic downturn I couldn't afford to miss any potential clients. "Speaking," I said.

"Ellie. Thank God you answered." A sound came over the line, a raspy gulp like the kids made when they were trying not to cry. My "mom sense" went on high alert, even though it wasn't one of my kids on the phone.

"Angela?" I asked.

"I need you to take the purse, the fake Leah Marshall—this is really important—take it to my apartment," she said. Her breathing was rough and there was a tension in her words, an urgency that had me sitting up straighter.

"Are you okay?" I asked.

There was a slight hesitation, then she said quickly, "Yes, I'm fine. Don't worry about me. Just take the purse, okay?"

"Sure," I said slowly. "I'm on my way to pick up my kids. I can drop it by there later—"

"No!" she said sharply, cutting me off. "You've got to do it *now*." Her breathing was ragged and her words were vibrating with . . . fear, I realized. My heartbeat sped up. I pulled off the road into a Publix and stopped at the far end of the parking lot with the van slewed diagonally over the parking lines.

"Do you understand?" she said, her voice tense. "You can't wait a minute. Take it now."

"Okay. I can do that. What's your address?" I asked, opening the van's console, where I keep a pen and notepad.

"Thank you," she said as she blew out a breath. "12989 Sea Water Lane, Apartment twenty-nine B."

I jotted the address down. "I was worried about you when you didn't show up last night and I didn't hear from you this morning. Ben, too."

"I'm sorry. I—," she broke off. "I'm sorry. Tell Ben, I'm sorry . . . about everything," she said, her last words caught up in a sob.

"Angela," I said, using the soothing voice I did when the kids were hurt or distraught, "where are you? I'm sure everything will be okay. Are you at home?"

"No. That's not important. What's important is you take the purse there and leave. Do you understand?"

Her voice trembled with intensity. "Don't stay. Just leave it on the porch and get out of there."

"Okay," I said, tapping the address into the GPS, which was still mounted on the window screen for the drive down yesterday. I put the van in DRIVE. "I'm turning around right now."

A dial tone sounded. I glanced at the purse, which I'd tossed on the passenger seat when I first got in the van. Why the panic, the fear? It was just a purse—and a fake one, at that. I hit REDIAL on my phone, but got a message saying the call couldn't be completed.

The GPS routed me inland along the highway and then south back toward the gulf. I made a quick call to Summer to let her know I'd be a little late, then called Ben. He didn't pick up. I was glad the route kept me off the busy beach road and I made good time, pulling into the Sea Water Garden apartment complex a little after noon. Located a few blocks inland from the busy beach road, the complex was misnamed because there wasn't a drop of water in sight, only a shopping center and a few gated neighborhoods with patio homes. Several high-rise hotels towered over the patio homes, cutting off any sliver of the gulf. The complex was well kept with spotless cream two-story stucco buildings topped with terra-cotta roofs. The "garden" part of the name was accurate. The grounds were lushly landscaped with fringy Pindo palms shading the walks, which were lined with the low-growing, sturdier Sago palms. Purple bougainvillea mixed with ivy trailed over the stucco walls, draping down to low-growing shrubs and flowering ground covers.

I couldn't find a slot near building "B" and had to park on the far side of the complex near the pool. There were several parallel parking slots running along the tall stucco wall that enclosed the property. My parallel parking skills were a little rusty, but I managed to pull into the space on my first attempt. I picked up the purse and hopped out of the van, feeling accomplished as I walked by the vine-covered wall that enclosed the pool. Through the wrought-iron gate, I could see a slice of blue water sparkling in the sun. It looked like the pool was only slightly larger than a hot tub, but I suppose if you were a few steps from the beach, you wouldn't need a big pool. I saw Ben under the residents' carport near a silver convertible BMW. The convertible's top was up and he was peering in the driver's window. I looked at the number painted on the ground, 29B. "Angela's car?"

Ben straightened. "Hey, Ellie. What are you doing here?"

"Angela called me and asked me to bring this by her apartment," I said, holding up the purse.

Ben closed his eyes for a moment and breathed out. "She's okay? What happened? Where is she?"

"I don't know. She wouldn't tell me anything. All she wanted to talk about was this purse. She said I had to get it here right away and leave it."

"Is she here?" Ben asked, starting toward the apartment.

"No. She said she wasn't home."

He took a step closer to me. It was already shady with all the palm trees and it was even dimmer under the carport. "She wouldn't tell me where she was and she sounded . . . ," I paused, trying to think how to sum up Angela's state. "Distraught" and "afraid" were the words that came to mind, but I didn't want to voice those words. "She was . . . upset," I said, knowing it was a pretty mild description, but I couldn't quite overcome those sheltering, big sister habits. Ben was already worried and I didn't want to add to his concern.

"Upset, how? Crying? Angry?"

I sighed, realizing that he wasn't going to let me gloss over her reaction. "I don't know her that well. I've only talked to her on the phone a few times, but I think today she sounded . . . scared." I watched his face and said, "You're really worried about her . . . that she's in trouble?"

He put his hands on his hips and stared down at the car as he said, "Angela's kind of like this car—you can't drive it slow, you know what I mean? She's crazy and fun and wild . . . I'm worried she got herself into something . . . over her head."

He blew out a sigh and nodded to the empty slot next to the car. "The neighbor just left and she told me it's been here all night—at least, it was here when she walked her dog late last night and early this morning."

"It's a nice car," I said, taking in the leather trim and sleek lines. "Are you sure Angela had money problems?"

Ben shrugged. "I don't think she's making payments on this. It was a gift from her dad."

"I guess she could always sell her car if things got really rough," I said as we walked to the apartment. "Her brother isn't here yet?"

"I don't think so, but let's check," Ben said as we walked up the curvy path and followed the little signs pointing us around the corner to Angela's building. "How did you get here so fast?"

"I didn't take the beach road."

Number twenty-nine B was a secluded ground-floor apartment on the end of the building, a prime spot. It shared a concrete patio with the opposite apartment, twenty-eight B, which had a pot of petunias beside its front door and a mat that read, "Wipe your paws." Angela's door, with only a dry, crinkled palm frond caught under the threshold, looked bare in comparison.

Ben raised his hand to knock on the door, but paused, then leaned closer. "That's odd," he said, pointing to several deep gouges between the door frame and the handle. He tapped on the door and it swung open.

"Is Angela messy?" I asked.

"Not like this," Ben said, carefully edging the door farther open with the back of his hand, revealing tumbled couch cushions and a lamp on the floor.

"Angela?" Ben called, and stepped slowly through the door.

"We shouldn't go in," I said. "We should call the police."

"What if she's in there? She might be hurt," Ben said. He didn't wait for a reply and shook my restraining hand off his arm. "Chase?" he called.

I followed him inside the small entry area. Ben stepped over a large leather cushion from the couch and moved toward the kitchen. From the entryway, I could see through an open door to a bedroom decorated with a feminine flare in shades ranging from pale yellow to deep gold. It was in even worse shape than the living room. Clothing hung from gaping drawers and was strewn across the floor. An overturned nightstand lay in the middle of the room and fashion magazines rested on top of everything as if they'd been flung into the air like oversized, glossy confetti.

A breeze stirred the lemon curtains in the bedroom, catching my attention. No one leaves their windows open in muggy Florida in July. "The window is open in this bedroom," I said as I stepped carefully around several throw pillows. Ben moved that way, too. I stopped on the threshold of the bedroom while Ben swept aside the curtains.

A pale gold comforter had covered the bed. It was piled on the floor, along with eyelet-edged sheets. It looked as if a small explosion had taken place inside the double-doored closet, scattering clothes, shoes, bags, scarves, and hats across the bedroom floor in front of the open closet doors.

Ben examined the window. "This is how they got out. The screen is outside on the ground." He turned from the window.

"But if the front door was already open, why . . ." I trailed off. "Do you think they were in here when we got here?" I whispered as I reached to pull my phone out of my purse. "They could still be outside."

Ben spoke softly, too, as he said, "You call nine-one-one. I'll call Chase." We both moved back to the living room. I pulled the purse off my shoulder, then stopped abruptly. "I don't have my phone. It's still in the van." I'd been so wrapped up in what was going on, I'd forgotten I was carrying the imitation purse. I'd taken off the Fossil crossbody bag when I climbed in the van. It was still there. Ben waved a hand to stop me. "Let's stay together. Chase still isn't picking up." He left a terse message, then dialed the police.

There was a sharp knock on the door and a voice called, "Hello?"

I twirled around and saw a teenage boy, maybe sixteen years old, in a T-shirt embroidered with the words *Costa Bella Flower Shop*, holding a huge bouquet of mixed flowers. "Delivery for Angela Day," he said, holding the flowers out to me. "Must have been a good party," he said, glancing at Ben.

The gorgeous arrangement of roses, lilies, lilacs, and

gardenias wobbled in midair as he held it out with one hand. I took them, but said, "I'm not Angela."

"But you are in twenty-nine B," he said, quickly consulting a piece of paper. "Enjoy." He gave a little salute as he turned to go.

A man in a pale gray suit shoved past the delivery guy. "What the hell is going on here?" he barked as he surveyed the room.

"Chase," Ben said, quickly crossing the room to him. "I just tried to call you."

Chase pulled off Ray-Ban sunglasses. "Oh. Ben, is it?" While his sister had golden blond hair, his hair was white blond and cut close to his head. A mustache and goatee framed his lower face and I wondered if he'd grown it to distract from his rather pointed nose. If he had, it didn't really work because the added facial hair only emphasized the feature and with his small dark eyes, he reminded me of a mouse.

"That's right." Ben handed off Angela's cell phone, then quickly introduced me and explained we'd found the apartment door unlocked and the place ransacked. As Ben explained, Chase made a quick circuit of the apartment, twirling his sunglasses by the earpiece.

"Ben called the police," I said.

He twirled the glasses faster. "Good. Good. That's good," he said, his dark gaze darting around the room. I got the feeling that he was anything but pleased. "Well, thanks for coming out to check on Angela. She'll turn up soon. She always does," he said, walking toward us, obviously intending to usher us out the door. It was the first good look I'd gotten of his face. It must have been the suit that gave me the impression of maturity. He was closer to twenty—maybe just barely that—than thirty.

I pulled the purse off my shoulder. "Angela called me and wanted me to drop this off—" I broke off and turned to the front door, which was still open. Outside, a high-pitched voice wailed, "Ohmygod, ohmygod, ohmygod. Someone help. She's dead."